ABOUT THE AUTHOR

Robert Laxalt's books have won critical
acclaim and awards throughout the United
States, the United Kingdom, Europe, and South
America. His book *The Basque Hotel* was
nominated for a Pulitzer Prize. *A Cup of Tea
in Pamplona* led to his being awarded one of
Spain's most prestigious literary honors, the
Tambor de Oro (Gold Drum), in 1986. Two
other novels have been selected for the New
York Public Library's Books for the Teen Age.

Laxalt has been a United Press correspondent, a Fulbright research scholar, a consultant
on Basque culture to the Library of Congress,
and a writer-in-residence at the University of
Nevada, Reno. He is the first recipient of the
Distinguished Nevada Author chair at the university. Laxalt is the author of twelve books
and numerous magazine articles.

The Governor's Mansion

. . . .

The Basque Series

. . . .

BOOKS BY ROBERT LAXALT

The Violent Land: Tales the Old Timers Tell

Sweet Promised Land

A Man in the Wheatfield

Nevada

In A Hundred Graves: A Basque Portrait

Nevada: A Bicentennial History

A Cup of Tea in Pamplona

The Basque Hotel

A Time We Knew: Images of Yesterday in the Basque Homeland
with photographs by William Albert Allard

Child of the Holy Ghost

A Lean Year and Other Stories

The Governor's Mansion

ROBERT LAXALT

The Governor's

Mansion

UNIVERSITY OF NEVADA PRESS • RENO • LAS VEGAS • LONDON

Basque Series Editor: William A. Douglass

The paper used in this book meets the requirements of American National
Standard for Information Sciences—Permanence of Paper for Printed
Library Materials, ANSI Z39.48-1984. Binding materials were selected for
strength and durability.

Library of Congress Cataloging-in-Publication Data
Laxalt, Robert, 1923–
The governor's mansion / Robert Laxalt.
p.   cm. — (The Basque series)
ISBN 0-87417-251-9 (cloth : acid-free paper)
1. Nevada—Politics and government—Fiction.   2. Basque
Americans—Nevada—Fiction.   I. Title.   II. Series.
PS3562.A9525G68   1994
813'.54—dc20   94-4858
                                                              CIP

University of Nevada Press, Reno, Nevada 89557 USA
Designed by Richard Hendel
Printed in the United States of America
2   4   6   8   9   7   5   3   1

For Myrick Land

One

1

I drove past the Governor's Mansion that day. Afterwards, I wondered why I had. That imposing white edifice was not a curiosity for me. Living in the same part of town, I had seen it so many times that I did not see it anymore. It was just a white space in the landscape.

The same applied to the capitol dome. I had grown up with it always there, looming high over the cottonwoods and tallest poplars of Carson City. When I was a boy and my parents had a little hotel with a false front and a handful of rooms on Main Street, it seemed that every time I looked up, there was the capitol dome.

Later, when we moved to a white frame house on the back streets, where we did the rest of our growing up, the dome was the first thing you saw when you walked out through the front porch. And later yet, it was straight down a wide street from my older brother Leon's modern ranch house on the outskirts of town. If you fired a cannon from Leon's entrance down the long street, it would have bored the capitol dome amidships.

As I turned off the lane coming down from the Sierra to the west, the Governor's Mansion was there in front of me. I examined it earnestly as if I were seeing it for the first time. I wondered why I had never attached any particular importance to it before and decided it was probably because none of its tenants had stayed around long enough to give the place a personality.

I suppose it really is an impressive building, especially for such a small state as Nevada. It is like something out of the deep South, with curving driveways and wide steps, fluted pillars and encircling balconies, tall firs and weeping willows, and down at the entrance,

· · ·

two old lampposts that we had probably swung on before they were salvaged and moved from Main Street to the mansion.

At that, there was one premonition that did cross my mind on the Friday when our lives were to be disrupted. As I drove down the shaded street that fronted the mansion, it occurred to me that we had surely been raised in the political heart of Carson City.

A few blocks down from the Governor's Mansion was the white house where Mark Twain had lived when his brother was secretary of state. The house was really the Orion Clemens house, but everyone had forgotten that long ago. Now, it was the Mark Twain house, which seemed to me unfair.

Orion had put up the house and also put up his brother, Samuel Clemens, who was usually unemployed in his Nevada days. Later, Samuel Clemens took the pen name of Mark Twain. He returned his brother's generosity by making fun of him in his writings about Nevada, never mentioning the one hell of a job Orion had done to get the state started. That was supposed to be the task of the territorial governor, James Nye, who had been appointed by Abe Lincoln. Nye took one look at the desert domain over which he was supposed to reign and promptly found more pressing business in the pleasure palaces of San Francisco in neighboring California. So, Orion had performed the task for him and found work for his brother, Samuel. After reading Samuel's observations about his brother, I could never again look upon Mark Twain with an objective eye.

Across the street, sideways from our family home, was a three-story house with a sweeping veranda. It contained an irascible district judge who stormed and fumed to his dying day. He was especially devoted to my brother Leon, suspecting, I am sure, that Leon would one day get into Republican state politics. The judge's advice to Leon was of a different kind of philosophical generality: "One lesson you will learn in this life is that a stiff prick has no conscience."

· · ·

4

Next to the judge's house was a slightly smaller but equally imposing white house occupied at one time by the state treasurer and later
by his son, who in time became governor, but as everyone in Carson
City knew, he was too kind a man for politics.

In an indefinable way, our family home fit in and did not fit in.
Outwardly, it had all the necessary trappings for the neighborhood.
It had been built the required length of time ago, somewhere between
seventy and a hundred years. It was white frame like nearly all the
houses in that part of Carson City. It was only a one-story house,
but it made up for that by the amount of ground it covered, half of a
Carson City block, which was smaller than big-city blocks.

The house was divided into two separate wings connected by a
foyer in front and divided in back by an alley. The house was filled
with a curious mix of early Mission and Victorian furniture, the
one distinguished by clean lines and the other by ornately carved
table legs and grained, white marble tops. Curved archways and lofty
double doors abounded.

The practice of building houses with two separate wings went back
to the early days, when out-of-town guests for formal parties and
balls could stay overnight if the hour got too late or the liquor flowed
too freely. The guests would leave carriages and stall their horses in
an immense barn that covered the back of the lot. When we moved
into the house, the barn was one of the first things to go. Cars were
coming into fashion and the barn really had no use except for the few
times when my father kept his horses there. From my point of view,
this was a huge loss. I think I thought more of that cavernous hay-,
grain-, and manure-smelling barn than of the house itself.

When the old barn went, my mother built a little Basque-style
stucco house with a red-tiled roof in its place, which absolutely did
not fit into the neighborhood architecture. Nobody protested because
it was the first new construction in Carson City since the Great De-

· · ·

pression had started. From my mother's point of view the little house brought in rent money, and that was first priority in those Depression days.

A state supreme court judge and his wife lived there for several years. He was a courtly man who always tipped his hat to my mother, but his wife was a social climber of the most vicious sort. She treated my mother badly, always trying to put her down by talking about the social life to which my mother was not privy. That didn't bother my mother at all, she being one of the few really proud women I have ever known. But the business about pretending not to understand my mother's English reached its intended mark. That, and some sidled remarks about my parents' having sold liquor in the little hotel on Main Street during Prohibition times. The judge's wife could not pursue this with too much enthusiasm, however, since the social crowd to which she and the judge belonged had been good customers for booze deliveries under cover of night.

The fact that my mother simply did not entertain people may have been one of the reasons why our house did not fit into the neighborhood. My mother felt she could not cope with the formal side of American society. She wanted station but she was unwilling to pay that much of a price.

But overshadowing that, I must believe, was her passion for privacy, which I have come to understand is very Basque. In all the years of our growing up, the only adults who ever saw the inside of our house were her few Basque friends, an occasional sheepman or sheepherder my father would bring by for a meal, and of course priests and nuns. However, she did not seem to mind our schoolmates stopping by to play a card game called solo or table tennis on the long Mission-style dining table, as long as they did not make a frequent habit out of it. Whenever she baked bread on a Saturday and the doughy scents wafted over the neighborhood, she could count on young company.

· · ·

The interior of the house had kept its original style, my mother having been exposed enough to city elegance in France to ensure that. Actually, the only radical disruption in the orderly placement of furniture and paintings and grand piano came from her penchant for religious icons. She left the living room pretty much alone, but every inch of available space in dining room and kitchen and bedrooms was plastered with Bleeding Heart of Jesus calendars and pictures and figurines of more saints than I had known existed. I have seen religious shops less well stocked than our house.

There was another incongruity that met me as I drove up to the family home on that Friday morning in June. Though I had seen it many times before, it never became commonplace. I would notice the incongruity every time.

Parked one behind the other in front of the house were Leon's long Cadillac and my father's pickup truck. There is no need to describe the Cadillac, but my father's pickup truck was something else. From front bumper to back, it bore the scars of ten thousand brushes with mountain and desert.

Sagebrush, manzanita, pine tree branches, and the sharp edges of rocks had all taken their toll. The wooden sheep racks in back were even more stripped of paint than the body, being less durable. The business ends of shovels, crowbars, and axes were held in place in the corners of the truck bed by tattered loops of cotton rope. And each individual board in the racks was wrapped around by mazes of baling wire. I sometimes thought that if the baling wire were removed, the pickup truck would die from sickness of soul.

· · ·

2

Later on in my brother's political career, a history professor told me that the quality of the *dramatically unexpected* seemed to accompany Leon Indart. It was not the kind of drama that is contrived or reckless and quickly forgotten. Things seemed to happen to him in a natural way that people remembered. When the quality developed into a sense, it was to stand him in good stead, because the dramatic is indispensable in creating a political aura. As time went on, a lot of it was by calculation because a politician becomes aware of the weapons he has at hand and uses them to his best advantage.

But in the beginning, at least, it was sincere and an unconscious thing. And it still was on the morning when Leon phoned me from his law office in Carson City, I having moved thirty miles away to Reno.

"Pete," he said, "you're coming over for lunch at Mom's today, aren't you?"

I said I hoped so, but there was a faculty committee meeting I would have to get out of.

"Well, make a point of it," said Leon. "We have a family matter to talk over."

A "family matter" meant it was not to be the usual get-together lunch. "I'll be there," I said.

Since World War II had ended and such things as university and law school were done with and we four brothers had settled into the pattern of our lives, it had become our custom to gather for lunch nearly every Friday at the old family home in Carson City. We pretended that it was the lure of our mother's French brandy pancakes that drew us, but actually it was a way of staying close to each other. As Leon said, "It's like going back to the womb." There, where we had

. . .

done most of our growing up, the house had been a fortress against the world. This is something the children of immigrants all know, or at least knew then when it was not fashionable to be the children of immigrants.

But it was something more than that. It came down to the fact that we four brothers could not live without each other. We did not enjoy anybody's company as much as our own. We never bored each other. If one of us was having a problem, he could count on honest advice from the others.

Yet, there was a restraint that went with it. The word *love* was never spoken between us and none of us would ever have admitted that we needed each other. Our wives, who were not first-generation children of immigrants, said that the relationship between the brothers was unhealthy and dangerous. In time to come, I thought they were right because for a while it seemed doomed. But in the end, the ties that bound us prevailed and what emerged was tempered and so better. It was also beautiful, and I know that those who have not known this kind of love have missed very much.

With our Friday ritual, perhaps we were trying to make up for the years of separation since we had finished high school in Carson City. War had separated us first, but we had come out of it relatively unscathed. Then, my three brothers had gone on to become lawyers. My mother had something to do with this. As an immigrant trying to cope with American ways of doing business, she had always wanted a lawyer in the family. Now she had three, and it was one of her homilies that they were all so busy she had to retain outside counsel.

One of our sisters, Suzette, had become a nun, which had not pleased my father, who saw it as a waste of a good woman. My mother swore she did not have a thing to do with it. I believe her. Suzette was always different. I remember too well the times when nobody could find her for such things as dinner, and our search would end

· · ·

in the darkened church where she was sitting alone. Our other sister had married an engineer in California. He was born of Italian parents, and his immigrant roots, I suspect, had a lot to do with her choosing him.

Like Suzette, the nun, my brother Gene had never married. Unlike her, he was a swinging bachelor lawyer with an office apartment at Lake Tahoe. He never did become attached to the law, mainly because of the Washington, D.C., influence. He had been sent to Europe on a cloak-and-dagger mission for Senator Pat McCarran and the Un-American Activities Committee, and that had spoiled him for a sedentary law practice. The story was cynically circulated in the legal fraternity that Gene ended every interview with a female divorce client by saying, "Now, let's lie down and talk about your fee."

Our youngest brother, Mitch, had just finished law school and gone into practice with Leon in Carson City. He was studious and had an astounding reservoir of information about the most unlikely subjects.

Once, that capacity of his had paid off for me. When Mitch had been a summertime caddy master at a Lake Tahoe golf course, he had noticed that one party of eastern golfers carried pistols in the pockets of their golf bags. With his enquiring bent, he found out their names.

Not long afterwards, one of them shot his partner in an argument. Not on the golf course, whose rules prohibited that, but in a gambling joint. The Reno newspapers carried the story as a simple shooting in which the assailant was one L. M. Strauss. Mitch knew better. He told me the assailant was better known in the East as "Russian Louie" Strauss, formerly of Murder, Inc.

I was a staff correspondent for United Press then. It was my first big story and the first time the state government knew about hoodlums expanding their territory beyond Las Vegas.

I even managed to get an admission of the shooting out of Russian

Louie in his jail cell in Carson City. It was so easy that my estimation of hoodlums went down considerably. Russian Louie tried to remedy his mistake by offering to buy me a new car. I can remember my exact words to him: "Thanks, but reporters don't do things like that." I have since learned better.

In spite of his bad handling of the whole affair, Louie actually won the legal end of it with a combination of a self-defense plea and a lapse of memory by such hoodlum notables as "Abie the Trigger" Chapman and "George the Professor" Kozloff. How I relished using those Runyonesque names in my news stories.

The hoodlum code of silence was a tactic the local district attorney was not accustomed to, and Russian Louie won his case. He did not win the Mafia end of it, however. He moved to Las Vegas and soon afterwards was invited along on a driving trip to Los Angeles by the man who, it was said, had executed "Bugsy" Siegel. Russian Louie never got to enjoy the auto trip. He was planted in the desert somewhere between Las Vegas and Los Angeles. I felt bad about that. He was my first hoodlum.

I did not suspect that the "family matter" had anything to do with politics because Leon had already had his taste of it. When he was only a year out of law school, he had had the audacity to run for district attorney in Carson City.

I say audacity because that was not the era of young politicians. Since first statehood days, the tradition was that no candidate was worth his salt until he was approaching middle age, and even then he needed tempering before the people would wholly accept him. I can remember hoary old politicians saying to me, "Leon Indart is a nice kid, but that's just it, he is a kid."

Except for winning, the experience was not a happy one. Following

· · ·

his instinct for confrontation even then, Leon had gone for election with an unheard-of approach—door-to-door campaigning. It was something none of the old politicians would have deigned to do. He met the arguments about his youth head-on by letting the voters size him up face-to-face to prove to themselves he was not still the gangly kid they had cheered for on the basketball court and football field. Law school had informed him about the things they wanted answers to, and combat in the Pacific had made him older than his years. Instead of a rostrum, living room and kitchen became his stump.

He had another ace up his sleeve. In that time, the young of Leon's age rarely got around to the business of registering and voting. That was another political tradition. They made up an ignored voting bloc, and Leon called upon their loyalties as schoolmates who had shared classes with him since day one, and teammates who were tied to him by the bonds forged by competition with the enemy.

The campaign was a growing-up experience for Leon in many ways. Before that, he had been an unquestioned leader, at least among those of his own age. But now that he had offered himself for public office, he found out what it was to be public property. All the little jealousies surfaced, and the backbiting was carried back to him by his loyal friends. He ran into the illogic of remarks like, "Leon Indart's not so much. I can remember when we got drunk together in high school." The immigrant label, his being a Catholic in a Protestant-dominated community with an old suspicion against Papists, and his being a Republican to boot all worked against him.

In the beginning, he was stunned and mad with the cold anger that was part of his makeup. It could have embittered him forever against politics and human nature. But losing would be worse. Lord, how he hated to lose at anything. I took this as a fault in him then. Now, I am not so sure. If you are in a fight, you go to win. Despite all the pap

· · ·

we are handed about the nobility of losing, the truth is that losing is ignoble in the eyes of the loser. Also, it hurts like hell.

Leon served only one term as district attorney and then "chose not to run again." But the experience of serving and the fruits of it were good. He made a reputation as a courtroom lawyer with such innovations as a blackboard on which he would write out a syllogism—two premises and a conclusion, the conclusion in this case being nontheoretical—ending up getting a verdict of guilty. He had learned that trick from his logic classes in a Jesuit university. Words were cheap, he knew, but the double impact of rhetoric combined with the written word worked like a charm with jurors. It was like taking them back to the classroom and the infallible teacher.

He confided to us that the reason he did not run again was that he did not like sending people to prison. That was probably true, but the main reason was that he had established himself enough to go in on equal footing in his father-in-law's firm. His father-in-law was one of the old school who felt that young lawyers should learn humility by being treated as lackeys. This attitude did not coincide with Leon's nature. He never could tolerate being second.

In the years to come, Leon made a lot of money. He was a lawyer's lawyer, one of those to whom other lawyers come for advice. He was strong in range and water law and the ranchers came to see him. When his father-in-law was appointed federal judge, Leon took over some of his choice clients. Then when gambling got to be a big business in Reno, the gamblers came to Leon, usually in income tax cases. For people who made a business of numbers, it was surprising how weak they were when it came to adding up profits correctly.

In spite of all this success, Leon was getting restless. At first denied a family, he and his wife, Janet, adopted three children and then predictably had three more of their own. So his family was complete.

· · ·

Then he built a ranch-style house and added a swimming pool and tennis court. So his home was complete. He liked to live well and he wore wealth in a natural way, as though he had been born to it.

But money as an end was not enough. He was bored with law and well on his way to getting fat, prosperous, and opinionated. He was pronouncing dictums that did not hold water.

I think this more than anything else was the final trigger. Something was happening within himself that was not good, and he had enough sense to recognize it.

3

"Holy Christ!"

"Don't swear, Peter," my mother said absently. But she, too, had been shaken enough to sit down suddenly at the lunch table, something she never did when there was still clearing to be done. "I don't understand, Leon," she said, having been only half listening.

"It's not complicated," said Leon. "The Republican party, or what's left of it in Nevada, is leaning hard on Tex Maynard to run for governor. But Tex won't go unless I run for lieutenant governor with him."

"That movie actor!"

"Silent screen movie actor," corrected Gene.

"Listen, Mom," said Leon. "Don't underestimate the man. He got to be lieutenant governor, didn't he?"

"But why does he have to do this to you?"

"Well, it's not exactly an insult," Leon said wryly.

"Leon," my mother persisted. "Politics is such a dirty business."

· · ·

Leon made a deprecating wave of his hand. "I've been hearing that old saw from day one. I don't happen to believe it."

I was looking at my mother in surprise. From the time we were children, I would have sworn that this was exactly what she had always had in mind for her eldest son. At times it had seemed to me that it was an obsession with her, to see her eldest son elevated to high station in life, and through that, her own station enhanced. Now, a wariness had come into her handsome face with its framing of graying hair caught up in a braided chignon in back. It was as though she were about to venture into troubled waters and was uncertain what they held for her, my father, and us. Much later I was to remember that look. Immigrant and unsophisticated, her instincts were better than ours.

"Excuse me," my father mumbled. "I have to get back to work." He rose from the table and went out through the kitchen. I could hear the slapping of gloves against his Levi's to knock out the wood chips and, a moment later, the sound of chopping from the back yard. It was a good sound that I cannot hear today without seeing his long, lean arms coming down with the axe to split a log cleanly in two. And the sound meant that he was home for a while between sheep-herding jobs. Age had treated him well, but in a different way from my mother. His hair was white, but blazing summers and frozen winters had failed to scar his bronzed face as they had so many other outside men. They had added a few crow's-feet at the corners of his gray eyes from squinting into the sun, deepened the lines of concentration on his brow, and carved deeper the curved lines that arced his mouth.

"Boy, what a reception," Leon said to the silence of the room. His eyes had gone cold.

Leon had two very expressive features about him, his eyes and

· · ·

15

his hands. His eyes were brown and deep set and totally revealing of what he was thinking. They could be commanding at one instant, warm when he was laughing, and frighteningly cold when he was angry, the last of which he learned to mask in politics. His hands were strong hands, but in a long-boned way. They worked in concert with the mood of his eyes.

I went out to the kitchen to get the coffeepot. When I came back in and poured coffee around, I glanced at my other brothers to see how they had taken Leon's announcement. Gene had pushed back his chair and was staring studiously at the table. His long legs and arms were crossed into themselves and his jaw was jutted out in concentration. The ash of his cigarette was lengthening dangerously. He had something to think about, all right, and we all knew what it was.

From behind his black-rimmed glasses, my youngest brother, Mitch, was regarding Leon without really seeing him. He blinked now, bringing Leon into focus. "What are the pluses?"

The coldness faded from Leon's eyes at the first question rationally delivered. "I don't see too many pluses," he said. "Except for the party. We couldn't be in any worse shape if we tried. From what Tex tells me, it's gotten so bad in Las Vegas that *Republican* is a dirty word down there. But if we let the governor's race go uncontested, the party might just as well have signed on for a mass suicide compact. Tex Maynard is the only logical candidate because he's been through the political chairs."

"If the party is in that kind of shape," Mitch said evenly, "how does he figure he's got a chance of being elected governor?"

"Don't underestimate that smiling cowboy," said Leon. "He's got a personal following that cuts across party lines." Leon turned to the rest of us. "How do you size it up?"

"I'm not sure," I said. "This state doesn't have a habit of turning

· · ·

governors out of office at the end of their first term. And Dean Cooper is a popular governor."

Leon broke into Gene's concentration. "Gene, how do you read it?"

"I think Dean Cooper would have to belt his wife in front of Harolds Club to lose this one."

"You've been listening to too many Democrats," said Leon.

"I don't listen to them," said Gene. "They listen to me." He added qualifyingly, "Well, some of them anyway."

The reason for Gene's studious concentration and long silence was a legitimate one. Over the last few years, all four of us had been skirting the edges of politics. In the beginning it was a haphazard drifting with no strong feelings involved. But Gene had gotten into it deeper than the rest of us. He was one of a cadre of young lawyers who had gone to law school in Washington, D.C., by way of a patronage job from Senator Pat McCarran, who was probably the most powerful senator in the United States. He had even taken on President Roosevelt in the battle over packing the U.S. Supreme Court, and won.

Gene was known as "one of Pat's boys." The patronage thing had been an effective political tactic for McCarran, and he had core lieutenants in every town in Nevada. McCarran was dead now and the obligation was gone. Still, Gene had been swept up in the postmortem continuity and was elected chairman of the Democratic Central Committee for the neighboring county.

Leon was on the other side of the political fence. He was a member of the Republican policy committee, which was a polite title for a squad of sharpshooters who aimed at Governor Cooper's Democratic administration.

I was a Democrat, too, but a halfhearted political party member at best. I had done political publicity and speechwriting for both Republicans and Democrats. My motives had been strictly mercenary.

· · ·

Political newswriters were in short supply and extra money was welcome to the family budget. Like a lot of newspapermen, I wondered at times why I had gone down the news road instead of becoming a lawyer, and rich.

As for our youngest brother, Mitch, he had studied the platform of both major parties in depth and then gone out and registered nonpartisan, finding no particle of difference between them. In time, he had become inured against Leon's labeling him as a political eunuch.

The family's political spectrum had merely provided fuel for good arguments around my mother's table, nobody taking it very seriously. But suddenly, on this day, politics was no longer a joking matter.

"If Tex Maynard thinks he's so strong," said Gene bluntly, "why does he need you?"

Leon spread his hands. "He's not that strong. All of us know that. He feels he can hold his own in the south, in Las Vegas, where the big votes are. But he needs an edge from the north to win, from Reno and the rural counties. He's convinced I can give it to him. I should be able to. The family's been here fifty years. We haven't welshed on any debts yet. Our family name is good. If we haven't made friends by now, then we've been living in a dream world."

Mitch changed the subject before Gene could say anything. "Our law practice is going to suffer if you have to start stumping the state," he said. "Our clients aren't going to like it."

"I'm not going to kid you," said Leon. "If I go, the big load would be on your shoulders. You'll have to hold down the fort."

Mitch retreated behind the barrier of his horn-rimmed glasses, but not quickly enough to conceal from me the impact of Leon's declaration. The prospect of dealing with Leon's tough-minded clients who would not accept inexperience as an excuse or tolerate any weakening of their defense had hit him like a truck. If they fired the firm, the responsibility would be his.

· · ·

"Have you told your family?" my mother asked.

"Not the kids," said Leon. "They're not old enough to understand what's involved, so there's nothing they can say that will influence my thinking. Janet says that if I make up my mind to go, she'll be there. She's not enthused. You have to remember she went through a rough time when her father got beat for attorney general."

Gene had had time to do his thinking. He uncrossed his long legs and reached for a cigarette. "This creates a problem for me with, pardon the expression, the Democratic Central Committee."

Leon had anticipated what Gene was going to say. "It's your decision to make, Gene," he said. "You have to call your own shot. I'm not going to pressure you. I know you're in a box."

"I could care less about the box," said Gene. There was a pause that was far too long for my tastes, but it seemed to slide right past Leon. Then Gene made his own declaration, the one that would change the course of his entire life. He was a figure of station, poised, I thought, for his own political career, respected for his leadership. All that was about to evaporate now. "I'll have to resign my chairmanship of the Central Committee."

Leon expected no less, and so he did not acknowledge it. He looked questioningly at Gene. "What's the problem then?"

"What bothers me is that it won't look good." Gene grinned, but it did not come off convincingly. "My former fellow Democrats won't take it kindly. They could hurt us in the press and alienate Democratic votes." He stopped, then added almost painfully, "You know, the thing about party defection."

It was the first practical dilemma in the tactic of juggling public opinion. Afterwards, we were to become pretty skillful in the game of political pragmatics.

"How do we meet it, then?" asked Leon, but he was talking to himself, not us. His gaze had turned inward. He had already removed

· · ·

himself from our presence, and in that isolation chamber his mind was already sorting out alternatives. I think that at that moment he established the habit that was to mark his political life—that of making instant decisions about problems that are usually talked and worried to death.

Leon leaned forward, his eyes engaging ours again. "Why not meet it head-on? Take the initiative away from them."

"You mean loyalty to his brother outweighs all earthly consider-ations?" At that moment I meant to be sarcastic, but it did not come off that way. Later, after I was caught up in the fever of the campaign, I was not so sure.

"Be frank with me, Gene," said Leon. "I have to know before I decide. Do you have political ambitions?"

Gene shrugged. "I thought I did once," he said. "But now, I don't think I really want to be out in front. I'm not cut out for it. My place is helping behind the scenes." He sounded so sincere that I will never be sure whether he meant it.

Leon folded his napkin with precision and placed his hands on both sides of it. "Well, the cards are on the table," he said, sweeping us with eyes that were already wide with the anticipation of battle. It had been a long time since I had seen that kind of excitement in his eyes.

"Now," he said after a moment, "it's my turn for a decision. I'll be honest with you. I can see more disadvantages than advantages in getting into the political pit. We've barely touched on the biggest minus of all. If I run, life will never be the same for us again. I could be in office for a long time. That will mean the end of our privacy as a family. We'll be public property from here on out."

My mother bent her head as if bowing to the inevitable. From the backyard came the sounds of my father chopping wood. They

· · ·

had the pure ring of detachment from the intrigues of the world. I remembered that later.

Afterwards, Gene and I lingered outside the house for a moment. I had planned on asking him if he had really meant what he said, or if he was sacrificing his own political career for Leon's ambition. But then I realized how unjust that question would be. The die was cast, never to be retrieved.

I asked instead, "What do you think? Is he going?"

"Of course he's going," said Gene.

When we parted, it occurred to me there was something we had not talked about. Leon had never once raised the possibility of defeat in his race for lieutenant governor. The omission was not inconsistent with who he was.

What children we were. Because we had grown up knowing politicians, we thought we knew politics. But all we had really known was the outward face of politics. We had seen the affable smile and felt the firm handclasps, but we had never seen the unguarded moment when the smile was gone and the bruising showed through, and we had not even wondered why these men grew old before their time.

We had seen the outward face, but we had never been privy to those secret rooms where that face was manufactured. We had heard the roar from beyond the podium, but we had never listened to the muted voices that dissected and plotted the oratory.

We had taken it for granted that a man in politics either wins or loses, but we had never considered that there is no middle ground in politics. We were in a game where there is a winner and there is a loser. To have almost won meant nothing but to have lost. A

· · ·

21

political man rises to the battle and survives, or he falls away into oblivion.

We learned that it was not enough simply to declare for office. That was only the beginning and the easiest part of it all. It was not enough to say, "I am a candidate because I believe . . ." and to think to yourself, *You must be able to see that I have strong beliefs.* But the electorate is not clairvoyant, and in every American there is a Missourian that must be shown the mule. From there come the interminable meetings in the secret rooms where the mechanics of the message are painfully hammered out.

We learned there was no escape from the circus that is American politics—the showmanship of billboards and signs and bumper stickers, the revival meetings that are called political rallies, the modulated voice of radio and the theatrics of television, and above all, the sustaining of momentum.

We learned the parry and thrust of infighting, that there was a right time to attack, a right time to defend, and, most important, a right time to keep still.

We learned that it was a time for the diminishing of ego, because every thought, word, and deed must become subservient to the campaign and all egos must be diminished in order to preserve the almighty ego of the candidate.

We learned that the electorate does not give a damn about issues, that a warm smile and a handshake, a good radio voice, and a television presence mean more than all the issues put together. We learned finally that there are no merits in campaigns, but only show biz.

We learned that a campaign means people—people to speak well of you, people to arrange rallies, people to put up signs, and people to pay for all this. And this last was the hardest of all, because for every one who gave you money out of good heart, with no strings attached,

· · ·

there was another who would consider it a due bill he expected to collect in time.

We were hurt when people we thought were friends suddenly took pains to avoid us, and it took a long time to understand that their pocketbooks were involved and that political party or a job in jeopardy could override the friendship of a lifetime. We were puzzled when others who had never spoken to us before now began to speak to us for an ulterior reason, the promise of reward.

And then there were the people who made it worthwhile, the friends who stayed by you at great risk and the ones who appeared out of nowhere, who believed in you and worked for you, who had everything to lose but would ask nothing in return.

For the first time, we felt the ridicule of opposition newspapers in public print for everyone to read and heard the private things about family that might have been whispered before in a few places but were now spoken aloud in many places, rumors embellished and rumors invented. And we endured the fury and helplessness of all this, because there was nothing we could do about it.

We learned what the testing by fire can do to men who live the intensity of six years in the six months of a campaign, who grow ten feet tall or diminish to nothing.

We learned that uncertainty and the intangible are the ghosts that stalk every campaign, and it is like fighting with shadows or walking in quicksand because you are never sure whether you are winning or losing or even know exactly where you stand.

What children we were. But, like children, we learned quickly.

· · ·

4

It was my first smoke-filled room, and Tex Maynard was there in all his radiance.

Tex Maynard had not become a silent screen idol by accident, and starlet Gloria Rowe had not singled him out for marriage by accident, either. He really was a striking figure of a man, tall with broad shoulders and narrow hips. He had sandy hair going very carefully to gray. Summer or winter, his face kept an astonishingly consistent tan. And he had one of the most beautiful smiles I have ever seen in politics.

His image was cowboy. I suspect that anywhere else except a western state, this would have been cause for amusement by the political hierarchy, but in Nevada it was not all that bad. In the huge chunk of ranching territory that the politicos called the "cow counties," the cowboy image had to work. But in Tex Maynard's case, it also seemed to work in the metropolitan centers of Reno and Las Vegas, and that is the proof of the pudding.

Tex's wardrobe was exquisite. There is just no other way to describe it. He wore tailored western jackets and tight-fitting pants that shone in the sunlight and handmade cowboy boots of the finest leather, done up in hues of purple and green and gold. No Nevada parade was considered complete without Tex Maynard.

As a one-to-one campaigner, there was no better. His dazzling trappings coupled with an innocent nature and a ready smile won him friends from the Las Vegas Strip to the raunchiest cow town. It was foregone that he would set women's hearts aflutter, but curiously enough, even the legitimate cowboys with sweaty shirts, faded Levi's, and worn-down spurs liked him. Tex had stumbled upon a political

· · ·

truth. If a person likes you he'll vote for you, and to hell with the issues.

That was where his qualifications for public office ended. Though he was the incumbent lieutenant governor, the president pro tem of the legislative senate, and the titular head of the Republican party in Nevada, I suspect that he had only the haziest notion of the workings of government and no notion at all of the legislation that went through his hands. He was good at playing poker, though, when the senate was in recess, and that endeared him to the senators from the cow counties and, naturally, Las Vegas.

His political speeches were written for him by a canny old newspaperman who in his wanderings had managed to work for every newspaper of note in the United States. The speechwriter understood his candidate. He made it a rule never to insert a word that went over three syllables.

However, there were times when the speechwriter, who was also Tex's campaign manager, could not protect his candidate. Once was when a statue of a Pony Express rider was being dedicated at Lake Tahoe, on the state line between California and Nevada. To dramatize the ceremony, the organizing committee had hit upon a unique format. A horseback rider from California was to make a dash up to the state line with honest-to-goodness Pony Express mail pouches tied to his saddle. In front of the reviewing stand, he would transfer his mail pouches to a waiting rider for the dash into Nevada. Naturally, the Nevada rider was Tex Maynard.

The first part of the transaction went off without a hitch. The rider from California pounded on lathered horse to the reviewing stand perched right on the state line, leaped off, and slapped the mail pouches on Tex Maynard's horse. Tex was ready and waiting in splendorous costume, astride a golden Palomino stallion with silver-

· · ·

mounted saddle, bridle, reins, and spurs. Putting the shining spurs to his horse, Tex stood up in the stirrups, doffed his hat, flashed his radiant smile at the cameras on the reviewing stand, and proceeded to gallop back into California. He was a hundred yards along the road before he finally heard the shouts of "Tex! you're going the wrong way!"

Nothing daunted, Tex reined his horse to a skidding stop, whirled him around, and pounded back in the right direction. When he passed the reviewing stand a second time, he stood up in his stirrups, doffed his hat, flashed his radiant smile at the cameras on the stand, and galloped into Nevada as if nothing unusual had happened. It was like a movie retake.

"Our eminent Governor Cooper," said George Friar to the newspaper in his hand, "is revealing his sensitive nature." Wagging his great head in mild disapproval, Friar went on, "His tactic is sound and to be expected. Tex, he is attacking your qualifications for the governorship. However, one would have thought he would approach the subject somewhat later and on a higher level."

We were gathered around a carved mahogany table in Reno's most luxurious hotel, built during World War II with a slightly dubious loan from the Reconstruction Finance Corporation, which is to say with taxpayers' money. The transaction was consistent with Nevada and nobody saw anything wrong with it, the prevailing sentiment established by silver-maned and now-deceased Senator McCarran being that it was the duty of every politician to sack the federal treasury for the State of Nevada. The meeting was an auspicious beginning for Tex Maynard's campaign for the governorship and my brother Leon's campaign for the lieutenant governorship.

When George Friar had done speaking, Tex Maynard winced and

· · ·

looked to his speechwriter for a translation. The speechwriter said drily, "He means Cooper is a hip-shooter."

Tex turned sulkily back to Friar. "What did he say about me?"

Friar intoned, "I quote our eminent Governor Cooper: 'We welcome the candidacy of the Republican opposition, et cetera, et cetera . . . but I seriously question the qualifications of a one-time silent screen star for the weighty responsibilities of the governor's chair.'" Friar lowered the newspaper gravely. "Translated," he said with a superior glance at Tex's speechwriter, "this means that our eminent governor is not only attacking your experience and mental equipment, but he is also dragging in by the heels the matter of your age, and conversely—it need not be explained—*his* youth."

Tex was genuinely hurt. I think it was the first time on his smiling road through politics that he had encountered a frontal assault.

Friar bowed his head commiseratively. "Well, at least he was not so gross and, I might add, unwise as to raise obliquely the question of your morals. To wit, your mistress. It's a pity he didn't. That would have cost him a bundle of votes."

Tex's eyes narrowed, his face hardened, and he made a motion as if to push his chair back from the table. Both the facial expression and the motion were flawlessly done.

Friar raised his hands in front of him. "Pardnuh, don't go for your gun. I ain't heeled."

Leon, who was sitting beside Friar, kicked him under the table. Friar flushed with embarrassment.

"Gentlemen," said Friar, "I kid you not. You may think me indelicate, but I tell you that we are in a tough political campaign and we had better put our cards on the table now. Anticipating the opposition is half the secret of this ball game, and honesty with each other is our only defense."

· · ·

Friar had abandoned the role he had been playing. He turned to Leon with steady eyes. "How about you, Leon? What can they hit you with?"

Leon had been listening intently to Friar. In this beginning time, he listened a lot. Not so, later, when he knew his way around. "Nothing," he said. "I'm clean."

Tex moved his chair back up to the table. He was clearly baffled. "What the hell am I supposed to do?" he said helplessly. "That sanitarium Gloria's in is a mental hospital, if you want to know the truth. She's been no wife to me for a long time, and she never will be because there's no getting out. But by God, I haven't divorced her and I never will." All the radiance was gone now, and he looked pathetic. "I'm a man and a man needs a woman. Can't people understand that?"

"We understand it," said Friar. "We understand it and we admire you for the way you've taken care of Gloria. Our eminent Governor Cooper also understands, and he, too, probably admires you. But that's not going to keep the rumor squads from using it against you. Don't kid yourself that the people won't eat up every bit of it. Mr. Average Citizen can cheat on his wife at the drop of a hat and manage to forgive himself just about as quickly. But he won't forgive it in his leaders." Friar chuckled drily. "Henceforth, Tex, thou shalt be denied the mortal feet of clay."

Whenever Friar lapsed into what Leon called his Gideon prose, Tex Maynard reacted with puzzled annoyance. Before he could look to his speechwriter, Leon interrupted. He had emerged from that isolation chamber of his mind. "I don't buy it, George," he said to Friar. "You're making too much of a production out of Tex's personal life. Cooper is too smart to use it publicly, and if his people do it could rebound in spades. Your Mr. Average American has a streak of fair play in him, too. He can get mad when the game isn't played by the rules. But I'll bet he secretly delights in seeing a little clay in the feet of his

· · ·

leaders. It helps him to justify his own departures from the straight and narrow."

This time, the speechwriter spoke without prompting. "That's for sure," he said, peering over his thin gold-rimmed glasses. "Look at Kennedy. He hardly left a broad unlayed on the Strip, and Las Vegas loves him for it."

Leon, who had never been an admirer of Jack Kennedy, said wryly, "I'm not taking it that far. There's such a thing as overdoing it."

Friar was regarding Leon with frank curiosity. "Not bad," he said, thrusting out his lower lip and nodding. "Not bad."

Out of all the people in the room, including Tex's speechwriter, George Friar was the only one who really knew the science of politics. Not the political science of the classroom variety—I have come to know that professors are the purveyors of astounding ignorance when it comes to the real workings of politics. Friar knew politics inside out.

George Friar came as close to being that muchly belabored type known as a self-made man as anybody I had ever heard of in this latter day. A product of an orphans' home who had been put out to work on a Nebraska farm, he had climbed the ladder all by himself through high school, college, and law school.

His obsession for politics had taken him to Washington, D.C., and, in time, to the inner circles of Republican national politics. In the Eisenhower campaign, he had debated against Adlai Stevenson, among others, and managed to come out with a whole skin. For that, he was named a deputy secretary of interior. When the Democrats took over the White House, Friar had packed his bags and come to Nevada to set up practice as an international lawyer, for which profession it does not seem to matter where one sets up shop.

Despite his imposing appearance—a trim mountain of a man with Ivy League attire, a rich speaking voice, and a presence and man-

· · ·

ner that reminded me of Jack Kennedy—he was never a candidate. He reveled instead in the tactics of politics. But mastery of the art of politics—and we know now that it does not change from New York to Nevada—more often than not robs a man. He begins with a native understanding of human nature and faith in it or else he will not even get off the ground at the outset. But he will lose that faith one day and the void must be filled with something, and that something is inevitably the stuff of cynicism.

I believe George Friar recognized that the process was already well along in himself. That was the real reason he left Washington. And it was why he saw what he did in Leon: the pure beginning before the impure bruising and compromises that were to come. And George Friar needed more than anything else to taste again of a pure beginning and somehow try to keep it that way for as long as possible.

"All right," said Friar after Leon's rebuttal of the argument about Mr. Average American. "I accept the minority report. Now, let's get down to whatever the hell we were talking about before we were so rudely interrupted. By me."

Which was the matter of a film retake for television of Tex Maynard and Leon filing as a team for the offices of governor and lieutenant governor, an act that had already been accomplished without a television camera anywhere in sight. They were rare then.

In this, Tex was in his element. His dejection vanished and the prospect of a camera appearance brought back the exuding radiance.

"Now, this is the way I've got it blocked out," said Tex. "We start the action with a long shot of the capitol dome rising above the trees. Then the camera moves in with a soft music background through the capitol grounds and up the stairs to the big doors. Fade. The next take is of me and Leon handing our filing fees to the secretary of state and shaking hands with him. That's important, because he's a Democrat. Fade. The camera picks up me and Leon walking together

· · ·

through the trees to the entrance on Main Street. Repeat soft music background. We stop at the entrance, smile at the camera, and shake hands. You know, wishing each other luck. Fade out with music."

I had been listening, entranced. "You mean you're not going to say anything to the television audience? No audio? No statement about what you have to offer to the people?"

Tex made a dismissing gesture. "It's not necessary," he said. "We can have the names 'Tex Maynard' and 'Leon Indart' and the slogan printed up in a slide for the end."

It came out before I had time to think. "For Christ's sake!" I said. "Do you know what you're doing? You're shooting a silent."

Tex Maynard's eyes narrowed, his face hardened, and he made a move as if to push his chair back from the table.

We shot the silent.

5

The sky overhead was a deep blue, spreading cottonwoods edged the manicured expanse of lawn, and the summer sun at noonday was blazing hot.

Against our will, we were reposing in various postures around the blue-green waters of Leon's swimming pool. The proper time for this sort of indulgence in Nevada would have been midafternoon, when one could swim and lie about without the danger of sunstroke. But this was the busy political season and we, or rather Tex and Leon, had to take every opportunity to work on different facets of their political image.

In this instance, the facet was suntan.

· · ·

In more polite regions of the country, a political candidate could inherit a tradition of conservative dress and glasses, cultivate a facial pallor, subtly penciled-in lines of exhaustion, and drooping shoulders, and so have his proper political image.

But in the West, and particularly Nevada, the absolute requisites of political image consisted of shoulders thrown back, a long stride reminiscent of John Wayne's, a firm handshake, steady eyes and a ready smile, and a suntan. Not just a hastily acquired and makeshift coloring of the skin, but a deep and convincing bronze. In the cow counties where the voters were legitimately bronzed from a lifetime of work on the open range, a candidate without a suntan was dead. Paradoxically, he would also be dead in Las Vegas, where the badge of position, power, and wealth was a suntan carefully cultivated on the golf course, by the swimming pool, or under sunlamps.

More rules applied in matters of dress. When in the rural counties, the candidate had to shed his usual clothes and substitute Levi's and cowboy boots. And in Las Vegas, he dressed in cool white shirts with personally monogrammed pockets, yellow or red seersucker slacks, and handmade loafers.

Tex did not really have to work on his suntan, since his was perennial. But Leon had spent too much time in his law office, and his tan, at the beginning at least, had been hastily acquired in stolen moments on his tennis court or by his swimming pool. He was tanned, but it was just not good enough for a candidate.

On that day, the searing rays of the noonday sun were not the only thing causing discomfort to Leon. His dark glasses concealed the bloodshot eyes of a king-sized hangover.

"If this is politics, you can have it," he said to the sky. "I'll be a goddamn drunk before this campaign is over."

Tex Maynard inclined his head toward Leon with a gratified smile.

· · ·

His long, muscled frame was reclining on a patio chaise and he looked out of costume in swimming trunks. "You mean you don't like to drink?"

"Sure I like a drink, but I'm not a fanatic about it," said Leon. "Every time I turn around, whether it's a Republican rally or a cow-town saloon, somebody is handing me a drink. I can't take it anymore."

"I'm mighty glad to hear you say that," said Tex approvingly. "I was beginning to think my pardner in politics had a small drinking problem."

"If I didn't before, I'm damned well developing one now."

Tex laughed in silvery tones. "And all the time you were just accommodating the voter."

"Fighting for survival," said Leon. "Every time I try turning down a drink from some seven-foot cowboy, it's at the risk of my life. They act like I've insulted them."

"There's a trick to it, you know," said Tex.

"What? Tell them I'm on the wagon?"

"No," said Tex. "Then they will think you are a temporarily reformed drunk."

"What I've made up my mind to do is tell them I'm a teetotaler," said Leon. "That way, I can salvage the Mormon vote at least."

Tex wagged his head wisely. "Politicians who don't drink make voters uncomfortable. You know the old saying: Never trust a man who won't drink with you."

"Then I'm dead in the water."

"I'm telling you there's a trick to it," said Tex with sly benevolence.

Leon raised his aching head. "Well?"

"The trick is to take one drink and sip it down until it's just above the halfway mark," Tex lectured. "You know, full enough that one look will show your host or a seven-foot cowboy that you don't need

· · ·

another drink. Never sip past that middle mark, though, or you're a target for another drink. Of course, you can't stay in one place very long or people will get the idea you're putting something over on them. You've got to keep moving, be it a political rally or a saloon. But the good candidate should keep moving, anyway, to cover as much ground as possible."

We were, or rather Leon was, beginning to master that tactic pretty well. He would invite a group of friends to his house and practice moving through them with a handshake and a little bit of conversation, and then move on. His friends were instructed to try keeping him in one place on any invented pretense. Leon's task then was to break away from them without antagonizing them or hurting their feelings. It was not an easy chore in any case, since he much preferred one-on-one conversation to brief encounters.

George Friar came through with the best solution of all, an old political trick of a constant escort or front man who would stay glued to the candidate's elbow. When a voter threatened to impede the candidate's progress too long, the escort would simply tug at the candidate's elbow and say, "Fred so-and-so needs to talk to you for a minute," and so extricate him. This stratagem would work better in theory than in practice, because Leon was genuinely interested in people. But the time would come when he would say to the escort, "I'm like the legendary old hooker, Dotty Calhoun. Just point me in the direction you want me to go and tell me what you want me to do." Prostitution having been an accepted institution in Nevada for a century, Leon's response would draw a laugh and a vote more often than not.

The problem of remembering names when one is meeting hundreds of people haunts all political candidates. The tried-and-true ploys imparted by an old political hatchet man for the now-legendary

· · ·

Senator Pat McCarran served Leon well. Before going into a new town or political rally or saloon, McCarran would send an advance man who would make a list of nearly everybody that McCarran would meet. The list would include not only the influential but also the little prospector or laborer who religiously frequented favorite saloons.

In a state with as small a population as Nevada, this tactic was logistically possible. The advance man would brief McCarran thoroughly on names before he came to a town and then stay close to McCarran's side in case he had to say, "Senator, you remember old Bill Muldoon. He's still prospecting for that lost gold mine in the Amargosa desert."

McCarran would clap the old prospector on the shoulder and come up with a cobwebbed old joke about the Amargosa River being so dry that jackrabbits carried canteens when they crossed it. McCarran went the advance man one better by declaring that he was naming Bill Muldoon the admiral of the Amargosa fleet. That declaration of course spread like wildfire through the ranks of miners all over Nevada.

McCarran established early on the legend of being the friend of the little man. Later, he was to solidify the legend with another affair having to do with prospectors. One day in his Washington, D.C., office, an aide handed him a crudely lettered note. It was from a prospector who lived in a shack in some godforsaken canyon. The note read: "Dear Pat. I have broke my chopping arm and cannot get in my winter wood. Your friend. Frank."

McCarran solved old Frank's problem by calling up a financier crony in Reno and ordering him to have a truckload of firewood hauled to Frank so that he could live out the winter. That story was repeated in every saloon in Nevada, except in Las Vegas, where it would not have been understood.

The second tactic Leon borrowed from McCarran in the matter of

· · ·

remembering names was simple but effective. Whenever Leon met a voter for the first time, he would use the voter's name repeatedly. The patter went something like this: "My name is Leon Indart. Good to meet you, Tom. Tom, tell me what you expect from the lieutenant governor's office. Be frank with me, Tom, because I'm going to be your next lieutenant governor and I need to know. Tell me what you think the issues are in this campaign, Tom. Thanks for the advice. I mean that, Tom."

Although Tex Maynard was invaluable in passing on campaigning hints, Leon never did accept one Maynard maxim: Never get pinned down on an issue. Whenever anyone asked Tex where he stood on an issue, he would respond, "Don't worry. I'm on the right side of that one." Then Tex would unleash that dazzling smile. The voter was blinded. Before he could recover, Tex had moved away to another group.

The only time it didn't work was in a mining town where a dirt-caked miner asked Tex where he stood on the Taft-Hartley Labor Act, which happened to be vital to the miners' livelihood. Tex's answer and the dazzling smile were not enough. Before Tex could make his getaway, the miner reached out a muscular arm and a grimy hand and literally pulled Tex back. Leon saved the day by making their position absolutely clear on Taft-Hartley, about which Tex had no understanding whatever.

Leon learned very early, however, that with the exception of the mining towns and Taft-Hartley, national and international issues were of no concern to the rural-county voters. Local issues was the name of the game: protection against overly stringent fish and game regulations; Washington, D.C., sticking its nose into local control of schools; and the federal government fencing off the public domain. One bow-legged old rancher from the Idaho-Utah-Nevada corner summed up local reaction to that: "This used to be open range. Now them govern-

· · ·

ment bastards has got everything parceled out. They wired a spring on the Utah line I always used. It won't stay wired long, I promise you. The law don't help us at all most times, and a Winchester under your leg is the only answer."

There were trying times in the rural counties. At the town of Fighting Hill, the old epithet of "tough town" had not altogether been discarded. The mayor had won his position not by campaign tricks but simply by being the toughest guy in town. He was a man named Casady, built like a chunk of concrete. He told us about his arrival in town.

"Well, I was a fighting man," he said a little sheepishly, "and my reputation had preceded me. I come to town with a saddle and wanted to see if I could get a car or truck of some kind, so I went to this garage. There were two brothers who owned it, and I did my business of trading my saddle for a beat-up old pickup with one of them brothers. It was all gentlemanly. But when business was done, the brother said to me, 'I hear you think you're pretty tough stuff.' What I didn't know was that these two brother garagemen were the town roughnecks. So, I figure out the situation quick and say, 'I'm tough enough to get by.' This one brother says, 'You don't look it to me.' So I take off my coat and say, 'All right, let's get it over with. Take your best shot.' So I whip him. Before it was over, I had to whip his brother, too.' And that was how the people of Fighting Hill started thinking I should be mayor."

Casady was regaling us with this secret of his political career when the swinging doors to the saloon flew open and a working man built almost to Casady's concrete proportions barged through the aperture, walked like a gorilla to the bar, and accosted Leon. "I hear you think you're pretty tough."

Leon bowed his head in weariness, but he was thinking all the while. "All right," he said. "You want to fight it out or drink it out?"

· · ·

The tough look on the laborer's beaten face dissolved into a grin, and he said, "Now, here's a man after my own heart."

Since the earliest days of statehood, politicians running for top offices were expected to ride horseback in Nevada's some one hundred parades for such occasions as Admission Day, the Reno Rodeo, Las Vegas's Helldorado, Fourth of July, and myriad local celebrations. Since nearly every U.S. senator, congressman, governor, and lieutenant governor in Nevada history had sprung from ranching roots, riding in a parade posed no problem.

For Leon, however, it did. Even though he had ranching credentials, "son of a pioneer livestock family," he didn't like horses. If this had become known in the cow counties, it would have been rank heresy. He would not have drawn flies, as the saying goes, in a population where people liked to say, "I learned to ride afore I could walk."

There was a reason, of course, for Leon's fear of horses. When he was twelve years old, a cowpony racehorse of my father's had run away with him. I had stood fascinated as my father's horse circled the block three times, passing me in a blur of sorrel horse and white-faced boy hanging on for dear life. The only reason Leon emerged unscathed was that the horse simply ran himself out to the point where he could barely stand. It took two of us to pry Leon's hands loose from the horn. He slid off the saddle, almost fell on his face, then rallied himself and walked away without a word.

I don't believe Leon had come nearer to a horse than a hundred yards after that escapade. Until, that is, Tex Maynard announced to him they would be riding side by side in the big Reno Rodeo parade. Leon blanched. "You mean ride a horse?"

"What did you think we were going to ride, burros?" asked Tex.

"In front of people?"

· · ·

"That's the point," said Tex. "Showing the people we are true sons of the West."

"Tex, I can't handle it," Leon blurted out.

Tex regarded him with incredulity. "What is your problem this time?"

Even though they were political allies, Leon did not dare to divulge his secret to Tex. Inevitably, the fact that Leon hated horses would leak out to the cow counties and he would henceforth be branded a traitor to the livestock gentry. Scrambling about for an excuse, he managed to seize upon something. "It's that old war wound, Tex," he said with no conviction. "You know I've got a bad back."

Tex waved the excuse aside. "It won't wash, Leon. Everyone knows you play tournament tennis."

"That takes a different set of muscles," said Leon, warming to his fabrication.

Tex chuckled. "The only muscles you'll be using on a horse will be your ass muscles. And if my memory serves me right, you were not shot in the butt."

Knowing that the trap had closed, Leon gave in. In the few days before the Reno Rodeo parade, I strapped a saddle and reins to a hidden fence rail on Leon's grounds and made him practice getting his foot into the stirrup in the old cowboy way—facing the rear of the horse in case it jumped out from under you, pressing the balls of your feet to the stirrup and taking the jolts with your knees—and showed him the proper way to neck-rein instead of pulling at one rein as if he were steering a plow horse. The only thing that was missing was the horse. Leon would not go that far. He was having a hard enough time steeling his mind against the moment of truth at parade time.

When the moment of truth did come, Leon faced up to it. He somehow managed to swing into the saddle without acknowledging

· · ·

to himself that there was a living, breathing horse under it. His face was drawn and pale, but he had fixed a frozen smile upon it. That smile never altered once throughout the parade.

As it turned out, all his courage and all our efforts were in vain. Roy Rogers himself could not have managed to ride as an equal beside the spectacle that was Tex Maynard—silver-mounted saddle on a golden palomino horse that pranced and tossed his silken mane, a red, white, and blue costume tailored and colored so subtly that one had a subliminal impression that he had seen the American flag go by. Riding frozenly beside him on a smaller and aged nag, Leon looked like Sancho Panza riding his burro in the shadow of Don Quixote.

Leon never rode in another parade. He confined himself to perching on the rear seat of a convertible. The word got out that Leon had been wounded in the back in the war. The aftereffects of that had forced him to give up one of his finest pleasures in life, riding horseback across the deserts and over the mountains. The rural-county voters believed it, and in time, so did Leon.

The only total catastrophe had been at the beginning of the campaign. Tex's silent commercial was bad enough, but at least his smile on camera salvaged something out of that debacle. Nothing, however, was salvaged out of the other debacle, which was Tex and Leon's formal announcement of their candidacy.

The credit for that one went to Leon. Truly impressed with the dignity of the offices they were seeking, he had insisted on a formal setting for the announcement. As George Romney did in Carnegie Hall in later years when he declared for president, Leon also rented a hall. He forgot it was not yet political season and nobody was interested in politicians.

The audience consisted of one television news camera, two radio microphones, one bored reporter, and a few drunks who wandered in off the street. The television news camera mercilessly panned the

· · ·

empty rows of seats and the likewise empty galleries, then zeroed in on Tex Maynard and Leon Indart standing at two of the loneliest podiums I have ever seen. All I could remember afterwards was the hollow sound of their voices echoing throughout that chamber of horrors.

I vowed then and there that if Leon's political career managed to survive this election, next time's announcement would be in a crowded corridor leading from his campaign headquarters office. If there were not enough radio or television reporters around, we would simply rent microphones for campaign workers to stuff in front of his face as he politely but insistently elbowed his way through hired bodies, creating that aura of excitement that surrounds "the man on the move."

But all in all, we had done more things right than wrong. At least in Reno and the small counties, Leon Indart was not a total unknown. Now was to come the trial by fire in that chaotic, formless crucible where all Nevada elections were won or lost: Las Vegas.

6

A hundred miles of blazing desert surrounded Las Vegas on all sides, but where we sat by poolside on the Strip it was like a lush tropical island. Far overhead, fronds of palm trees waved gently in the oven-hot but not unpleasant afternoon breeze. Exotic flowers and emerald green grass bordered the winding walkways that led to the azure waters of the swimming pool. The pool was freeform and immense and inviting and absolutely devoid of swimmers.

The palm trees were imported. The flowers were imported. The

· · ·

grass was imported. The water was imported. Even the guests were imported. They lounged in chaises longues at poolside, sipping occasionally at tall, cool drinks and chatting in New York accents that revealed old relationships. The plate glass doors of the hotel-casino swung open almost constantly, letting escape the intoxicating monotones of roulette and craps dealers and the metallic sounds of whirling slot machine reels.

Balding, gray-fringed heads, crepey skin, sagging muscles, comfortable rolls of fat, all burned purple and black by the desert sun. No youth permitted here, except for statuesque blondes with bikinis stretched to the breaking point over flaring hips and overflowing breasts. The time of anorexic figures and small breasts had not yet arrived. No wives permitted here. Only mistresses.

"Everybody in Las Vegas is out to take you, one way or another," one of the reclining figures proclaimed. "And some are more adapt at it than others."

"The word is 'adept,' " said a man called Max.

"That's what I said. 'Adapt.' "

The loudspeaker interrupted incessantly, bringing conversation almost to a halt. "Page for Abie Werner. Page for Moe Shapiro. Page for Samuel Golden. Page for Paddy O'Hara."

"How did that Irish mick get in there?" my companion asked.

"Page for Frank Costello. Page for Lucky Luciano," the loudspeaker interrupted. There was a slight ring of doubt in the loudspeaker voice, as if it knew it was being put on.

"Some wise guy," said my companion, Roger, "ringing in those Sicilians."

Roger's wave embraced the aging men with their young mistresses at poolside. "The raison d'être for Las Vegas, as you can plainly see, is for guys to come here with broads, not their wives," said Roger. "Some of those guys are my friends. We grew up together on New

· · ·

York's East Side. I know their wives from the time we were kids. You got to remember that manners apply here, too. I can say hello to my friend, but *never* to his broad. If my friend wants to introduce me to his broad, that's his business. But don't force the introduction. That's bad taste in Las Vegas."

Roger's spelling out the rules of proper conduct in Las Vegas made sense to me. I remembered a Reno gambler, originally from Detroit, telling me how it was back there. "If a respectable guy came to my gambling joint at night in Detroit I could talk to him. But if I ran into him on the street next day, I didn't even nod my head at him. That was the rule in Detroit in them days. Probably still is," he said.

Roger was lecturing me on how Leon's campaign aides were to act in Las Vegas. Tex Maynard already knew how, having lived there for years. We were all ensconced in the Desert Inn. Wilbur Clark's Desert Inn to be exact. "The name's just for show," Roger said. "Wilbur owns next to nothing in the D.I., actually. He's just the front man with a proper Anglo-Saxon name. It's going to come as a hell of a shock to him when he finds out." Later, when the Kefauver crime committee investigated Las Vegas, Wilbur finally found out. It came as a shock to him, all right. Almost mortal.

The Desert Inn was our fortress, and its real owners were Moe Dalitz and Ruby Kolod. A mile away down the Strip, Governor Dean Cooper and his campaign team occupied another fortress, called the Sands. In an election year when everyone was running for everything, candidates for lesser offices occupied the lesser hotels. The arrangement was very much like castles in Spain, occupied by local monarchs. When candidates got up in the morning, they could look out the windows of the various presidential suites at the enemies' fortresses and contemplate what cunning strategies were being hatched there.

· · ·

My new friend Roger had worked for Moe Dalitz and Ruby Kolod, but he had quit them, so he said, to join Leon's campaign because Leon looked like a comer in politics. The inspiration for the resignation was pure, so Roger said. Perhaps Roger knew the real reason he had joined our campaign, but he wasn't showing, as the saying went in Las Vegas. The truth of the matter was, as we learned later, that Moe and Ruby liked the odds on Tex and had met and talked with Leon and liked what they saw. They ordered Roger to quit his executive job with them and join Leon's campaign for proper instruction of the candidate to Las Vegas's special rules of conduct.

"All the time I worked for Moe and Ruby," Roger droned on, "I never stole from them. I never asked them for a thing. They've bought me two drinks in ten years. I know they're supposed to be syndicate, but they don't play dirty with people who don't play dirty with them. Since I've been with Leon, my wife has become a political widow. I've been putting out fires that that little shit, pardon me, that our *illustrious* governor Dean Cooper has been planting all over Las Vegas. My work keeps me out at night, but that doesn't mean I fool around with the broads. I got a good wife. Cooper and his people can't hit me on that one."

Listening to the sagas of Las Vegas, I was learning far more by way of political involvement than I had ever learned as a United Press correspondent—about the mores of so-called hoodlums in particular. As reporters, we had listened to a lot of rumors and reported them as fact. In that time, a reporter could write practically anything he wanted about hoodlums and have no fear of a lawsuit. The hoodlums shunned the legal limelight like poison. The reporters threw ethical responsibility out the window and wrote as much purple prose as editors would swallow. The stories about Mafia members in Las Vegas had a little credibility, though, and that came via official arrest

· · ·

records in New York, Chicago, Detroit, Miami, and so on. The fact that few of the arrests ended in conviction was seldom reported.

Starting with proven hoodlums such as Bugsy Siegel, the syndicate—as it was called before the word *Mafia* came into style—managed to get legal gambling licenses before state government or the citizenry ever learned the true identity of the casino owners. Even Las Vegans refused to believe they were gangsters. Starting with Siegel's plush Flamingo, the pleasure palaces went up. Every mob family was represented in the "open territory" of Las Vegas by a hotel—Thunderbird, Desert Inn, Sands, Sahara, Riviera, Dunes, Royal Nevada, New Frontier, ad infinitum. Their owners were syndicate stars like Little Moey Sedway, Gus Greenbaum, Charlie Fischetti, Joe Batters, and, my favorite hood name, Jake "Greasy Thumb" Guzick.

It took thousands of people to build the palaces, and thousands more to staff them afterwards. Unemployment was nonexistent, the local economy was booming, and the old guard was making a ton of money.

The old guard staunchly defended the casino owners, describing them as "ideal citizens." The owners gave freely to civic, fraternal, and religious causes, asking only that their contributions never be attributed to them, which of course assured that they would be. All those rumors and stories about their being gangsters were thought to be fabrications. It was a common boast that not one casino owner had even been cited for a traffic violation.

"Well, you know where he got the moniker of 'Bugsy,'" Roger said. He was discoursing on Bugsy Siegel, the first top-line hoodlum to set up shop in Las Vegas. Siegel and Roger had grown up together in New York. As Bugsy prospered, he moved into New York's Waldorf Astoria, which he liked so much he decided to build his own Waldorf in Las Vegas. "It was because he was nuts," Roger went on. "But nobody,

· · ·

not even Lucky Luciano or Frank Costello, ever called him Bugsy to his face. They called him Benny."

Roger was uncertain whether to say what he wanted to say. "Bugsy was a psychopathic murderer. He had gotten away with so many gangland executions that he felt murder was legal, as long as it was done by him. He was the vainest man I ever knew." Roger shook his head in wonder. "He dressed like a million dollars. Tailor-made suits, monogrammed shirts, handmade shoes, you name it. When he opened the Flamingo he even made the janitors wear tuxedos. He couldn't stand the slightest blemish on his face. He would run to the doctor if he had a hickey. So it was very disturbing to me to see that newspaper picture of him sprawled back on a sofa with two big bullet holes in his face, and blood all over."

Roger sighed as if he were bearing the burden of the world on his shoulders. Then he brightened. "Well, I still say he was the founder of Las Vegas. They should build him a statue and put a historical marker in front of the Flamingo hotel."

In the beginning, at least, the casino owners shied away from political involvement like poison. Back home in Detroit or Chicago, campaign contributions were never made by check, but in cold cash. The "big bills" were slipped to the candidate by hand in utter secrecy. Nobody ever knew about them except the giver and the taker. Back home, the gamblers could pick the candidate of their choice with the unspoken assurance that they would be left alone to follow their illegal pursuits without being hassled by the authorities.

But out here in the unsophisticated frontier of Nevada there were no secrets, and never had been, especially when it came to political campaign money. The news would be all over the state in a week. Here in the West, it had to be out in the open and the syndicate didn't know how to handle that. The syndicate was confused and so were Nevada politicians.

· · ·

In the early days of statehood, campaigns were bankrolled by Virginia City mining barons and, later, livestock barons. For a few decades, livestock barons changed their minds about backing candidates who turned out to be disloyal to the range. The barons bankrolled themselves into the governorship and the U.S. Senate. In our time, politicians relied on backing from successful businessmen, utilities, banking, and ranching. The silver and gold veins had petered out, and mining was not to be relied upon any longer.

Now, suddenly, the big money was in gambling, but politicians were wary about taking a penny of it. Gambling wasn't legalized in the true sense of the word. In the lawbooks it was "a tolerated nuisance" and had come into being for the state's economic survival when mining withered and died. It was neither a nostalgic frontier vestige nor proof of the "live and let live" liberality of Nevadans. The truth of the matter was that back of the main-street gambling joints, Nevada was more conservative than New England. Hence the wariness of politicians and the syndicate alike about a public marriage.

I was certain the syndicate would not stay confused long. Just a while back, underworld executions had been the order of the day and were on my beat as a reporter. The hoodlums had turned Las Vegas into a shooting gallery by bringing their old feuds with them to Nevada. That and greed, each Sicilian and Jewish *family* trying to make as much as possible in this blessed environment of open gambling. When the FBI and congressional investigating committees got into the act, the gangland executions stopped overnight.

Top syndicate leaders in the East, like Lucky Luciano and Frank Costello, could see that their Nevada confreres were killing the goose that laid the golden egg. A meeting of national and local syndicate bosses was held, and what was whimsically called a Purity Code was adopted. Nobody was to be killed within the borders of Nevada. A marked man could get on an airplane in Las Vegas in total safety.

· · ·

When the plane landed in Chicago or Miami, the code was in effect no longer. The marked man knew he was fair game. How he coped with that was his worry.

Along the Strip, everyone smiled at each other to show they were one big happy family. When a new hotel-casino opened, it was considered good manners for all the owners on the Strip to go to the opening and lose "a few big bills." Five thousand dollars was an average offering.

The heat died down and the casino owners went back to making their ton of money. The syndicate knew that the FBI was still watching them, however. They had a fair hunch the FBI suspected that only half of casino winnings was being kept in Nevada. The other half was being transported in black handbags to points east and south. Not a single courier had as yet been arrested, because no laws had really been broken. The money was laundered and unmarked and it was no crime, federal or local, to fill one's handbags with hundred- and thousand-dollar bills and take a plane trip to visit a poverty-stricken aunt in New York.

The FBI, which knew, and state government, which did not know, had not solved this problem of "skimming" off the top. Within Nevada, in fact, *skimming* was a vague word and practice that only a few people in the know had heard of. The citizenry had not the least inkling of how they were being cheated out of taxes on undeclared gambling winnings. The syndicate did not like the FBI's snooping and knew that sooner or later, the FBI would spring the trap on skimming and so educate the citizenry of Nevada and possibly antagonize them so much they might force gambling licenses to be revoked. This was the main reason the syndicate wanted politicians on the home front to turn their heads when the money was being counted.

"One big piece of advice I give to you to give to Leon," said Roger in affirmation of what I had been thinking. "Tell him to abstain from

· · ·

riding a white charger into Las Vegas. The Strip hates knights worse than they hate wardens."

I sensed at this poolside interlude with Roger that the smart money on the Strip was on Tex and Leon. They had, I think, already tagged Leon as the one who would go further in politics than his running mate. But Leon was not to be taken for granted, it seemed. He was not now, nor would he be later, a patsy. The syndicate were practiced people-readers who rarely made a mistake in judgment. Roger transmitted the syndicate's reading with a single story.

"So Tony Dragna . . . he's one of the old-time hoods out of New York," Roger related, "comes up to me and says he would throw his weight and his money to Leon Indart but by God he was going to get a gambling license out of him when he got to be governor. Then he tells me I had better intercede with Leon when the time comes. So I tell Tony Dragna, 'No.' And he says, 'You know, there are ways to take care of you and a governor, too.' And I said to him, 'If Leon Indart gets to be governor one day, and you go into his office with a threat like that, he will throw you out personally.'"

Roger shook his head with weary impatience. "These old-time hoods," he sighed. "The only language they understand is 'buy or kill, buy 'em or kill 'em.'"

Our bedrooms were clustered around a circular parlor in the presidential suite on the top floor of the Desert Inn, compliments of the management. A round table of outsized dimensions had been moved into the center of the parlor.

There was a campaign headquarters on Fremont Street in downtown Las Vegas. This was where Republican women volunteers held a telephone bank to answer questions about where Tex Maynard and Leon Indart stood on issues, talked to drop-ins from the street, and mailed out campaign propaganda.

· · ·

In actuality, the headquarters was the suite we occupied and the immense round table was where the main business of the campaign was conducted. It was here that strategy was worked out, Governor Dean Cooper's record was scrutinized and attacked, Cooper's countercharges were answered, public-opinion polls were analyzed, radio and newspaper ads were approved, political spots were worked out for that new medium—television—and expenses were weighed against the campaign war chest. It was also the place where I was to punch out campaign propaganda disguised as news releases. I could not concentrate with all the activity at the round table, so I had moved my portable typewriter into the privacy of my bedroom.

I had worked out the body of my story, but could not settle on the right wording for the lead. I decided to seek help from the round table.

"Governor Dean Cooper's fiscal policies are leading the state to . . ." I read aloud. "There I'm stuck. '. . . to the brink of bankruptcy.' No, that's too strong. '. . . to the verge of financial chaos.' No, that's too fancy. Give me a hand, you guys."

George Friar lifted his massive head from his strategy sheets, lowered his Ben Franklin glasses further down his nose, and dictated, "Governor Dean Cooper's fiscal policies are leading Nevada . . ." he paused for dramatic effect, ". . . to a state of Godless Communism."

"Don't, George," I moaned. "I'm fighting a *Herald* deadline. I need a lead quick."

". . . to the brink of insolvency," said Peck Poulson, our political poll expert and the newest addition to our team. He was a slight man who pursed and unpursed his lips and blinked his eyes rapidly when he spoke. But there were no quirks in his mental makeup. He had a mind as cold and unemotional as a computer. An array of pages torn from a legal-sized pad and covered with figures was spread around him at the table like a fan.

· · ·

My brother Leon's entrance interrupted the exchange at the table. He stripped off his summer-weight sport coat and loosened his narrow necktie, both considered proper afternoon wear in Las Vegas. Yellow cashmere sweaters and purple slacks had just begun to appear, but they were not for candidates for public office.

Leon was tired but in good humor. "I must have shaken a thousand hands today," he said, and added as if he had just scored a coup, "and I just had a drink with the nicest man. He wants to help us. He's one of the owners of the Tropicana. He's with us. People and money."

My brother Gene, who was stretched out nearly asleep on a long sofa, said, "How much money? Did he name a figure?"

Leon's expression became irritated. "We didn't talk money. I don't want to talk money until I've got some things straight in my head."

"What about votes?" said Peck, the poll taker. "Tropicana. Let's see. That's five hundred employees right there, if he passes the word." Peck paused and said cynically. "And if they can read the ballot."

"What's his name?" George Friar asked quizzically.

"A Mr. Alderman," said Leon.

"Would his first name be Willie?" I asked from the doorway to my bedroom.

"Yeah, that's it," said Leon. "Willie Alderman. Why? You know him?"

"No, I don't know him. I don't think I want to know him."

Leon looked at me wordlessly, as if not wanting to hear what was coming.

"Willie Alderman, in the former circles he traveled in," I said, "was better known as 'Icepick Willie.' He got the name in New York's East Side, where he was a hit man for the mob. He had his own particular way of making a hit. It was really cute. He would invite the hit to a drink at a bar, preferably unpeopled. When his hit had had a few, Willie would drape his left hand over the guy's shoulder, in good

· · ·

51

fellowship. Then, holding the hit firmly with his left hand, he would ram an icepick into his ear with his right hand. Right into the brain. No blood. No nothing. Then he would tell his friend the bartender that his companion was drunk and "help" him out of the joint. The bartender didn't say a word, of course."

"You mean he's a gangster?" said Leon.

"Hoodlum," I said. "Gangster is out of style."

"Bullshit," said Leon with a withering look at me. "That's newspaper bullshit." He crossed the parlor to his bedroom, slamming the door behind him.

"My God," I said. "He doesn't believe there are such things as hoodlums outside the movies." George Friar and Peck Poulson were looking at the table, intent on their strategies and statistics. "Well," I said to them, "let him find out the hard way."

7

It took one more incident to convince Leon that there were such things as hoodlums in Nevada, and that Las Vegas had more than its proper share of them.

He did not mention his new relationship with that "nice man" Willie Alderman for some time. Knowing Leon, I knew he was sorting fact from fiction in his mind, trying to convince himself that he had not made a grievous error in judging people.

The conclusions he came to surfaced one day when we had gathed for a strategy meeting at the big round table in our hotel suite. "I've been thinking things over," he said, "and I don't see the justification for tagging Las Vegas casino owners as gangsters or hood-

· · ·

lums or whatever it is they're supposed to be called. They oper-
ated gambling joints in Detroit and Miami, wherever, and because
gambling was illegal there, they were called hoodlums. By the same
token, we never called our homegrown variety of gamblers 'hoodlums,' because gambling was legally permitted here in Nevada. That
makes for a contradiction in my book. Why should we call Moe
Dalitz and Ruby Kolod and, yes, Willie Alderman hoodlums any
more than we call Harold Smith a hoodlum because he runs Harolds
Club?"

Leon paused for a long moment before he tried another "conclusion" out on us. "The same goes for the girls," he said hesitantly.
"Prostitution is legal in Nevada. We don't point fingers at our mad-
ams in Reno and the boonies, so why should we single out the joints
here for running girls? That's hypocrisy if I've ever seen it. If Moe or
Ruby or Alderman were peddling dope, then I'd go along with you
and have nothing to do with them. But they're not, so I'm going to
accept their support. I'm not talking money now. That we'll have to
judge when the time comes, and I hope it never does. For now, we're
keeping it to people and votes. If Moe and Ruby take us around to
meet their pit bosses and dealers, cocktail girls and waitresses, I'll
do it. They're voters just as much as the Daughters of the American
Revolution."

I winced. "I wouldn't make that comparison publicly if I were you."

There was an audible sigh of relief from our poll taker, Peck Poulson. For the first time that I could remember, he did not purse his
mouth or twitch his eyebrows. "For a while there," said Peck, "I was
afraid you were going to ice the casino workers, too. In which case,
our campaign would be dead in the water and I would walk right out
of this room."

Tex Maynard had joined us for the strategy session. "You're making
sense now, pardner," he said to Leon. "These eastern hombres who

· · ·

own the joints are no different than we are. We got the breaks being born West, and they didn't. What did my good friend Jimmy Durante tell us the other night? If he didn't have a talent for vaudeville, he could have ended up in the hoosegow with the rest of his street compañeros."

Leon broke in, using his pontificating voice this time. "Sometimes I've thought that if our immigrant dad had decided to set roots down in New York instead of going west to be a sheepherder, we . . ." He looked squarely at me and said, ". . . would have been born in a ghetto and ended up in jail."

Knowing the wilderness creature that was our father, I considered Leon's words foolishness and was about to say so. But everyone at the round table was nodding his head sagely as if he had heard the gospel according to Saint Luke. There wasn't a word I could say then about Moe and Ruby and the syndicate and what Roger had told me about Tony Dragna's "buy 'em or kill 'em," so I seethed in silence and bided my time. As it turned out, I did not have to wait long.

Charlie Baron with his crooked half smile, slicked-down black hair, and black eyes always reminded me of dancer Gene Kelly. The only problem was that Charlie Baron's black eyes were neither Irish nor artistic. They were glittering hard and they never missed a thing.

Charlie Baron was a dapper dresser with suits so expertly tailored to his slender frame that nobody would suspect he was carrying a gun. But he was, and I could attest to that. Charlie Baron was a *greeter* instead of a partner at the Desert Inn only because he couldn't get on the gambling license. He had come to Nevada just after the licensing gates began to close up. Hoodlums like Bugsy Siegel, Moe and Ruby, and Icepick Willie Alderman had managed to come in under the wire, before the state began asking probing questions about backgrounds of prospective casino owners.

Like Bugsy, Charlie Baron had been a mob hit man. Unlike Bugsy, Charlie made the mistake of almost being convicted. The publicity about his trial had gotten a lot of national news because it dealt with a Chicago mob killing, which automatically called up memories of the celebrated Al Capone era.

In a curious sort of way, Charlie had been discriminated against. When Leon took up campaign residency at the Desert Inn, he met Charlie Baron and heard his story. Leon was sympathetic and promised Charlie he would look into his dilemma after the election. Never having been so considerately treated by a political candidate before, Charlie Baron then and there became Leon's friend for life. There wasn't anything in the world he wouldn't do for Leon Indart, he told me over drinks at a private cocktail table in the Desert Inn lounge.

Charlie Baron leaned forward to tell me this. Since the table was small and circular, he also had to lean sideways. A small, flat, James Bond–style automatic tumbled out of its shoulder holster and landed soundlessly on the carpet. Charlie was not a bit embarrassed. He leaned over to pick up his automatic, grinned, and said, "Pardon me. My gun." He put it back in its holster and went right on with his conversation.

There were five of us for dinner that night in the Desert Inn's gourmet dining room—Tex Maynard and Leon, George Friar and I, and Charlie Baron. Tex was attired in fairly formal fashion to match the elegance of the dining room—a silk shirt with sterling silver tabs, a braided leather string tie with silver tips and a massive turquoise and silver cameo, a fawn suede leather coat with a western yoke, and a pair of hand-tooled lizard cowboy boots with silver toes. Everyone in the dining room seemed to know him. At least, they smiled

· · ·

and waved and called out his name. Tex smiled gently and dazzlingly back, nodding his head at each hello. I would have sworn his sandy hair had been dusted with silver specks, but upon closer inspection, the glinting lights were only reflections from his costume.

As always, Charlie Baron was host and an informed gastronomic guide. Escargot in bubbling garlic butter, frog legs or flaming steak Diane, white and red French wines, and palate-cleansing sherbet made their stately way onto the table.

Jackie Fields stopped by to say hello in a hoarse voice. Tex Maynard greeted him with, "Howdy, Champ." Jackie smiled a crooked smile and shook hands all around, but gingerly, as if his hands were paining him. He reminded Tex and Leon of their promise for a seat on the state athletic commission that governed big-time prizefights in Las Vegas.

Jackie Fields's face was a mess. His nose was spread all over his face, he had cauliflower ears, his brows were crisscrossed with fight scars, and he had a glass eye. When Jackie moved away, Charlie Baron shook his head sadly. "Before Jackie got into the fight game," he said, "he was the best-looking boy in Chicago. He was a real Adonis." Charlie's eyes brightened, "Lord, how he could fight."

So fighting had been Jackie's passport off the streets and out of jail, I had to tell myself. Jimmy Durante was a born entertainer and Jackie Fields was a good fighter. But not good enough. A top contender, he seemed always to fall short of being champ.

Like Charlie Baron, Jackie Fields was a greeter at the Desert Inn. But Jackie had no aspiration for a gambling license and a piece of the action. All he wanted was a spot on the athletic commission. Jackie Fields wanted respect more than he wanted money.

In deference to the dinner, conversation was small talk until dessert was done and espresso and French cognac were being savored. Leon

· · ·

had seemed preoccupied during dinner and Tex Maynard's practiced eye had not let it go unnoticed. "Something chewing on you, pardner?" he said.

Leon sighed. "Chewing is right," he said. "A piece out of my hide every day. Romaine just won't let go with that damned column of his."

Charlie Baron had fallen silent. The flashing smile had given way to an expression I hadn't seen before.

Hank Romaine was the publisher of a scrappy newspaper that as a wire-service reporter I had taken a liking to. I liked Hank Romaine, too. He looked a little like Jack Dempsey, whom Leon and I as kids had often seen with our father when Dempsey was fighting or promoting big-time fights in Reno. I made the mistake of telling Romaine that once, and he had repeated the observation ad nauseam in his column.

But the main reason I had taken a shine to Romaine was that he had figured prominently in the Arms to Israel movement. On one voyage to Israel, the old wreck of a cargo ship he had managed to rent had run into a storm. Overloaded with guns and ammunition, it had begun to sink and the captain was prepared to abandon ship. The captain finished that voyage with Hank Romaine's pistol at his head. Romaine's detractors in Las Vegas scoffed at the story, claiming it had been concocted. But the fact remained that Hank was the only man in American history ever to be convicted of breaking international law. He was convicted, but never went to jail. All that happened was that he lost his voting rights. His detractors called him an ex-con and said the only reason he shipped arms to Israel was that the Israelis had made a better offer than the Arabs.

The rival newspaper couldn't go that far, but it could with impunity remind its readers that Hank Romaine had come to Las Vegas with Bugsy Siegel and worked for him as a flack. Certainly, Romaine had

· · ·

worked for Siegel, but he claimed he was just an unemployed news-paperman trying to earn enough money to stay alive. I never did find out what the real story was.

"What's Romaine saying about my *friend?*" Charlie Baron asked George Friar in a husky whisper.

"That he doesn't deserve to be lieutenant governor," said George Friar. "He's too young and dumb."

"He said *that?*" asked Charlie Baron.

Tex's drawl was a chuckle this time. "Didn't I tell you why Romaine's shooting at you?" he asked Leon.

Leon reacted as if he had absorbed too many surprises already in Las Vegas. "Go on," he said to Tex.

"Because he wanted me to choose him as my running mate," Tex Maynard said triumphantly. "It's just sour grapes, pardner."

"Well, that answers that," said Leon. "But knowing the motive isn't going to stop him from committing the deed. He's got me targeted and I don't like it. People believe the guy."

"Is he worrying you that much?" asked Charlie Baron.

Leon nodded. "He is worrying me that much."

Charlie Baron's black eyes brightened to a glitter and his flashing smile returned. "Don't worry, Governor," he said, using the special name he had for Leon. "Don't trouble yourself about it one more minute."

Leon regarded Charlie Baron with justified apprehension. "Why?"

"Because I'm going to disappear him," smiled Charlie.

"You're going to *what?*" Leon said in a tight whisper.

Charlie made a dismissing gesture with his hand. "You know," he said. "Disappear him." Charlie groped for an explanation and settled on, "Make him not be."

Leon finally understood what Charlie Baron was saying. He held up his hands palms forward between him and Charlie Baron. "No,

· · ·

that's all right, Charlie," he said shakenly. "Don't do that. I'll handle him myself."

Charlie was downcast. "Well, all right," he said. "If you say so." His brows narrowed. "But if you need a piece, just ask me which kind. I probably have one."

He probably did. George Friar and I had been to see Charlie once in his apartment. The place was an arsenal. There must have been at least five hideaway guns in every room, behind and under couch cushions, in desk drawers, in the Frigidaire. I even found one in a hollow book I had pulled down and replaced hurriedly in the bookcase.

Tex Maynard was grinning broadly at Leon, and George Friar was choking on his cognac. I neither said anything nor looked at Leon.

Hey, good-lookin'. You're lookin' down. A lay is the thing to change your luck. Gambling or politics.

I promise I'll cover you up when I leave. Wouldn't want you to catch a cold and my vote at the same time.

You're not going to get by working this casino once. This is a twenty-four-hour joint, so that makes it three shifts of shaking hands per day. That's what most politicians think, anyway. For a seat on your gambling commission, I'm going to let you in on a secret.

Actually, there's two more shifts inside a shift. You can recognize the locals by the fact they only gamble one buck a pop. Conservative you might

· · ·

say, trying to make money but don't know how to ride their luck. They hang around for a couple hours and go home.

Then comes the tourists' shift. They try a bet for kicks, then another and another, until they are over their heads. Most of the time they go under, get panicky, and start losing their heads and their money badly and quickly. Don't waste your time on them. They don't vote.

Last come the high rollers. They wait until the others are gone, late at night, so they don't have to rub shoulders with the cheapies. They always know how many aces and faces have passed. And they know their luck. They're sharp. If they start to win too big, the pit bosses bring in the heavy artillery: the deuce dealers—the guys who jabber and talk while they're cheating. When they show their act, the high rollers hang it up. That is the time to hit them for a handshake. A vote maybe and a few big ones for the campaign pot for sure.

I'll tell you how girls get into this business. First, you win a beauty contest in your hick town in Kansas and you get stars in your head. Then you go to Hollywood to become a star and find out the place is jammed with girls who won beauty contests in some other hick towns, and one out of a thousand can even get a part in some Grade Z flick. Then you hear Las Vegas which is next door in Nevada has opened the door to women dealers. So you put out your last savings your folks sent you from Kansas, and you get on a bus and go to Las Vegas. You learn to deal but you're not even good enough to handle cards quick and right. You lose your job and there's no money left. You're having a drink to ease the pain and some bartender tells you, "It doesn't have to be, you know. You got good looks and the body to go with it. Just charge some snakey new clothes and come on down to the Strip one night." So you say to yourself, "What the hell. Why not?" The first time is the hardest of all, but then the money starts rolling in, and pretty soon you're not only out of debt but you've got expensive clothes and a neat car. Then it starts getting to you, unless you're a nymph by nature,

· · ·

which most of them are. It is rotten, utterly. Your score goes away feeling macho, and all you get out of it is another nail in your coffin. You can't go back home again, because sure as hell you are going to run into someone you saw in action. So you become a Las Vegas hooker for good. I don't even want to think what happens after that. It is rotten, utterly.

I know now we were always looking for something . . . and that something was love. It wasn't for the money alone. We even believed we would find love. But it always turned out to be a sordid experience. You wake up in the morning knowing you haven't found it, found the love you were looking for. With a man, making love is more of a physical thing than anything else. With a woman, it has to be more. But it's never there. It's a fruitless quest, and yet you keep hoping and looking. The man goes away satisfied and proud of himself, or ashamed of himself if he's made a woman do something he wouldn't ask his wife to do for him at home. You have to make love out of love, or else it's a terrible thing. I've seen the other side of the mountain, the other side of many mountains. The rainbow is never there.

This is the way it went for Leon. From morning to night and then half the night. Shaking hands until his fingers swelled and had to be soaked in salt water. Making small talk until his voice gave out and had to be brought back with sprays. Three hotel-casino shifts a day and then some on the Strip, and half a dozen casinos along Glitter Gulch in downtown Las Vegas where neon went to die.

Leon met them all. Hard-eyed dealers and see-everything pit bosses surrounded by craps tables, roulette wheels, and twenty-one tables. Security bruisers who watched for the pit boss's head gesture and thought nothing of escorting a crossroader—a cheater—into a soundproofed room and smashing his fingers to a pulp with hammer blows on a chopping block so that he would thereafter have trouble

· · ·

handling a knife and fork much less performing sleights of hand. Jaded or about-to-be-jaded cocktail waitresses with long legs "up to here," who spent their day "eight hours on their feet and four hours on their back" by order of the boss. The end-of-day shift and dusty laborers with hard hands at the gates to magnesium plants on the outskirts of Las Vegas. Engineers with preoccupied expressions and clean white coveralls keeping watch on the turbines far below that impossible wedge of concrete and steel and a million tons of water that was Hoover Dam. Sunburned farmers with clean-smelling earth staining their hands, working in the little Mormon farms outside Las Vegas.

Confronted with this confusing array of voters, the candidate wondered if he had lost his mind in trying his hand at politics, or if his ambition were up to the challenge. One way or another, he learned a lot. A political campaign is the surest way to learn human nature. Before it was all over, Leon could judge for himself who would vote for him and who was against him. He said, "If I lose this campaign, I'll be the best damned lawyer in this state. Neither judge nor jury will ever kid me again."

Las Vegas was a neophyte politician's nightmare because there seemed to be no uniformity about the place. Unlike in the rest of the Nevada towns, which usually had a singular character to them— such as mining, livestock, or railroad—a solitary political pitch and posture didn't work for Las Vegas. There were too many diverse voting blocs in the city. But if one took the time to dig through several layers of earth and demographics, he could find out what Las Vegas was all about and choose which pitch would work with which group.

First, back about two centuries ago, there had been the Indians— pueblo-building Anasazi. They had vanished into mystery. Anthropologists cared, but as far as the politicians went, nobody knew for

· · ·

sure what happened to them, or gave a damn, because vanished Indians don't vote.

Then came the Spanish explorers, who rested between desert crossings at the springs and fed their horses in the meadows for which Las Vegas was named, and then moved on in their fruitless quest for those fabled cities of gold they called Cíbola.

Then came the Mormons, the ever-colonizing Mormons sent out a century ago from Salt Lake City by Brigham Young. The Mormons didn't have a habit of vanishing, except for a while when Brigham Young called them home at the time he declared war on the United States, and they still don't. They put down roots along the banks of muddy little rivers, dug for wells, planted crops, built neat and spartan houses out of adobe or wood, actually made polygamy work in a one-husband-and-three-wives household, practiced abstinence from alcohol, coffee, and tobacco with reasonable success, and discouraged westbound wagon trains from settling by turning loose their sharpshooting Mormon mounted battalion.

But neither their inhospitality nor their marksmen could stop the inevitable iron horse and its contingent of roughnecks and Chinese coolies. Las Vegas became better known as a Union Pacific railroad stop than a Mormon colony. Under the stern scrutiny of Mormon elders, the roughnecks had their choice of correcting their ways or getting hung. For the most part, they chose the former course. Their progeny formed a voting bloc that a pro-labor stance appealed to. The quiet Chinese, who had invented patience, simply outwaited the Mormons and, with their laundries and restaurants, made peaceful coexistence. The roughnecks did not make a unified voting bloc and the Chinese coolies didn't vote.

At first, neither did the Mormons. When Nevada became a territory and then a state, the Mormons' allegiance was still with Brigham

Young and the church. But when the Mormons did decide to have a voice in state elections, they were a cohesive force to be reckoned with. A candidate had better be a Mormon or have morals to match theirs or he would never see a Mormon X on a ballot.

The first really big thing that happened to Las Vegas was the decision to build Boulder Dam. Nearly a thousand hungry Depression workers came from all parts of the United States to the dam site, willing to do any kind of work, even clinging to the nearly sheer walls that rose from the Colorado River. When the dam was completed, most of the workers stayed in Las Vegas and its surrounding galaxy of small communities. They opened up little stores or became saddlebag lawyers, car dealers, and even bankers—and had a monopoly on that. Poor no longer, they backed candidates who were anti soak-the-rich in political posture.

The building of Boulder Dam, later renamed Hoover Dam, brought the first blacks to Nevada. They came from the economically busted East and South, working at anything to make a buck. They segregated themselves into what was to be called Westside Las Vegas, put down their own roots, and registered Democrat. The second wave of blacks came when the next big boom hit—Bugsy Siegel, his successors, and a dozen hotel-casino pleasure palaces. The blacks worked as kitchen helpers, janitors, and groundskeepers. They rented rooms and apartments in Westside and in time built their own houses and registered Democrat. The political axiom then and for a long time afterwards was that a Red Chinese fighter pilot could get more votes in Westside than a Republican. A candidate needed only one political pitch on the Westside: Run Democrat.

Another wave of humanity came to Las Vegas with the hotel-casino boom. They held positions that needed expert training and attitude. Their precise and proven loyalty could not be found in Nevada, so

· · ·

the hoodlums brought them along from their casinos and gambling joints in the East and South, mainly Detroit and Miami. They were the dealers, pit bosses, and security people. The dealers seemed all to look alike, unblinking little men with deft and delicate fingers. They taught locals the tricks of the trade in dealing cards, spinning roulette wheels, and handling dice. At first all of them were men, but after a while the doors were opened to women dealers, who were probably more adept pupils than their male counterparts. The first pit bosses were imported, too. They also resembled each other, with ever watchful eyes set in poker faces. The security men bore a certain similarity also. Where they had come from, they had been brawny bouncers in loose-fitting suits. Now they wore uniforms, but that did not conceal their street-schooled brutality.

Almost to a woman, the cocktail waitresses and freelance hookers came from Los Angeles. Pretty girls with corn-silk hair and blue eyes who had been high school prom queen in some little town in Texas or the Midwest, tawny-skinned Mexican maidens from the Southwest and Mexico, saucy French creoles from New Orleans—all had gone to Hollywood to become movie stars. When they learned that at least a little acting talent was also necessary, along with good looks and shapely figures, they tried the worn-out old way of trying to screw themselves to stardom. They couldn't go home as failures, so they became streetwalkers. When they heard about the money that working girls were making in Las Vegas, they moved almost en masse to Nevada to freelance along the Strip or Glitter Gulch downtown. The law didn't bother them because prostitution was, of all things, legal in Nevada. The girls had found their true home. For the time being, anyway.

The entire contingent of dealers, pit bosses, and cocktail waitresses wanted only two things from their political candidates: Keep gambling and prostitution legal, and leave me alone. I don't care whether you're Democrat or Republican, as long as the management likes you.

Blazing August heat. Banners and bunting. Football goal posts wrapped in red, white, and blue. Papier-mâché elephants. Brass bands tuning up. Blue and gray crossed belts. A fifty-foot-high American flag. Hot dogs and beer. Republican fat cats at a thousand dollars a pop for the war chest. Party workers with little hand-held American flags. Newspaper cameras lined up like artillery pieces on the wooden platform. The announcer exhorting the crowd.

Tex Maynard leading Leon Indart through the crowd. Tex seeming to know everyone there by his or her first name.

A deafening clap of applause when Tex Maynard mounts the platform in his cowboy boots and takes the microphone. Tex's handsome, chiseled face and his rich, slow drawl, mixing Republican clichés with western humor. Another burst of applause when Tex waves good-bye and walks off the platform.

A spattering of applause when Leon Indart is introduced. Whispered questions that carry. *What's his name? Where's he from? Carson City? The capital? Never heard of it.*

Thank God for Tex. Without him, the Republicans couldn't win an election for dogcatcher. Without him, Leon wouldn't have a chance.

And then, three days later, when Tex was leaving his mistress's apartment, and Leon, five hundred miles away, was sitting on his heels staring at the flames from our father's cookfire high in the Sierra, Tex Maynard dropped dead.

· · ·

9

At ten thousand feet, on the peak of a mountain, the wind can take the air out of your mouth so completely that you cannot breathe. Every few minutes, we had to duck down into the narrow cleft behind the rock barrier to fill our lungs. Even if we had wanted to say anything, we could not have made ourselves understood over the roaring of the wind. That wind was blowing our minds and our bodies clear of casino smoke and perfumed scents and the insincere accents of politics.

Leon and I and our father stood side by side, looking out upon the descending slopes and ravines of evergreen forests and manzanita brush, and beyond that to a few hundred miles of desert mountains and flatlands covered with sagebrush and studded by round clumps of piñon pine. Off to the north, the Truckee River wound down from the Sierra through the cottonwoods and elms and stately buildings that made up Reno. Directly below us, reduced to miniature by distance, the white capitol dome protruded through the trees that covered Carson City like a canopy, as though reminding us of work yet to be done.

With the wind tearing at his thick white mane of hair, our father resembled an angry patriarch with a cragged face and streaming locks when he turned toward us. He had unslung from his shoulder the canvas bag that contained our lunch and held it out to us in a wordless gesture. We nodded wordlessly back and hunkered down on our haunches in the hollow behind the rock barrier.

The fare for lunch had never changed since we were kids helping our father with his bands of sheep in these very same mountains.

. . .

Bread and cheese and wine. *Ogi eta gazna eta arnua.* It was one of the few phrases left to us from our childhood Basque. The rest we had left behind when we went to school.

My father reached into the pocket of his Levi's jeans and came up with the yellow, bone-handled knife he had carried all his days in America. With his work-hardened hands, fingers twisted and scarred by ropes and wild horses, he opened the knife to expose the long thin blade, sharp as a razor. He had used the knife for everything from punching holes in leather straps to castrating lambs. He used it now to cut off chunks of bread from the round sourdough loaf and thick slices of the Monterey jack cheese that emerged from the canvas bag. He handed around the bread and cheese, and then set down between us the goatskin wine gourd we called a *chahakoa* in Basque. In between mouthfuls of sourdough bread and cheese, we could reach for the *chahakoa,* raise it above our heads and squeeze jets of red wine into our mouths in the old way. It occurred to me that eating lunch was something like a ritual, performed to remind us of what we had come from.

The sheep were gone now, and we seldom came to the sheepcamp located in a big hollow of ground far below. Our father sometimes came alone, however, to chop up lightning-blasted trees for winter wood for the whole family and occasionally to fish for little trout in the creeks fed by springs and still-melting snowpacks, but mostly to wander his old rangeland and see what the winter had done to the earth and the trees and plants now left ungrazed. He knew every rock on the mountain.

The day before, our father and Leon and I had made the ascent from the main highway to the high camp, a dozen miles of steep and tortuous dirt road, to the reassuring whine of compound gear in my father's old pickup. We had penetrated the forests of tall trees and the

· · ·

groves of aspen whose ten thousand leaves danced and trembled in the slightest breeze like a multitude of fairies.

From the beginning, the main sheepcamp had been situated in the same hollow of ground. It was a huge hollow that served as bed ground for a band of a thousand or more sheep. The sheep would be trailed slowly to the hollow each day at dusk, with even the lambs, rambunctious at daybreak, dragging their feet after the day's feeding. In these mountains, a ewe had to travel far to fill her stomach with grass and browse. It was not like the green mountains of perpetual grass in my father's homeland in the Basque Pyrenees between France and Spain.

My father had always pitched his tepee tent at the lowest edge of the hollow, so that he could look out even in the moonlight to see if a bunch of sheep led by an errant black ewe had wandered away, or to hear an attack by a nocturnal coyote or a mountain lion. Then it was time for sheepdogs, pretty much wild themselves, and the crash of a carbine reaching out toward coyote or cat, usually with no luck.

The bedrolls had been tumbled into the back of the pickup, held in by scarred wooden stock racks. Sleeping bags had not yet come to mountain dwellers. Our bedrolls were still made up of woolen blankets laid and cinched into envelopes of heavy canvas that could keep out rain and snow.

Always before dusk fell and suppertime came, we were under strict orders to make our beds ready. This meant chopping off great armloads of pine and fir boughs and laying them down in our sleeping spots with the chopped ends pointing out and the soft ends pointing inward, so that one would awaken at dawn with the scent of newly cut pine suffusing him.

While we were laying out our bedrolls over their mattresses of green boughs, our father started dinner in the cookfire. The cast-iron dutch oven rested securely in the curved fire-iron shaped like a giant's hairpin. The fire-iron in its turn was balanced firmly on flat-surfaced stones on either side of a deep bed of coals.

Dinner fare had not changed from early days, either. My father had greased the black interior of the dutch oven with olive oil until it shone. Lean lamb chops went in first, and then in succession sliced green peppers and onions, a few cloves of garlic, and finally potatoes cut into chunks. Each ingredient added its singular aroma to the dutch-oven dinner, bringing back more memories.

My father's scarred tin plates had been heaped full, and in the cool of evening, steam rose from them in heavenly vapors. We sat around a familiar and grease-spattered square of canvas that served as our tablecloth on the ground. In the middle of the square was a big plate of sourdough bread cut into generous slices, and beside it, the goatskin *chahakoa* filled with wine.

We made small talk fit for eating a lunch that did not need words, by habit avoiding two subjects. One was the brothers' shared guilt that at least one of us had not followed my father in the sheep business so that he would not have had finally to sell his livestock in that postwar time of few trained herders. It was just too much work to run so many sheep alone. The other subject was something we had always assumed our father had no taste for: politics. Nevertheless, we were in the middle of a campaign and the talk had to swing back to it sometime. It started at our high, wind-buffeted lunch with an amused remark by Leon about how well or badly Tex Maynard would grace that Georgian edifice, the Governor's Mansion.

To our astonishment, our father said, "He won't be the first cowboy to live there. It's just a house like any other, after all."

Something in the way our father phrased it made Leon regard him curiously. "You mean you've been inside the mansion?"

"Well, I had to if I wanted to see Balzar," my father said.

· · ·

Leon and I were silent, and then Leon asked, "You mean Governor Fred Balzar?"

"People didn't call him that then," my father said matter-of-factly. "They called him 'Bucky.' He used to be a buckin' hoss rider, you know, and like Pat McCarran, he was a good-hearted man, but he would fight you in a minute. You appreciated a man like that."

We did not know. We knew Balzar's name only because he had been the governor who had legalized gambling and prostitution in Nevada. "What did you talk about?" Leon asked experimentally, as if he expected my father to say "politics."

"Oh, his sickness a little," our father said. "That's why he was in bed. But that was just manners. Bucky wasn't the complaining type."

"What else?" Leon asked, fascinated.

"Oh, about something that happened when we was young together in the deserts," my father said. "He never could get it off his mind."

Leon nodded impatiently, as if urging our father on.

"In them days," our father said. "There was strangles going around the wild hosses. Ranchers were afraid their broke stock would catch it from them. Strangles makes a hoss choke to death. You got to shoot him to put him out of his misery. Also, to protect your own hosses."

Our father fell silent as if the conversation had ended. "Something must have happened," I said, almost impatiently.

"Oh, it happened, all right," my father said. "I had gone to town for a buckboard load of provisions and things for the ranch and I had tied my best saddle hoss in back so's he could follow. The tie-rope got tight, as they will do, and my hoss jerked back and broke it and ran away into the desert. Bucky Balzar was out checking his stock when he saw this hoss running like crazy and tossing his head. So he shot him, thinking he had strangles. He could never get over shooting my best hoss."

This time, it really was the end of the conversation as far as my

· · ·

father was concerned. When it became obvious that he wasn't going on, Leon said, "That's all?"

My father's brow wrinkled. "That's enough to talk about. It ain't every day your best hoss gets shot."

"Someone coming," my father said. "In a hurry." Standing in the hollow with his back to the roaring gusts of wind, he was looking down the mountain we had climbed that morning, following the switchback trail that deer had cut over God knows how long a time. A trail through the twisted bushes that covered this slope like a jungle had been necessary even for them. On our climb, we had stopped to rest when we topped the first crest and came into the little meadow where last winter's snow still lay in the deep hollows. Leon and I had a halfhearted snowball fight to remind us of the snowball fights we had there in midsummers when we were kids.

My father was looking far beyond the manzanita slope, over the deep forest that descended to the paved main highway a dozen miles away, to the point where the narrow dirt road left the highway and began its winding, impossibly steep climb to our father's old sheep-camp.

Tracing by memory the twists and turns of the dirt road, I could see no movement whatever. Sometimes, I swear our father had the long sight of an eagle. Then finally, through a window in the forest, I saw a flash of red. I followed that by memory to where the next aperture would be and caught enough of a glimpse to recognize Abner's pickup truck. Abner was in a hurry, all right, but I had no fears about his losing the road. He had been raised on a ranch in Oregon and he knew mountain driving. Later, he became a fighter pilot with nearly enough kills to make him an ace. On D-day alone, he had flown nine missions from England to France before getting hit and going down

· · ·

in the English Channel. Despite all the impossible activity the Normandy invasion consisted of, a boat had spotted his dye marker and his rubber raft and plucked him out of the water.

After World War II, he had tried his hand at many things: sports announcer, rodeo shows, disc jockey, and psychological warfare for the Army in the Korean War. He was made to order for a political campaign strategist, and he obviously did not lack for courage. Leon had seen those ingredients in a hurry and now Abner was solidly in the inner circle of our campaign. He did everything from voicing radio spots to arranging political rallies. "It's Abner," I said.

"We better head down," said Leon soberly. He was already anticipating trouble.

We reached the sheepcamp almost at the same time. Leaving his engine running, Abner stepped out of the pickup truck almost too deliberately. His face was set in a rigid mask and his habitual expression of amused tolerance of life was gone. He wasted no time in saying hello. With his worn Levi's and dusty cowboy boots, he approached Leon as if he were bent on a shootout.

"Tex Maynard is dead," Abner said in a low, controlled voice. At the question in my eyes, he said, "No, nobody killed him. He just dropped dead. Heart attack."

After one faltering moment so fleeting that I wasn't even sure I had seen it, Leon was up to Abner in his composure. One could almost watch him withdraw into that isolation chamber of his mind that only he was permitted to enter. Of the turmoil and thoughts that must have been churning inside him, I could only guess. He looked straight ahead unseeingly, then took a deep breath and let it escape. It was a reaction to crisis I was to become familiar with in the political time to come.

"Okay. So we go it alone."

· · ·

Abner made a short, curt nod of approval. I turned and headed toward my clothes sack and bedroll which were resting on a barely used bed of fragrant pine boughs.

Leon and I threw our gear into the back of Abner's pickup. When I looked back for the last time, it was to see the tall figure of our father staring after us. I stuck my arm out the window and waved good-bye. He did not wave back. He was not the kind of man to delude himself. He knew that days like this, in the company of his sons, would be few and far between. If he could have foreseen that this was one of the last days he would spend with his oldest son in these mountains, he would have been lonely indeed.

10

"Now cracks a noble heart. Good night, sweet Tex. And flights of angels sing thee to thy rest!"

There were East Side New York accents, I swear, in the sniffles of the black-suited contingent that occupied the velvet booths on one side of the Tropicana showroom. The mourners on the other side of the showroom were made of sterner stuff. Their taciturn western faces showed only creases carved by desert sun and mountain cold, and no emotion whatever. They had come to Las Vegas from every corner of Nevada to pay their respects to their Republican leader, Lieutenant Governor Tex Maynard. If they felt sorrow, they would not reveal it for a eulogy delivered by a Democrat, Governor Dean Cooper.

"Them's the prettiest words I ever heard," sniffed a New York ac-

· · ·

cent from the casino contingent. "That governor is the best genius I ever saw."

George Friar and I exchanged glances of incredulity. I could not believe what I was hearing. Governor Dean Cooper was actually cribbing from *Hamlet,* and getting away with it. There wasn't even a credit line to Horatio, the slain Hamlet, or Shakespeare. The expressions on the casino contingent's faces showed they were hearing Shakespeare for the first time and that henceforth the famous words would be attributed to Governor Dean Cooper.

It had been unbelievable enough when we had landed in Las Vegas and been told that Tex Maynard's funeral was going to be held not in a church or mortuary, but in the Tropicana hotel showroom, on the main stage at, no less, rehearsal time. The dancers did not like their stage being usurped. From time to time, the back curtains parted to show a long-legged chorine in form-fitting leotards, and once a male dancer with hands on hips, tossing his chin.

Tex's silver-mounted casket was situated on center stage and tipped forward so that Tex was looking out upon the audience, or in this case, congregation. He had been dressed in a black silk tuxedo with silver-tipped shirt and lapel tabs, a black western string tie with a silver throat clasp, and cowboy boots covered with more silver inlays than leather.

On the right-hand side of the stage stood the Tropicana's glittering showtime podium and behind it stood Governor Dean Cooper holding his written eulogy. There had been quite an argument about that, the Democrats feeling that it was more proper for the governor to eulogize the lieutenant governor than for his running mate on the Republican ticket to do so.

The casino contingent's side of the showroom was seated according to station in resort hotel hierarchy. Owners ranked according to their "points in the joint" occupied booths from left to right on eye level with Tex Maynard's face, upon which propriety had thankfully won out. The mortician had wanted to set Tex's face so that his famous dazzling smile and shining white teeth would be revealed.

The funeral was like a showtime performance, which it actually was in a curious way. When we first came in, the ushers who met us at the entrance were the maitre d's from the Strip hotels. A maitre d' would ask the number of mourners in any given group, raise his right hand and spread his fingers in the time-honored signal to the waiters below, then hold up one, two, three, four, or five fingers to transmit the number of mourners to the waiters. They being so deft at it, I have never been sure whether tips were passed in exchange for good seats.

The row of booths directly behind the Strip hotel owners was occupied by their hulking bodyguards.

"Let four captains bear Hamlet . . . I mean Tex . . . to the stage!" Dean Cooper's sonorous voice rolled on. The bell captains in the casino contingent looked at each other, thinking they had been given instructions. They were confused, since Tex was on stage. "He's already on stage," one bell captain said in a loud whisper. His fellow bell captains shrugged and decided not to make a move. They could not know the governor was quoting Horatio.

"Take the bodies, such a sight as this. Go, bid the soldiers shoot!" Simultaneously along bodyguard row, hands dived under black coat lapels for automatics tucked into shoulder holsters. The only soldiers the bodyguards had heard of, outside of wartime, were Mafia "soldiers." Charlie Baron jumped to his feet, waving his hands frantically at bodyguard row. "It's all right! It's all right!" he hissed in a harsh whisper. "It's all part of the act!"

After a moment, the bodyguards opened their collective mouths in an "O" of acceptance and pulled their gun hands out from under coat

· · ·

lapels. And so was averted what might have been a massacre to rival St. Valentine's Day.

There was no doubt in anybody's mind that Governor Dean Cooper had scored a coup by being chosen to give the eulogy at Tex Maynard's funeral. It had not been by accident. Dean Cooper was a wily politician. Tex wasn't even cold before Dean Cooper moved. Tex had only one living relative, his institutionalized wife, silent screen starlet Gloria Rowe. The couple were childless. Dean Cooper, by virtue of his position as governor, cut through the rules that bounded her seclusion and arranged a private interview with Tex's wife. Gloria Rowe was touched, and without protest gave the governor written permission to eulogize her husband, his lieutenant governor.

Leon was left out in the cold. Still virtually unknown in Las Vegas, he could have gotten immense public exposure if he had been the one to eulogize Tex Maynard. Leon not only did not get that vital exposure, but the public impression was that he had been publicly snubbed. He had been relegated to nothing in the public eye. Even at the funeral, Dean Cooper had made sure that our group, headed by Leon, was seated in the lowest possible row. Tex's lidded eyes looked right over our heads as proof of Leon Indart's demotion.

Governor Dean Cooper did not miss a trick. When his eulogy had been delivered, he suddenly materialized at the entrance to the showroom. There, like a pastor, he shook hands with every mourner and in unctuous tones thanked them for the homage they had paid to his lieutenant governor and loved friend, Tex Maynard.

When he shook Leon's hand, he leaned forward and whispered in his ear as though consoling him for the loss of his running mate. "Sorry you have to eat shit," Governor Dean Cooper whispered.

· · ·

"You're going to have to be quicker on the trigger or you won't even win lieutenant governor."

It was Leon's turn to lean forward, smile, and whisper into the governor's ear. "I'm not running for lieutenant governor," Leon whispered. There was an instant of unguarded elation in Dean Cooper's face. Plainly, he thought Leon was dropping out of the election race altogether.

"I'm going for your job," said Leon.

It was at that moment, I am convinced, that Leon made his decision to run for governor. He had to have been thinking about it in flashes during the furious hours since we heard of Tex Maynard's death. With Tex gone, Leon had been cast adrift.

Added to that was the problem that there was no Republican well enough known to challenge Dean Cooper for the governorship. Hank Romaine, the flamboyant publisher of the *Las Vegas Herald,* had the audacity to run, but he would not have drawn five votes in Reno and the cow counties. He was just too much New York, and now, too much Las Vegas. Still, there was no predicting where Hank's ego would drive him.

If the top spot on the ticket went forfeit by lack of a candidate, that would spell the end of the Republican party in Nevada for a long time. Someone with stature had to run. I suddenly remembered an exchange between Leon and George Friar. It was in the campaign car that picked us up at the Las Vegas airport.

In a matter-of-fact voice, without elaboration, Leon had said to Friar, "You're the only one, George."

Friar had shaken his leonine head. "You're making me bigger than I am."

The exchange had gone right past me, but now I could decipher

· · ·

it. Leon and George understood without words. The question of who was going to run for governor had been lying quietly in the back of both their minds. It did not need to be spelled out.

Something else transpired here, too. With all his stature and Washington, D.C., experience, political expertise, and eloquence, I had wondered before why George Friar had never run for office. Now I knew. It was what he had really meant in the luxurious Reno hotel room when he teased Tex Maynard about mortal feet of clay. George Friar did not have the courage to risk defeat, I realized for the first time. It must have hurt like hell for him to admit it. The knowledge did not make me feel less for George Friar. It made me immensely sorry for him. He would always be the king maker, but never the king.

The jaws of the trap must have been closing in on Leon from that moment on. It was a death trap. To run for lieutenant governor and win had seemed improbable. To run for governor and win was impossible. I damned Dean Cooper in my private heart. If he hadn't rubbed Leon's face in it, we would not be in the death trap now.

That whispered exchange between the governor and Leon had not escaped George Friar. When we gathered glumly around the strategy table in our Desert Inn suite, George leaned back in his chair and looked at Leon. "If we were having trouble raising the money to run for second spot, where in hell do you think we'll get it to run for governor?"

"What? What? What?" squeaked our numbers expert, Peck Poulson. "What are you talking about? *Governor!*"

Leon regarded him kindly and said in a voice that was aimed at reassuring his numbers man, "Peck, I have no choice. I have to go. Either that or the party loses the governorship by forfeit. It's nothing personal. I like Dean Cooper's style. In fact, if we weren't at total war politically, we would probably be good friends."

· · ·

"You can't win!" squeaked Peck. "You don't have a snowball's chance in hell! An unknown beating an incumbent governor?" Peck paused for breath, realized he had lost his cool, and fell back on his specialties—numbers and historical statistics. "It's never been done in the history of Nevada."

"What's happened in the past doesn't concern me a bit," said Leon. "The present does."

"I'll run a poll right now," said Peck. "That'll prove it to you."

Leon held up his hand, palm outward. "No," he said emphatically. "Any poll right now would show me getting whipped out. That would demoralize the troops and make hay for the newspapers if it leaked. Wait one month. That's the poll I want to see."

Peck nodded in surrender. He could see the sense in that.

"I'm not so sure about his whipping me," said Leon. "I was looking right into his eyes when I told him I was going for his job. He didn't have time to cover or even think about the possibility I would be the man." Leon paused and his brows contracted. "You know something? He's scared of me."

Jim Murphy was a diminutive man who for some reason didn't look short. I think it was because of his wizened face, a cynical twist to his lips, horn-rimmed glasses, and curling black hair already wound through with gray. He had been a reporter for the *Los Angeles Times* when he was given an assignment to cover a story in Las Vegas. He hated the town instantly and intensely, so much so that he moved to Las Vegas and got a job as a reporter for the *Las Vegas Tribune,* the biggest paper in southern Nevada. He did it so that he could find more reasons to fire his hatred of Las Vegas.

Jim Murphy had been assigned to cover Tex Maynard and Leon Indart's campaign. His presence was welcome because his heretical one-liners were a leavening factor in our conversations. He rarely repeated himself: "Las Vegas has a scale of values like a slot machine."

· · ·

Or, "You can always tell who the leading citizens of Las Vegas are. To a man, they hate wardens."

Jim Murphy had been listening to the exchanges about Leon running for governor. He regarded Leon quizzically. "You've got a death wish," he said. "You remind me of Napoleon losing half a million men in Russia because he had an image problem."

Leon's feelings were not hurt. He even grinned at Jim Murphy. "Do me a favor, Jim. Don't use that one when you write my announcement story. It's liable to catch on."

"I won't use it," said Jim, but not placatingly. "For the simple reason that the average reader of the *Las Vegas Tribune* has never heard of Napoleon. Or Russia."

A quiet man named Bill Skinner had joined our campaign team. He did not look like a dangerous man, but as an FBI agent he had been the prime mover in jailing three Mafia family bosses in New Jersey. He knew the background of every hoodlum with a gambling license in Nevada, and he knew how to dig out information. Leon had brought Skinner out from Washington for exactly that reason.

"I've got a job for you, Bill," Leon told him. "We've got to know how much Dean Cooper has in his war chest, particularly in campaign money from the casinos. It won't be in checks. It'll be in cash. Have you got any pipelines into the joints?"

Skinner nodded his head. "Yeah, but I won't have to use them for this one." He paused. "What I'll do is find out how much newspaper space and how much radio time he bought for his campaign against Tex. If your instincts about him are right, he'll keep the ads and spots and just change the name of the opposition."

"What about television?" asked George Friar.

"I think he's afraid of it," said Skinner. "It's too new and he can't know how many people are out there. But I'll check his time buys anyway."

· · ·

"How about our buys?" George asked.

Peck Poulson's skeletal thin nose pinched. "Pretty skimpy. Tex told me he had a bundle in pledges," said Leon.

"That doesn't mean it'll come to you," said Abner. "Need I remind you that our cowboy has ridden off into the sunset, taking his pledges with him?"

George Friar's thick eyebrows raised in inspiration. "But you're assuming that Tex is dead and we can't identify with him any longer."

Everyone's head turned towards George Friar. He cleared his throat and said, "Tex Maynard is not dead. We are going to resurrect him."

11

The faint drone of a propeller-driven passenger plane flying high overhead did not interrupt the oratory and ground sounds below. A dog barked. Two dogs barked. An automobile horn revealed an angry driver. A bird twittered.

There was a burst of applause, the clearing of a throat, and then eerily came the unmistakable western voice with its touch of Texas drawl not successfully erased. It was the voice of Tex Maynard.

"I will tell you again, my fellow Nevadans. Not only you faithful Republicans gathered here in Las Vegas for this campaign kickoff, but you Democrats out there who are with us in your secret hearts.

"The two-party system is nearly dead in Nevada. The Democratic party pirates who run the state are getting away with murder, because there are so few of us to stand up to them and shout, 'You are committing wrong!'

"The issue in this campaign is not only our incumbent governor's

· · ·

liberal attitude toward crime, his liberal policy of early parole that is emptying out our prisons and unleashing dangerous criminals into our neighborhoods so that our women and children are afraid to walk by night, it is something more important. The concept of the loyal opposition con . . . con . . . con . . . conceived [Tex Maynard's wily old speechwriter had chosen the wrong word there] by our forefathers, Thomas Jefferson and George Washington, is almost dead in Nevada.

"But me and my loyal compañero, Leon Indart, are fighting to keep it alive. My compañero is not well known here in southern Nevada. But he will be. He will be, I promise you. North and west and east in Nevada, Leon Indart is very well known. He comes from pioneer stock. He comes from ranching stock. He comes from immigrant stock, just like you Italians and Jews [Tex and his speechwriter had had different opinions about using the word 'immigrant']. I give you Leon Indart."

There was a burst of applause, the clearing of a throat, the twittering of a bird in the pause, and then Leon came on. "Thank you, dear friend Tex . . ."

"Cut!" Abner's voice came over the intercom. He was speaking from the control room where he and a bespectacled little engineer with earphones peered out from the glass cage that was the control room. The engineer was surrounded by turntables with acetate discs, his glasses reflecting little colored lights emanating from the big panel in front of him, a panel filled with dials and flickering needles. The engineer's hands seemed to be moving in all directions as he observed the dials and turned knobs.

Leon stood alone in front of a portable microphone on the studio stage. He was plainly irritated.

"You are not in a courtroom," Abner's voice came in reprimand over the intercom. "You are standing on a platform in the middle of a playing field in Las Vegas. The people in the second row can't

· · ·

83

hear you. You have to aim for the back row, fifty yards away. Shout. Wave your arms if that will help you to get excited. Project! Project! Project!"

With a hundred halts and dubbings and soundtrack inserts, so went the re-creation of Tex Maynard's and Leon's canned radio announcement. It wasn't a spot announcement. It was a full-dress performance that consumed a half hour of air time. Abner had had incredible luck in his search for someone, anyone, who had taped the open-air Republican rally in Las Vegas and gotten Tex Maynard introducing Leon Indart. He drew a blank at the most logical source— radio stations. Then one engineer remembered that a civilian amateur had asked for his advice on how to operate a little home-recording set. Abner had tracked him down and we were provided with the essential ingredient in raising Tex Maynard from the dead.

The re-creation of the Las Vegas Republican rally speech was vital to the campaign. Elaborating on George Friar's inspiration, Abner had booked time on every radio station in Nevada. Nearly every cow town or mining town possessed one radio station with a monopoly on local listeners.

Political spot announcements on radio were nothing new. But the timing was. The practice had been to book one or two spots during prime evening listening hours. The rest of the day was ignored. Leon had asked, "If we're going all-out radio, let's aim for the guy driving to work, the guy going home after work, the farmer and the rancher and the miner all alone out there in the boonies, except for their radios." Abner's eyes brightened as the idea grew. "How about the housewife home on the ranch alone or with the kids all day long?"

It had to be done quietly and on credit, because our war chest was small and not likely to get bigger following Tex's departure. But radio time was cheap for the off-hours. Before two weeks were out, Abner had shotgunned the air time of every radio station in the state, ex-

· · ·

cept in Las Vegas. We could not risk a leak there that would upset our strategy. Something else would have to be cooked up for the southland. I saw the pondering light come on and stay on in Leon's eyes. He was on his way to solving the Las Vegas problem.

But on the night of his first radio performance, he was simply tired and confused. After three hours, we sat in the empty studio and listened to the finished tape—complete with overhead airplane, traffic sounds, barking dogs, twittering birds, invented applause, and the ghost of Tex Maynard speaking against the background music of "Cool Water" by the Sons of the Pioneers. The resurrection had been accomplished. All that Leon could muster was to shake his head and say, "I'll never believe in anything again."

Later on, when we were jaded and politics was no longer fun, I would recall that lament of innocence.

12

Without design, our family home had become headquarters north for the campaign. Perhaps it was because our getting into politics had started here at one of my mother's French pancake lunches when we brothers got together on Fridays. Perhaps because the family home had been our stronghold growing up.

It was a combination of these, surely, but I believe the real reason was that truth had always been spoken here in times of big decisions—college and war and career. As for now, we had already come to know that truth was the rarest commodity in the political campaign.

People wondered why Leon's law offices had not been made head-

· · ·

quarters in Carson City. That was impossible. By agreement, our youngest brother, Mitch, was holding down the law practice. But if Leon were around the premises, it was inevitable that he would encounter a client of the firm who considered his personal troubles more important than politics and would insist on getting counsel from Leon alone. Mitch was hollow eyed with exhaustion, with little to offer in the way of political advice.

Leon's modern ranch house was out of the question, too. With swimming pool and tennis courts, it had too many attractions for youngsters and others not so young. Their shouting and screaming was not the problem. Little ears were. Kids raised in a political town such as a capital seemed to have an instinctive talent for eavesdropping.

Seasons had changed since that summer's day when Leon put the question to family. On the drive over from Reno, the valleys I passed through had begun to turn tawny as a lion's coat. The giant old cottonwoods covered Carson with a gold and green umbrella, early falling leaves clattered with the slightest breeze down the back streets, and the Virginia creeper that enclosed the screened front porch of the family home was turning red. The capitol dome that before had always just been there suddenly became a symbol of our aspirations.

One thing was missing, though. Leon's Cadillac was parked again in front of the house, but our father's scarred old pickup truck was gone. It was absent often these days as the political meetings grew more frequent. I did not have to wonder where our father was. He was in the mountains.

My mother, however, was in her element. Not because of the prestige of her son running for governor, but because her sons were around so often these days. She pampered us as if we were still children. She was pouring fresh coffee for Leon when I came in. Leon was

· · ·

presiding in his usual place at the head of the dining room table. As far back as I could remember, my father had shunned that authority chair like the plague, so Leon as eldest son filled it in the Old World Basque tradition without even knowing that it was one.

This was to be money-counting day, with no coffee klatches or speeches for Leon. He was casual in the tennis shirt and shorts he had worn for a match he had played early that morning. When it came to exercise, he was rapidly becoming a disciplinarian in order to burn off extra pounds and the nervous edges from campaigning. He looked tanned, leaner, and fitter than in the days before his decision to get into politics.

There was a long yellow legal pad covered with figures in front of him. He was studying it as he talked. "In a political campaign, everyone is trying to inject his thinking, his ideals, and his gripes into the candidate," he said to no one in particular. "In any campaign, there are a thousand candidates without portfolio using the real candidate as their conduit. The big problem is trying to stay your own man."

Leon had taken to soliloquizing, not because he suddenly thought of himself as a philosopher and sage, but in order to use us as a sounding board for his frustration and discoveries about human nature. Here in the family home, he could vent his anger in a safe haven.

"I will tell you one thing," he went on. "A campaign is the surest way to become a people reader. It's a great lesson in finding out who your real friends are, and the ones who never were. When you say, 'I hope I can count on your support,' it's the moment of truth. Look into their eyes. Feel what's really coming through that handshake. Make your ears pick out the guarded statements, the sincere smile or the concealing smile."

One didn't need to be clairvoyant to know where all this was coming from. It was a new ball game now. Leon wasn't running for

· · ·

a mere lieutenant governorship. He was running for "the big one," as the gamblers put it. Tempers had changed. Things had suddenly become deadly serious and people were revealing themselves. "If he's honest with himself," Leon said, "the candidate has to know best whether he's winning or losing. I know I'm on the downside now. But *they* are not sure out there. Ever since we started the shotgun radio barrage of Tex and me, they're just a little apprehensive that I might win, so they can't stiff me cold. They're afraid too. I'm talking about those bastards who want something out of me. They want cushy jobs. Sure we lost all the money in the campaign can when Tex died. His money pledges went with him. But we won something, too. We're free of God-knows-what-commitments he made to people I don't want around me.

"I'll give you an example. One of Tex's commitments was to a caboose swamper, for a seat on the Gaming Control Board. He is not a man to be trusted. He sneaked into the legislature just to shake down the lobbyists. Tex got ten big bills, ten thousand dollars, for that commitment. Not from the swamper's pocket, but from a guy who wanted a gambling license. You know who that payoff guy was? Tony Dragna. The swamper wants to know if I'm going to honor Tex's commitment to him. I told him I'm starting with a clean slate. He says he wants Tony Dragna's ten big bills back. I told him to go to Tex's campaign chairman, and good luck, because he's going to need it." Leon wagged his finger at us sagely. "There are a dozen like him who have hit me up for a seat on the Gaming Control Board. If I put them on, they'll shake more money out of the license hunters than there is in the state treasury."

"Licenses for dollars is not a bad idea," said my brother Gene. "We ought to dangle a few out there and see if we get a bite." Gene had come in while Leon was talking. His expression was sour. He poured

· · ·

himself a cup of coffee and lighted up a cigarette. "That son of a bitch," he said, taking an envelope out of his inside coat pocket and tossing it to Leon. Embossed in gold lettering in the return-address corner of the envelope were the words *Silver Lode Casino*. "A lousy five hundred dollars from one of the bastards you made a millionaire."

"Casey?" asked Leon.

Gene nodded. "None other," he said, his voice thick with sarcasm.

"All right, what happened?" Leon asked Gene.

"I told Casey I had come to pick up his campaign contribution," said Gene. "Casey squirmed a while and said, 'Leon doesn't have a chance. I can't afford to antagonize the governor.' I told him, 'Don't kid yourself. Leon is going to be the next governor.' Casey digested that for a while. Then I said, 'For Christ's sake, Leon made you a millionaire.' That nailed him. He took the big checkbook out of his drawer and wrote out a check. For five hundred dollars. I said, 'What's this? A down payment?' Casey said, 'No. That's what I gave to the governor's campaign.' He knew I knew he was lying, that he had given Dean Cooper five *big* bills, five thousand dollars. I didn't say a word. I decided then and there you would want to hear what happened. So you've heard. What do you want to do with his check?"

"Send it back," said Leon. "In pieces."

"With a note telling him what we think of him?"

"No note," Leon said. "Nothing." He got up and sat down at the chair beside the telephone. "I wasn't going to make this call," he said. "But I'm just in the right mood now."

"Who are you calling?" Gene asked.

"Denny's Club," Leon said. "Denny himself, in fact." Denny, or rather his canny old father, had started the whole phenomenon of gambling joints. The old man was a wizard, but his son was weird. He wore green eyeshades and garters and he hired and fired according

· · ·

to his whims. One week, he would fire all redheaded women dealers. The next week, all the blonde dealers. The girls were hard put to keep their hennas ahead of the game. When wigs came in, it was a godsend.

In later years he wrote a book, or rather his ghostwriter did. Comparing it to the Bible, he forced all his employees not only to buy the book but to read it. If they couldn't answer his questions on content, it was their ass, as the dealers put it. It is the most memorized book in the history of Nevada.

There was a moment's pause and then Leon said, "Denny?" Leon waited the dramatic moment and then said, "I understand you are telling people that we don't want a Catholic in the Governor's Mansion."

There was a silence. Leon covered the phone with his hand and said to us, "Denny seems to be having some trouble swallowing." He uncovered the phone and we could hear Denny's strangled denial piping through the receiver. "All right, I accept that, Denny," Leon said. "Let me tell you something. There *is* going to be a Catholic in the Governor's Mansion. That Catholic is me, because I am going to be the next governor of Nevada." Leon covered the telephone again and said to us, "He believes me. He believes I am absolutely right." After a silence, Leon said, "Denny, I want you to be the first to know that as governor, I will consider it a matter of first priority to see that the state tax commission collects that sixty thousand dollars you owe our state in sales taxes." There was a very long pause this time, presumably strangled, and then Leon said, "Denny, I hope too that it can be explained. For your sake." Leon nodded at Gene and said to Denny, "That's very generous of you. My brother Gene will be around tomorrow to pick up your contribution to my campaign." He hung up the phone and returned to his seat at the head of the dining room table.

· · ·

"Collecting that sixty thousand dollars in sales tax *is* going to be one of my first orders of business. Sawdust-joint gamblers are so damned arrogant. They think they can get away with anything."

From the foyer, there was an excited outburst of conversation and the sound of a family voice too long unheard.

"Talk about the Catholic Church and you get a nun," Leon said in a changed voice. He rose to his feet and strode out through the tall double doors that separated the dining room where we were meeting from the living room and the foyer.

The arrival of our sister Suzette was not unexpected except to my mother. Because he was not sure if he had convinced the mother superior to permit Suzette to come home, even for a turnaround visit from Las Vegas, Leon had not raised the slender hope to our mother. It wasn't until we heard Suzette's voice that we knew she would be at the family meeting. The mother superior played her cards close to her chest.

There was still a problem, however. Nuns of the Holy Family order were still bound by the rule that they could not visit even family without a companion nun being present. The companion nun was there right on schedule and by the rule book. From what we could see of her face, encircled by starched white headband and severe, full-length black habit, she looked not only inevitable but formidable. Her disapproval of the warmth of our embracing Suzette registered clearly on her face.

Without invitation, the nun companion prepared herself to sit down at table. That she had been told by the mother superior that the family gathering would be about politics was all too clear in her demeanor. But when it came to wiliness, Leon was one step ahead of the mother superior. He had taken our mother aside for an instant during the interlude of welcoming Suzette home.

· · ·

Before the companion nun could sit down, our mother took her by the hand. "You have to see my roses," my mother said. "They're St. Theresa Little Flower roses, you know." The companion nun opened her mouth to protest, but it would have taken a sterner character than even she possessed to turn down our mother. She was a woman from whom invitations were commands.

As soon as we heard the front door close, Leon gestured with both hands for us to sit down. He wasted no time with formalities and got down to business in a hurry.

"You've been hiding your talents behind that habit, Sue," he said in a low voice. "My informants tell me you've got the Indian sign on each and every gambler in Las Vegas, especially the ones with a bad reputation."

Suzette smiled disarmingly. "I know where their soft spots are," she said. "They may be dangerous to each other, but not to the people outside. They're not as bad as you think. They come from families like ours. They respect nuns. They go to church, Jewish or Catholic or whatever. And they're open-handed with their contributions . . ." She paused so briefly that if we had not been her brothers, we would not have noticed. ". . . to the Church."

Leon shook his head firmly. "Sue, don't even think I would ask you to raise a dime for my campaign," he said. "Never in God's world would I ever lay that on you." He collected his thoughts and went on hurriedly. "But I am going to ask you to do something for my campaign. You're a hell of a lot better known in Las Vegas than I am, do you know that?" He shushed Suzette's response by crossing his lips with his forefinger. "I want you to organize a task force of nuns to blanket Las Vegas with my name, that I'm an honest man, and most important of all, that I'm your brother."

Suzette pursed her lips. "Let me think," she said. "I could get in trouble."

· · ·

"I'll help you organize your thinking," said Leon. "Is the mother superior for me in this election?"

"Of course she is," said Suzette. "She hasn't said it right out. She can't go that far. But from little remarks and the look in her eyes, I know she wants you to be governor."

Leon leaned back in his chair. "That solves your problem right there."

Suzette nodded, uncertainly at first and defiantly at last. "It does, Leon," she said. "I'll do it for you and for the family. But you've got to let me organize the nuns in my own way."

Leon put his hand over his heart. "Cross my heart, Sue," he said with conviction. "I won't interfere. I won't mention it to a soul. Not even Pat Calanan."

Suzette smiled. "Oh, I wouldn't mind your telling Pat Calanan. He's a good Irish Catholic. He's got a heart as big as his purse, and he doesn't mind giving of both."

There was the sound of approaching voices from the foyer. My mother's tour of the rose garden with the nun companion was over.

"Dear Sue," whispered Leon with a grin. "I've got a feeling you're going to be my secret weapon in Las Vegas."

13

"Now, remember. When you get off the plane, turn left and walk into the propeller. It's the only way you'll come out winners in Las Vegas."

The voice came from somewhere behind us in the line of disembarking passengers. Las Vegas had grown but it still wasn't big enough

· · ·

to warrant more than a short stop by the single canvas-and-glue airline making the Los Angeles–Reno run.

It was late September, but stepping out of the plane onto the tarmac was like walking into a blast furnace. Bill Skinner was waiting for us at the bottom of the stairway. Unable to bring himself to dress either Las Vegas or western style, he had on a conservative gray business suit and a snap-brim hat. He looked unmistakably like what he was, a former FBI agent. George Friar had added another dimension to Skinner's demeanor. "He looks like he's shadowing himself."

"Find out anything?" Leon asked as our leather heels clicked on the new tile of the terminal.

"Tell you in the car," mumbled Skinner. He was never much for talking when walking.

Leon's face and name identification were getting better. The first time we came to Las Vegas, no one we passed in the terminal knew who he was. That was to be expected from the California high rollers who came to gamble. But when airport employees, locals all, didn't recognize a candidate, it spelled bad news. This time, a surprising number said hello or howdy.

"Cooper's taking as much as they'll give him," Skinner said when we were out of earshot of passengers and airport personnel.

"He's not being very smart," said Leon. "Where he sits now, he doesn't need big money. How much is he taking?"

"One thousand minimum from the sawdust joints," said Skinner. "Five to ten big bills from the carpet joints."

Leon whistled. "That's just plain dumb. Ten bills will get you one big due bill later on."

The core contingent was sprawled around the Desert Inn presidential suite that was headquarters south. Our numbers man, Peck Poulson, was poring pen in hand over tiny figures on his inevitable

· · ·

yellow legal pad. His mouth was working more than usual. Abner looked simultaneously pleased and baffled. The rural radio barrage had caught the governor napping, and Peck's polls showed Leon well ahead of Dean Cooper. That was the reason for Abner's looking pleased. What was baffling him was the problem of how to crack the Las Vegas vote. George Friar had made a swing for money through the rural areas at the height of the radio barrage. He was burned deep bronze from summer and autumn sun, but that was good news. It showed he had talked to ranchers where it counted—on horseback while they were checking cattle in the deserts and mountains. Farm-bred and Interior-trained in Washington, D.C., George could talk their language.

Nobody in Dean Cooper's camp could match that act. As George Friar unfailingly pointed out to ranchers and cowboys alike, Cooper was a town boy who wore horn-rimmed glasses but still couldn't tell one end of a cow from the other. He used a similar analogy for sheepmen and sheepherders, saying with a smile that if their governor would only eat a few mountain oysters now and then, he might grow some balls, but the awful truth was that he had never tasted a mountain oyster in his life.

Jim Murphy listened with his reporter's sardonic contempt to George Friar's tale of his wanderings. *He* was the classic town boy, hating horses and cows and especially John Wayne movies. He looked quizzical when George Friar mentioned mountain oysters. With malicious glee, Friar explained to Jim Murphy what mountain oysters were—lamb testicles. Friar then launched into an exaggerated description of how testicles are separated from their owners, the lambs, by a traditional method—pulling them out of the lamb's scrotum with one's teeth. Jim Murphy walked out of the meeting. Which was just as well, because Leon wanted to talk money.

· · ·

"Okay," he said, spreading his hands palm outward in a firm demand for silence, "this is how we're going to handle campaign contributions."

"What campaign contributions?" asked Peck. "Our money's drying up. We're damned near broke."

"Peck," said Leon with a note of irritation in his voice, "you are an incurable crepe hanger. Don't worry. The money will come. I can feel it. Things are about to turn."

"For the edification of town boys like you," said George Friar drily, "it's market time on the range for beef and mutton. We'll see hard money from the ranchers instead of talk and promises. It should start coming in regularly now. Not big, but big enough, and steady as a rock."

Peck nodded, looking mollified for the time being.

"This is how we're going to handle gambling money," Leon said firmly, spacing his words for emphasis. "We take no more than one thousand dollars from each casino—carpet joint or sawdust joint."

"That's suicide," squeaked Peck. "Take what we can get. We can squeeze a lot more than that from the carpet joints."

"And we can get a lot more due bills at the same time," said Leon. "If we win this campaign, I don't want any gambler telling me how much I owe him in special treatment. This way, I can tell anyone who calls in a due bill, 'You didn't give any more than a hundred other gamblers did.'"

"There goes the campaign," my brother Gene said. "I saw Willie Alderman for lunch today. He wants to make a contribution of fifty thousand dollars. Fifty bills will almost carry us through."

"If I take that," said Leon, "I'll never be able to call myself my own man again. I'd rather borrow the money from the bank even if it takes ten years to pay back."

· · ·

"That's not what Cooper is doing," said Peck maliciously. "I hear he's taking it with both hands."

Leon shook his head. "That's what I can't figure out. It doesn't make sense. Dean Cooper is a smart guy. He knows due bills like that can kill a governor."

George Friar had been absorbing the exchange quietly. His granite face was that of a man on the verge of a discovery. "You're right," he said, his chin resting on his clasped hands. "It doesn't make sense." He lifted his gaze and said directly to Leon. "I think I know why. You were right back there at Tex's funeral. He is afraid of you. He is really afraid of you." George paused for dramatic effect. "Governor Dean Cooper wants to bury you so deep that you will never raise your political head again. That's why he's taking with both hands."

"And that explains a mystery," said Abner. "Dean Cooper has bought nearly every minute of prime time from here on in."

"On radio?" asked Leon.

"Of course on radio," said Abner.

"What about television?"

Abner shook his head. "It's too new. It's untested. The pros say television can sink a man faster than it can make him."

"Maybe so," said Leon, and then cut off the exchange. "Abner, let me try something out on you. I've got an idea about media."

Leon turned to Gene. "Give Willie Alderman a call," he said. "Tell him thanks but no thanks. In a nice way."

"You're making a mistake," said Gene.

"I'm not minimizing your coup," said Leon. "Actually, you've given me one of the keys to unlocking this campaign. I'm delighted that our governor is taking it in with both hands. I'm so pleased that I think we ought to help him out."

The table turned its collective head and regarded Leon as if he had

· · ·

lost his mind. He met their gaze steadily. "Who is the most vindictive, vengeful, ferocious, and unrelenting hoodlum in Las Vegas?"

"Tony Dragna," said Bill Skinner quietly.

"If Bill Skinner says it, it's true," said Leon. "And who hates the FBI and J. Edgar Hoover more than anyone in Las Vegas?"

"Tony Dragna," said Peck. "But I don't get what you're driving at."

"You will," said Leon. Without looking directly at our brother Gene, Leon said, "Call Pat Calanan. Tell him I need to talk to him. Today."

When Gene had left the table, Peck said, "I still don't get it."

"I think I'm beginning to," said George Friar.

Gene had stopped just short of dialing Calanan's private number at the Shamrock, his Strip casino. "He'll be seen, coming up here."

"Pat Calanan doesn't care if he's seen," said Leon wearily. "Everyone knows where he stands in this election. He's made sure of that, personally."

Calanan was Irish through and through. He was also a philosopher, which is why I liked him. He was a square-built man with an Irish mick face and shrewd blue eyes, and when he sang, it was in an Irish tenor. If anyone had called him a philosopher, he wouldn't have known what they were talking about. He was a street kid out of New York and the roughness of that upbringing still showed. That did not seem to make any difference in Las Vegas. During the mob's early shooting-gallery days in Nevada, it was said that Calanan ordered his share of shooting. But when the Purity Code was adopted by the syndicate bosses out of the East and South, Pat Calanan put away his guns, simply because the Purity Code made sense. Whenever a new casino opened, he was there with the proper courtesy loss of five thousand dollars in his pocket. Pat Calanan was exactly what he was and Las Vegas accepted him for what he was, a man of no surprises.

Once when Pat and I were having a drink and I was lamenting about where we stood then in the campaign, Pat said, "Son, you better

· · ·

learn it sooner than later. Life is never 100 percent. It's 60-40. If you come out on the 60 end, you're winners." I never forgot that. It has given me peace of mind in times of rage at the breaks the world was dealing.

Another time, when Pat had just sold a gambling joint he owned, Leon asked him what he was going to do now. Pat said, "Wait until I see their money. I think clearer when I get money in the bank."

There was a call from the front desk, and Leon went to the door to greet Calanan personally. While Pat returned Leon's handshake, his sharp blue eyes flickered over the room. Pat wanted to know exactly what he was walking into.

The rest of the inner core had found errands to run. Leon asked George Friar, Skinner, and me to stick around. It was too early in the day even for the sundowner habit, so Leon poured us soft drinks. We gathered around a long coffee table in a corner of the suite.

Knowing how Pat Calanan disliked foreplay, Leon came straight to the point with the same questions he had asked Bill Skinner. "Who hates the FBI worst in town?"

Pat didn't have to reflect long. "J. Edgar isn't winning any popularity contests in Vegas," he said. "But for pure hate, it has to be Tony Dragna."

Good old "buy 'em or kill 'em" leaped to memory from my poolside interlude with Roger, seemingly so long ago.

Leon was looking at Calanan for elaboration. "Tony Dragna is a mad dog," Pat said. "I get the creeps even being in the same room with him. The son of a bitch is crazier than hell."

"What if I let leak that I was thinking about taking a public stance against J. Edgar Hoover and the FBI?"

"Tony Dragna would love you," said Calanan. He was going to add something, but he caught himself. He was observing Leon with narrowed eyes.

· · ·

"Would Tony Dragna love me fifty thousand dollars worth?"

"Yeah, yeah," said Pat, "but I'll give you fifty thousand if you *don't* take a public stance."

"For the sake of argument," said Leon. "What if I took Dragna's money and backwatered?"

"You would find out what a mad dog looked like. Close up."

"Would Dragna shoot me?"

Pat thought that one over. "My first thought was 'yes, he would shoot you.' But even Dragna isn't crazy enough to shoot a candidate for governor. I think."

"What if he offered fifty big ones to Governor Cooper if *he* promised to take on the FBI?" Leon asked. "Would Cooper take it?"

"That's what the word is. Plus he has a hate on for J. Edgar."

"What if Cooper started to back down on his promise?"

"Tony Dragna is the only one with balls enough to tell Cooper he'll shoot him if he doesn't come through," Pat said, and then added, "But Cooper wouldn't back out."

"Why not?" asked Leon, poker faced.

"Because nobody can be sure what Dragna will do, and Cooper likes living better than dead."

"Right on the button," interjected George Friar.

Leon grinned apprehensively at Pat Calanan. "As my friend, Pat, could you find it in yourself to hint to Dragna that the governor will take on the FBI publicly for fifty thousand dollars?"

Pat Calanan sighed. "Well, I'll try it. But sure as hell, Dragna will smell a rat. And Cooper will know for sure he's being set up. He may be a prima donna liberal, but he's no crook."

14

In the few short years that television had been around, at least in
Nevada, it was ignored as a political medium. Political advertis-
ing amounted to televising a slide on election eve, with not even a
photograph of the candidate to accompany the VOTE FOR . . .

Perhaps it was because politicians did not want that kind of close-
up scrutiny. But that is cynical, except in a few cases where politicians
were what they looked like—downright untrustworthy. Photos on
campaign cards, if they were used at all, either did not exist or were
touched up by an artist with an airbrush. Probably, though, the reason television was ignored was that it was an untested medium, as
Abner had said.

For us, television was a hunch that effectively turned the campaign
around. And live television at that, without scripts or touched-up
photographs. With all his courtroom experience behind him, Leon
was a natural for the TV screen. Against all arguments, he had Abner
book daytime hours five days a week, aiming for an unheard-of audience—housewives.

He chose early afternoon when children were at school and the
housework was done, an hour when relaxation was possible. Also, it
was a cheap time-buy.

Leon sat on a stool and talked in a conversational tone, occasionally getting up to point at a candid snapshot pasted to a wall. The
effect was that of a neighbor who had just dropped in for a cup of
coffee. When the camera moved in close, it revealed the serious eyes
that exuded sincerity, a crew cut, and what housewives came to call
his "charming smile," where his eyes crinkled nearly shut with good

. . .

humor. Also he wore a sport shirt instead of the mandatory necktie.

With the candid photograph accompaniment, he talked about his own family of wife and six children, three of them adopted and three of natural birth. Candid photographs of the three adopted children, complete with freckles, were particularly effective, revealing without saying it that Leon had a soft spot for children.

"This is Sally," he would say. "She's coming on twelve. The other night, I asked her if she had given any thought to what she wanted to be when she grew up. She said, 'Yes, Dad. I want to be a substitute teacher.' I suggested she go for broke and become a full-time teacher. She said she'd think about it, but 'full-time teachers work so hard and look so tired.'" That story of course made the rounds and won over a goodly number of schoolteachers.

When the time seemed right, Leon did not waste the opportunity to make political points. "The governor is taking credit for our population growth," he said, smiling. "Well, he's not going to take credit for my six children."

Leon talked about our family of six brothers and sisters, and our parents with good faces, and often showed pictures: My mother with silver-streaked braids wound in a chignon, standing in front of the old-fashioned family home in Carson City, snippers in one hand and roses in the other. Thanksgiving and Christmas family dinners were cooked by her in that house. My father in the mountains, his bronzed and sun- and wind-creased face and white shock of hair tossed by the wind. Lambs gallivanting on a summer snowbank on the slopes of a high peak that overlooked our sheepcamp. The camp itself with its worn canvas tepee tent and a bedroll peeking through, showing graphically that we came from hardworking earthbound stock. A shot of Leon right after World War II, relief cap still on his head, holding a tin cup while my father poured him coffee from a blackened campfire coffeepot. Leon was emaciated from his combat service in

· · ·

the Philippines, but he did not mention that. The photograph spoke for itself. Leon had served his country in time of war.

Another time, he commented on Dean Cooper's trotting in Democratic dignitaries from Washington, D.C. "We don't need the advice of out-of-state politicians to tell us how to vote," he said. A close-up picture of our sister Sue, her face confined by starched white linen headband and the black hood of her nun's habit, said without words that Leon came from a family where religion was important. By this time, Suzette's troupe of political nuns had begun to make a bridgehead for Leon where it counted, among the Catholics. And finally, Leon told about how our parents were immigrants who had come to America to seek out and work for the opportunity they had been denied in the "old country." That poignant story had a solid impact with Las Vegas's goodly quotient of Italians, French, Jews, Spanish, and even Scandinavians and Anglo-Saxons—not only on the foreign-born immigrants like our parents, but on their progeny, on Leon's generation.

After one week, Leon's show became a television event equaling the standing of any soap opera. Telephone lines hummed as one housewife called another to tell her not to miss *Leon's Hour,* as it came to be known.

The political momentum didn't stop there. It was a truism that housewives talk to their husbands when they come home to dinner from work, and husbands do listen to them. In a very short while, Leon's face and name were bywords in Las Vegas and its satellite communities.

That *Leon's Hour* was a political coup of major proportions revealed itself in the faces of Governor Dean Cooper's campaign staff and precinct workers. At first they had laughed outright at Leon's homespun approach to politics, which of course should be dealt with on an elevated plane. Then, as word got around and the momentum

· · ·

built up, Governor Cooper's campaign people began to show fury in their faces and reactions. Before two weeks were over, they were frothing at the mouth.

Dean Cooper tried to emulate Leon's approach, but it died dead the first night. Traditionally well groomed, hair a respectable length, and always wearing horn-rimmed glasses, his image was scholarly. Now, he changed to crew cut and contacts and then discarded his necktie for a cowboy hat and neckerchief. Leon commented wryly on his television show that Nevadans were getting confused as to what their governor really looked like. With the aid of a wig, Cooper promptly went back to his scholarly image and stayed there. With only prime time and one child as his ammunition, he also ran head-long into competition from people's favorite programs, thus earning him nothing by way of votes.

The governor and his backers were learning a lesson. But so were we. There were innovations to be made in the staid traditions of the political campaign game. We did not deceive ourselves. This innovation was born out of a hunch and a small war chest that could not afford prime time. It could have backfired.

George Friar's pronouncement on the innovation that worked was, "What our eminent governor can't seem to realize is that the laws of politics have existed forever. They are subject to change only after the change has been tried and tested. Just like that little military hand-book for infantry that we went by in World War II—everything there evolved from thousands of formulas tried and tested. What you have done here, Leon, my friend, is test and prove one more formula to be added to the handbook."

Leon mumbled something about George's Gideon prose. For him, a natural political animal, it was all part of the new game he was learning to play.

· · ·

15

The first hint we had that Leon's folksy television show was beginning to turn the campaign around was when Diamond Tooth Muller came to visit.

Diamond Tooth did not bother with such needless amenities as invitations. He just knocked one day at the door to our inner sanctum suite in the Desert Inn. The unmistakable figure framed in the doorway might ordinarily have gone unnoticed, melted into the woodwork. Diamond Tooth was a slight, thin, drooping man who looked as harmless as harmless could be. He was anything but that.

When Diamond Tooth smiled, his whole being lighted up. The afternoon sun coming in through the windows glinted dazzlingly off the diamond set squarely between his upper two front teeth. When the light was right, one had to shield his eyes to protect himself from the glitter.

Diamond Tooth Muller was by profession a political hatchet man. He was skilled enough at his profession that it was a political axiom that he was not a man to be taken lightly. I thought his reputation was exaggerated but I had never voiced that opinion to Leon. Now, I was curious to see whether Leon would even let Diamond Tooth in the door, and if he did, what the outcome would be.

"Diamond Tooth!" Leon exclaimed. "What a surprise!"

Diamond Tooth looked puzzled. "Why a surprise?"

"Well," said Leon, also looking puzzled. "This is the enemy camp for you."

Diamond Tooth shrugged impatiently. "Let's talk."

Leon actually sat him down at what had come to be called the Round Table. Our pollster, Peck, joined us without invitation. Peck

. . .

was simply not going to let an opportunity pass to see what the opposition had to say. George Friar was already at the table. He turned his writing pad on stratagems over so that Diamond Tooth would not see it and leaned back to listen. My brother Gene, who was taking the campaign very seriously, would not grant Diamond Tooth the compliment of joining the table. He sat where he was, reading what Jim Murphy had to say about politics in the *Las Vegas Tribune*. Skinner also chose not to join the table. He turned his chair around so that all Diamond Tooth could see of him was his back. But nobody in the room was fool enough not to know that Skinner, in the best FBI tradition, was listening to every word. Skinner did not take much stock in eye-to-eye communication. He preferred to listen to exchanges for tone and real meaning.

Leon was an eye-to-eye kind of people reader. He sat directly opposite Diamond Tooth Muller, his fingertips touching to make a tent. His face was impassive, neither antagonistic nor friendly. "All right," he said. "What do you want to talk about?"

Diamond Tooth cleared his throat. "I'm doing a pretty good hatchet job on you."

"Such as," said Leon.

"For example," said Diamond Tooth, "that rumor that as governor, you would oppose civil rights legislation."

"I didn't think that was so original," said Leon. "I'm a Republican, and Republicans are supposed to be against civil rights from the cradle on. You didn't change any votes on that rumor." Leon paused and said with almost a grin. "Now, if you had started a rumor that I was in favor of civil rights legislation, you would have cost me some conservative votes."

Diamond Tooth Muller nodded in appreciation. "Not bad," he said. "You've missed your calling."

Leon would not let the civil rights issue end right there. "To set the

· · ·

record straight with you," he said to Diamond Tooth, "I happen to be for civil rights because I come from a minority people. Heavily. Who do you think it was that went to Harold Smith and told him privately that if venerable old Harolds Club dropped its color ban, the other gambling joints would rethink their position?"

"You should have kicked that loose to the press," said Diamond Tooth.

"No," said Leon. "Nobody would believe it anyway, and those who did would think it was political expediency."

"How would you like to go into business together?" said Diamond Tooth. "With your brains and my hatchet, we could make a fortune."

Leon grinned and then got serious again. "Let's get down to business," he said. "Why are you talking to us?"

"I want to go to work for you," said Diamond Tooth. "I'll be your rotten rumor guy against Cooper."

"But you're on Dean Cooper's payroll."

Diamond Tooth shook his head wearily. "Oh, Leon, I'm disappointed in you. Everyone knows my hatchet is for hire."

George Friar nodded his head pendulously. "A new experience for me," he said. "I thought I'd heard them all."

Leon was grinning openly now. "Give me a sample," he said to Diamond Tooth. "What rumor would you start about the governor?"

"For example," said Diamond Tooth, "civil rights again. I'll start the word that Dean Cooper has changed his position. He will not introduce civil rights legislation next session of the legislature."

"And what will that accomplish?" said Leon.

"It'll turn the liberals against him," said Diamond Tooth.

Leon shook his head. "You're missing the point again, Diamond Tooth. You should know that no matter what, liberals always go back to the womb come election time."

Diamond Tooth again nodded in appreciation. Leon stood up.

· · ·

"Sorry, Diamond Tooth," he said. "No deal. Go back to the Cooper camp and do what you're getting paid for."

George Friar had been waiting. "Diamond Tooth," he said, "you must read more about political campaigns and the uses of subtlety in the past. I am reminded of William Allen White's repeated comment in the *New York Times* about a politician whom he hated. White's victim happened to be a teetotaler. Whenever the victim addressed a gathering, William Allen White would write: 'So and So addressed a gathering at such and such a place. He was sober.' Before the campaign was over, the whole country thought So and So was a drunk."

Diamond Tooth did not take offense. He got to his feet. "I get it," he said. He shook Leon's hand and smiled. "No hard feelings," he said. The afternoon sunlight was coming in the window at exactly the right angle. Diamond Tooth knew it and Leon knew it. George Friar did not. He received the full force of the glitter as payment for his erudition.

When Jimmy the Greek came into our lives we knew for certain that the campaign we were in had become a horse race. Up to now, Jimmy the Greek had not deigned even to admit that Leon existed, much less that he was a legitimate contender for the governorship. This omission applied not only to his weekly newspaper columns on politics in the *Las Vegas Herald,* but what was far worse, to his role as oddsmaker for everything from sports to politics.

Jimmy the Greek's real name was James Snyder, which definitely was not Greek. It also was not nearly as rememberable as Jimmy the Greek. So he dropped his real name, using it only in legal situations. Starting from his youth in Hot Springs, Arkansas, which was a hoodlum spa hangout, Jimmy had already built a considerable reputation as an oddsmaker. The reputation did not spring from guesswork and luck, but from doing his homework. That and a shrewd ability to see through façades and know who was a winner and who was a loser inside. This combination made him an oracle of no small stature. "I never book losers," was an often repeated line in his columns and he was just about right. In appearance, Jimmy looked Greek all right, with thick black hair, fleshy face, and oily skin, but he more resembled a benevolent Buddha looking down upon the world with oblique eyes and a wise, knowing smile.

Unlike Diamond Tooth Muller, Jimmy the Greek did observe the amenities. He called to ask if he could talk privately with Leon in our Desert Inn suite. When he knocked at our door and it was opened unto him, his bulky frame filled the doorway. He was built like one of the linebackers he wrote about.

But Jimmy diminished in size and ego with Leon's answer to his introduction, "I'm Jimmy the Greek. You know my game."

Leon nodded. In Jimmy the Greek's column a week ago, he had predicted that Governor Dean Cooper would clean what's-his-name's clock. "I know you're a good columnist, but your reputation as an oddsmaker is going to get blown to hell damned soon."

Jimmy the Greek was taken aback. Never having met Leon before, Jimmy fixed his "boring through the façade" eyes on him, and made up his mind then and there. We did not know it then, but Jimmy the Greek was going to become a fixture in our camp for a long time to come.

"Fair shot, Governor," said Jimmy. "I had it coming." He put out his fleshy hand and Leon shook it. Leon ushered him to the end of the long room and they had their "private talk" out of our hearing.

"Our eminent governor will win votes on this one," said Jim Murphy. "Why didn't you beat him to the punch?"

"Is this on or off the record?" Leon asked.

"On the record," said Jim Murphy, peering over his glasses like a

· · ·

ferret ready to pounce. "After all the clichéd political garbage I've had to write about between you and Cooper, *the issue* finally emerges. And I'm ready and waiting to cover it."

I will never be sure whether Leon recognized what Jim Murphy already knew. But when Leon heard the words to come, he recognized the truth in them. How many times this would happen, the real issue of a campaign coming out of nowhere when all the worn-out issues of economy and growth and crime had been exhausted—the real issue that was unplanned and unexpected but so apparent when it finally surfaced.

Leon's retreat into the isolation chamber came and went in a matter of seconds. "You're wrong, Jim," said Leon. "You've been talking to the wrong people. Every one of the quotes you've read me comes from the Strip, where, in your own words, they don't like wardens. The FBI and J. Edgar Hoover even less."

"So," said Jim Murphy. "They happen to vote, too, on the Strip." He qualified himself. "Unless they've had their voting rights revoked."

Leon had put on his lecturing voice. "Get off the Strip, Jim," he said. "Talk to the real people, the working stiffs. You'll find out they still believe in the Boys Scouts of America, their church and country, and yes, the FBI and J. Edgar Hoover."

"You skipped Thomas Jefferson," said Jim Murphy. He put his pencil down beside his pad. "For the sake of my story, will you part that American flag you've wrapped yourself in and give me a quote I can use?"

"That's my quote," said Leon. "You have my witnessed permission to use it."

"You're shooting yourself in the foot," Jim Murphy almost shrieked. "You don't respond like that to a governor taking a swing at the FBI."

But Dean Cooper's criticism of the FBI had been indecisive, and

· · ·

Leon knew it. I watched his face. He knew something Jim Murphy didn't, that Cooper's quote on Hoover and the FBI had been a slap on the wrist. Leon made a decision in his own mind. He was going to provoke the governor into all-out war with the FBI and Hoover.

"Okay, Jim," said Leon. "Here's the rest of the quote: 'I am appalled at Governor Dean Cooper's vicious attack on the FBI and J. Edgar Hoover—a man and an institution that will go down as the most heroic and courageous crime fighters in our country's history.'"

"I can't believe what I'm hearing," said Jim Murphy. "But I'm writing it down." He stopped writing long enough to look at Leon. "You do know you've lost the election with those phoney patriotic words, don't you?"

Leon snapped his fingers. "Add this, Jim: 'If, as the FBI and Mr. Hoover say, gambling winnings are being skimmed off the top in Las Vegas and smuggled to known syndicate figures in other parts of the country, I as governor will bring to bear every weapon at my command to revoke the gambling licenses of those who have been involved.'"

"It's been nice knowing you," said Jim Murphy, stuffing his pad into his coat pocket.

· · ·

16

I will never understand why Governor Dean Cooper responded as he did to Leon's position on the FBI. Cooper was no dummy. He was an intelligent man, a tested politician, a former district attorney and a trial lawyer who knew human nature from having to deal with juries. Still, he reacted as if he had been prodded with a hot needle, and thereby he set in motion the factors that proved to be the turning point of the campaign.

I have to think that it was Leon's homespun television pitch to housewives that drove Dean Cooper into pushing the panic button. But even that was a contradiction. The governor had to know there was little merit in Leon's corny stories about his kids. Leon did. Afterwards, he let slip a remark that set my vision straight on all runs for office: "There are no merits in a political campaign. It's all show biz."

Jim Murphy wrote his story about Leon's promise to bring "every weapon of the governor's office to bear" in revoking licenses of gamblers involved in skimming profits off the top. Dean Cooper went through the roof, calling Leon a traitor to Nevada. Leon responded that it was the people of Nevada who were being cheated when gambling winnings went uncounted and untaxed. If Governor Cooper was going to let that practice go on, Leon as governor sure as hell would work with J. Edgar Hoover to put a stop to it. That was money our underfinanced schools could use. Leon said his first order of business as governor would be to meet face-to-face with J. Edgar Hoover and the FBI to come to an understanding on jurisdiction. Dean Cooper compared that to Leon's meeting with Hitler, and he likened working with the FBI to working with the Gestapo.

Even the Strip recoiled at that one. As the argument between the

. . .

governor and the challenger grew more heated, the silence from the Strip grew deeper. The casino owners did not approve of Leon's position. Neither did they believe he would do anything to hurt them mortally. But they knew one thing: Governor Dean Cooper had gone too far in calling Hoover a Hitler and likening the FBI to the Gestapo. Some of them suddenly decided to go fishing at remote lakes in Michigan. Others sailed to the South Seas. Those who were left developed sealed lips. This was a politicians' fight they wanted no part of.

Jim Murphy was in seventh heaven, covering the governor's attacks and Leon's "responsible" stance and statements, as he described it. Jim Murphy even conceded to us that it was the governor, not Leon, who had made a bad error in judgment. Not only in attacking Hoover and the FBI, but in giving Leon that one gift an incumbent should never give a challenger—a forum from which to speak. The governor was giving Leon more exposure than he could have bought with a million-dollar war chest.

When that message finally got home to Dean Cooper, it was too late. Instead of pulling in his horns, he pulled out all stops. He formed a squad of political sharpshooters from Las Vegas, Reno, and even the cow counties to take pot shots at Leon, the rationale being that Leon would be forced into scattering his fire and so diffuse himself hopelessly. Leon sidestepped that strategy adroitly by saying he was not running against the sharpshooters, just Dean Cooper. When Cooper could summon enough courage to attack him personally, then Leon would answer. He added that the governor was "a big boy now, able to fight his own battles instead of relying on political stooges." That ended the sharpshooters' squad.

The governor and his strategists then hit on the idea of celebrity endorsements for Dean Cooper. Sammy Davis, Jr., was the first to cut radio and television spots. It might have worked except that

· · ·

Sammy Davis referred to Nevada's eminent Governor Dean Cooper as "a swingin' cat." That sank Sammy Davis as a political asset. As for the governor, he did not recover from that description for a long time.

Good old "Hoss" from the television show *Bonanza* was next up, exhorting Nevadans to vote for his "podnuh." All the lovability Hoss had earned in *Bonanza* converted to "What's that carpetbagger doing getting mixed up in our affairs?" Hoss was fired.

Governor Dean Cooper's celebrity endorsements died with Leon's well-circulated and righteous comment: "Nevadans don't like out-siders telling them how to vote." If Nevadans did before, they didn't now.

17

There was nothing out of the ordinary in the manner in which Bill Skinner opened the door to the suite and crossed the mock foyer. Nor was there anything different in the way he was dressed, in conservative gray suit and the fedora hat he had worn since FBI days in Washington, D.C. His expression was, as usual, unrevealing.

Yet, something *was* different. It emanated from him from the instant he walked in. Everyone in the suite felt it. George Friar in the corner of the parlor room reached up to take off his thick horn-rimmed glasses and hold them aloft. Abner, our media man, set down the newspaper he was reading and raised his head. His eyes were suddenly alert. My brother Gene changed from a prone position to a sitting position on the couch. Peck looked quizzically over his rim-less glasses. Leon, at the Round Table, stopped writing the speech he was roughing out. He leaned back and put his elbows on the arms of

· · ·

the chair in which he was sitting and regarded Skinner silently as he approached.

I remembered afterward that it was like a pantomime. Nobody paid a greeting, nobody said a word. Nobody got to his feet. Most important, nobody approached the Round Table to interrupt the whispered conversation between Skinner and Leon. That conversation lasted longer than anyone would have anticipated. When it was over, Leon leaned back in his chair again, his glasses riding low on the bridge of his nose, his mind retreating into that interior cocoon. Whatever Skinner had told him, it elicited neither disappointment nor jubilance.

Finally, Leon sighed and said in a voice intended for everyone gathered in the suite, "Take us through it from the beginning, Bill."

Wordlessly, everyone made his way to the Round Table and sat down. Skinner looked down at his hands for a long moment as if he were gathering his thoughts. When he raised his eyes, it was to meet the combined gaze of the core campaign group.

"I got a call a week ago from my informant inside the opposition's brain trust," he said. "The name of my informant is my business, nobody else's. The information I received was that Governor Cooper had made a personal call to every individual in his heavy-contributor force. He was summoning them to a private meeting in the Governor's Mansion. The key line in each call was this: 'This campaign isn't going as well as it could.'"

The table was silent, absorbing the import of those words. Nobody needed to be instructed about what the words added up to.

"The governor's first call went of course to the richest Mormon banker in Las Vegas. This call was important in more ways than money. It meant that our Mormon banker had erred in assuming that his flock was solidly behind him in his support of Dean Cooper. It also meant that our Mormon banker had erred again if he thought

· · ·

115

he had any influence with the . . . ." Skinner paused, but he could not bring himself to be so proper as to use the words *gaming casinos*. ". . . gambling joints on the Strip, to which he had been making big loans."

Skinner glanced at his wristwatch. "That meeting in the Governor's Mansion began at ten o'clock this morning. It lasted two hours. It was supposed to include a post-business-talk luncheon, but there was reportedly little appetite for that after the governor opened his remarks with these words: 'I'm going to need every bit of your help in every way—not only money but the whip hand—or else we're lost.' "

Skinner paused again to let that statement sink in. It did not take much effort to imagine the stone visages and the veiled eyes fastened on the governor when he uttered those words. There would have been mumbled phrases like, "You can count on me, Governor." Or, "I've never backed out of a fight yet and I don't intend to start now." That, or utter silence and monosyllabic good-byes as the governor's big-money task force trooped out of the mansion.

Skinner looked at his wristwatch again, then at Leon, but this time it was for a reason. "Any minute now, you should be getting some interesting phone calls."

As if on cue, the telephone rang. When nobody reached to pick it up, the telephone kept ringing. There was shrill desperation, it seemed, in that incessant ringing. Finally, my brother Gene picked up the telephone. "No, it isn't Leon," Gene said curtly. "It's his brother." There was a sputtering on the receiver. Gene covered it with his hand and said to Leon, "It's for you. Opposition high roller number one."

Leon took his time picking up the receiver. "Yes, Norm." Leon held the telephone in the air so that everyone at the table could hear. "Leon. I want to help your campaign in any way you choose," Norm's voice shrilled. "You name it. I'm there. I believe in you, Leon."

Leon lowered the telephone. "Thanks for your faith, Norm. Your

· · ·

help and your money weren't there when I needed them." Leon thought a moment, and then said contemptuously, "I don't need them now, when the battle has been won."

No sooner had Leon hung up than the telephone rang again. But this time it was the manager at the switchboard in the lobby downstairs. He had called to say that he was in a quandary. There were at least twenty urgent telephone calls backed up and he needed to know in which order Leon wanted to receive them. Leon thanked him and took the receiver off the hook. "It's poor politics," he said, "but I want no ties from false friends at the last minute." He was silent for a long, long moment, and then he said, "Poor Dean Cooper. He couldn't see those bastards were in it for themselves. Not because they believed in him." His gaze swept the table. "Do me one favor," he said. "Don't ever let me kid myself like that."

George Friar made a sound of mingled exultancy and contempt. "Congratulations, Governor, on the victory awaiting you. And felicitations for your state of mind. Save your compassion for those who have earned it. If the tables were turned, Dean Cooper and his minions wouldn't be weeping crocodile tears for you."

There was a blaze of anger in Leon's eyes, but Friar cut him off. "I signed on here as a hired gun, Leon," he said. "And that's what I aim to be for as long as I'm around."

Before either Leon or George Friar could say another word, Gene picked up the telephone and called Jimmy the Greek on his instant line. "Greek," Gene said in an overloud voice. "What's this business about Cooper calling a secret meeting of his heavies?"

Skinner was regarding Gene as if he had betrayed a confidence. Gene pointed surreptitiously at Leon and George Friar. Skinner got the point that Gene was fending off a fight, nodded, and said nothing.

"Oh, you know," said Gene. "Sorry, Greek, but the line has been tied up." The Greek's accented voice was indecipherable. "Jimmy,"

· · ·

shouted Gene. "I'm passing you to Leon." He did, and said for our benefit, "Jimmy just heard about it, but he hasn't got the sources we have." He nodded his head towards Skinner. "He'll make book, though, that the ball game's over and we've won."

There was a sharp, insistent rapping at the door. Leon covered his free ear with one hand and signaled to George Friar to answer the knock. George got up with obvious reluctance and crossed the foyer to the door.

It was Jim Murphy, for once stripped of his cool. "Of all the dumb stunts," he shrilled at George Friar.

That served to divert Friar from his postponed argument with Leon. "What've we done wrong now, Jim?"

"Arson!"

"I don't think I heard you right."

"Arson! At the last minute, too. You had a chance of winning. Until now!"

George Friar laid one bear paw on Jim Murphy's shoulder. "Control yourself, Jim," he said. "But first, explain yourself."

"Burning signs! Where do you keep your white sheets? I knew in my heart you guys were Ku Kluxers!"

Jim Murphy was unintelligible, but George Friar had been around long enough to catch a glimmer of what he meant. He held up a hand to silence Murphy. "I know what you're trying to accuse us of, Jim," he said. "There's been a big fire in an abandoned warehouse full of political signs saying RE-ELECT GOVERNOR DEAN COOPER. Am I right?"

But Jim Murphy had leaped one step ahead of George Friar. "You wouldn't know about that fire unless you had a hand in it!"

"Let me instruct you about political life, son," Friar said to Jim Murphy. "When the opposition can't find anyone who will post their

· · ·

signs in their yards, they gather them up, put them in an old ware-house, set fire to them . . . and *blame the opposition!*"

Jim Murphy was silent, thinking about what George Friar really meant.

"You mean it's all over?"

"Yes, Jim," said George Friar wearily. "The campaign's over."

18

Election night remembered meant many things to many people. I suppose it has always been like that, evoking disparate emotions that are too contradictory to be voiced for a long time, until the impact has finally hit home.

For Leon, it meant that he had been elected governor of a state. For his campaign workers, it meant victory against overwhelming odds, and for that they had earned every bit of the jubilation that the night held. For my mother, it meant loss, regardless of Leon's assurance. For my father, it meant confusion and dismay and flight to the mountains when a reporter named Si Price, one of the jackal breed that every press corps must endure, pummeled him with prob-ing questions. From that night on, the scarred old pickup truck with its tangled adornment of baling wire was never seen again when strangers' limousines and Cadillacs and Continentals were parked in front of the family home.

For me, election night was a harbinger of things to come. It was the night when the treasured privacy of our family was violated, per-manently.

· · ·

The emotional roller coaster of election night began even before 6 P.M., when the polls closed and the first results came trickling in. Leon's private election line to headquarters south, our suite in the Desert Inn in Las Vegas, had been installed in the "other side" of the house, the wing that had been reserved for guests in horse and buggy days. Skinner was holding down the Las Vegas end of the private line, both to phone voting returns directly to Leon and to keep watch for any chicanery at the polls.

Leon's private headquarters room was the nerve center, protected by a buffer of two big rooms, a parlor in front and a bedroom in back. Two television sets had been installed, one a jarring presence in my mother's gracious living room and one in the parlor of the wing. These were for campaign workers and supporters invited to the house to share the evening with the hoped-for governor-to-be.

Another telephone line had been added to the one already in place in the nerve-center room. That was for Peck, our numbers man, whose poll watchers were stationed in key counties throughout the state. That faithful standby, the radio, was also located in the nerve center as a backup in case the television signal failed, which was not uncommon in those days.

The same arrangement was repeated on the family side of the house, except that the bedrooms were sealed off from everybody except members of family. That was a Basque custom so iron bound that even Leon did not dare suggest making them accessible to outsiders. Nosey women, old and young, were politely but firmly turned back at the bedroom doors. They had enough to look at, anyway. It was legend that few outsiders had ever seen anything of the inside of the house. Now, they were prying everywhere, not interested in returns, but in the mix of early Mission and Victorian furniture, family pictures, and the religious icons that brought smirks to the hard mouths

· · ·

of wealthy, political-minded dowagers who had joined the campaign when things began to look promising.

My mother's long dining room table was laden with hors d'oeuvres and French wine cooling in buckets, while side tables held stronger stuff—whiskey and mixes. Not a beer can was to be seen. She would not tolerate that next to her cherished crystal and china. It was a mistake, as the breakage counted up the next day proved, but my mother winced in silence instead of complaining. After all, it had been for her eldest son.

That night was everything an election night should be. Early returns showed Leon and Dean Cooper neck to neck. Then Dean Cooper surged ahead in Las Vegas country and the cheers turned to moans. Then Leon came up neck to neck again when Reno country returns came in. Leon moved through the rooms every so often, but always when he was down in the returns and the *troops* needed cheering up. Finally, Leon began to creep ahead, almost invisibly at first and then visibly in a slow surge that could not be stopped. Leon had once said to Jim Murphy that the small counties were the backbone of the state and Murphy had responded, "Yeah. The lower extremities." At the *Las Vegas Tribune,* Murphy would be eating his words just about now.

In the end, Leon was right. Reno country and Las Vegas country balanced each other out and the swing vote came from those far-scattered polls in the boonies. Leon had seen and exploited their potential. The incumbent governor, Dean Cooper, had not. From that election on, save one, no candidate for major office in Nevada could ignore the cow counties. They were looked down upon no longer.

Dean Cooper had been around long enough to see the handwriting on the wall. When the rural vote became so lopsided as to be unbeatable, he telephoned Leon personally on his private line. We

· · ·

were to learn later that Skinner at the Las Vegas suite had given Dean Cooper the unrevealed number. Leon covered the receiver with his palm and said commandingly to the shouters surrounding him, "It's the governor." A sudden, awed hush fell upon the nerve-center room, a hush that spread swiftly throughout the house. "Thank you, Governor," Leon said with an altogether new note in his voice. "Nobody can say we didn't keep this one above the belt." Even after the connection had been cut, Leon took a long time in hanging up the telephone. He was staring at it as though he could not really believe the message it had carried to him. Then he turned to us, his face pale and drawn, and said, "The governor has conceded."

He recovered himself in the bedlam that followed. A sip of champagne brought the color back to his cheeks as he toasted his campaign helpers. A sip was all that he could risk. For him, election night was far from over. His car was waiting outside with the engine running. That would be for the dash across Washoe Valley to Reno and the crowd of supporters that awaited him there. With Reno country having backed him so strongly, that victory party would not be easy to escape from. Then on to the airport and the flight to Las Vegas in a Lear jet, piloted by inventor Bill Lear himself. The flight did not offer much of a respite. It was like being shot out of a cannon. The little jet zoomed toward an apex in the sky and then began its descent to Las Vegas.

Leon could not have imagined the proportions his Las Vegas reception would reach. The welcoming crowd had pushed clear to the runways, filled with screaming Las Vegans who had voted for him, and with as many band-wagon others who had not. They broke through the police cordon Skinner had arranged, and lifting Leon to their shoulders they carried him through the airport terminal to the convertible cavalcade outside. On its way through Glitter Gulch, the motorcade was tripled by tourists who didn't know what all the

· · ·

honking and shouting and horn blowing was about, but didn't want to miss a parade. There was another victory celebration, hastily organized at the new convention center, and then the motorcade, quadrupled in size by now, made its deafening way up the Strip. When it passed the Desert Inn, our personal headquarters, we covered Leon with coats and blankets and smuggled him out of his limousine. Nobody seemed to miss his presence. They were more interested in yelling and drinking their heads off.

When it was all over and we had managed to creep into the headquarters suite, nobody had energy enough to say a word. We sprawled on the chaises and armchairs and stared numbly at each other. After a while, my brother Gene got up and went to the bar. He returned with seven glasses—one each for Leon, George Friar, Peck, Skinner, Abner, me, and himself. He made another round with a bottle of champagne, but there were no toasts, just glasses raised feebly in the general direction of everybody.

Out of the bedlam we had been through this night, all that I could clearly remember was the scene I had walked in upon in my mother's bedroom. She had managed to spirit Leon there before he could leave. I remember that she was beautiful with her gray-streaked auburn hair braided on her head and the single cameo brooch on her black silk blouse. She was holding Leon's hand in both of hers, and she said, "I don't want to lose you, Leon."

"You're not going to lose me, Mom," Leon said hurriedly.

My remembering was interrupted by a quiet knocking at the door. I crossed the foyer and opened the door in irritation. Would this night never end?

Two men were standing outside the door. Two other men were standing on either side of the hallway behind them, their backs to the walls, one watching backwards and one watching forward. They were bodyguards, big and burly and stone faced.

· · ·

Of the two men at the door, I had met one. He was Ruby Kolod, short and round and jovial and one of the syndicate owners of the Desert Inn. The other man was also a syndicate owner of the Desert Inn. I had never seen Moe Dalitz in person, but I had seen newspaper photographs of him. He was thin, with a lined face, slicked-down gray hair, and dead blue eyes that were as cold as chips of ice.

"We came to congratulate our candidate," said Ruby.

Two

19

My hand stopped involuntarily on its way to reaching for the doorknob. Leon did not ask why. I supposed it was because he was sharing the same sensation as I. Being about to meet an American legend face-to-face gives one pause.

The double doors were of dark, polished wood and the upraised lettering on one of them was modest enough to be inauspicious. I don't know what I had expected it to be—red, white, and blue, and perhaps ornate enough to match the script of the Bill of Rights—but the letters said simply:

DIRECTOR

FEDERAL BUREAU OF INVESTIGATION

From the moment Leon and I and our companion from Nevada had climbed the steps that mounted to the Department of Justice, housed in a typical Washington gray stone building, nothing had been as I had anticipated. The front doors opened onto a reception room with a marble floor and, off to one side, a single desk to receive visitors. The young man seated behind the desk was dressed in a dark blue suit, white shirt and black tie, and black shoes. Everyone we met during the next several hours was dressed the same way. I had genuinely expected uniformed guards armed to the teeth to be stationed in the reception room, but there was only the young man. Still, I was certain there had to be electronic surveillance and agents with sophisticated weaponry watching us from somewhere. After all,

. . .

the Department of Justice was the nerve center for crime detection in the United States.

Something else pervaded the atmosphere here, and that was silence. The young man at the reception desk spoke in a subdued, quiet voice. The guide who materialized to lead us into the interior of the building spoke in the same tone. Even the tread of our shoes upon the hallway carpeting seemed hushed.

Things began to pick up when we entered the director's outer office. There were display cases with guns, knives, brass knuckles, and shoes with hacksaw blades concealed in their soles—all of which had figured in famous FBI cases of the past. Another display case bore outsized cartoons from vintage newspapers. A somber list etched into one wall bore the names of FBI agents who had been killed in service.

Keeping to the FBI's heralded code of racial equality, there were two black agents stationed at the door to the director's inner sanctum. "Mr. Hoover will see you now," one of them said, and he ushered us through the private entrance.

J. Edgar Hoover's formal office was spacious and sumptuous with an immense mahogany desk and plush chairs. Strict protocol had been followed. The agent who escorted us deftly made sure that Leon was in the lead. Hoover rose and came around the desk to greet him.

"Governor," he said, "I can't tell you how pleased I am that you won the election."

J. Edgar Hoover was taller than I had imagined. He stood six feet tall, but his fleshy face seemed to diminish that. It wasn't flesh of the mushy variety. Once, it must have been made of hard stuff. In newspaper photos and newsreels his eyes protruded, but in actuality they were lidded. His hair was black with a dash of pronounced white at the temples. He was meticulously and expensively dressed in a dark blue suit, a white shirt with long collar tabs, and a wide black tie. The uniform started here.

· · ·

After shaking hands with me, he turned to our companion from Nevada, a banker named Art Jones, and smiled broadly. They were old friends from American Legion days and it was Art Jones who had surmounted the difficulties of getting a governor from the notorious gambling state of Nevada together with the director of the FBI. Leon had so met his promise to the voters of Nevada, but that was incidental to the main business at hand. Nevada with its syndicate infiltration was in deep trouble.

"I trust your trip was pleasant," Hoover said. "And . . ." He paused, choosing his word, ". . . unobtrusive."

The trip had been unobtrusive, all right. But it had not been pleasant. The first blizzard of winter had made it impossible for Leon and me to fly out of the Reno airport. A military bus, hastily called, took us through a blinding snowstorm to a naval air station in a more sheltered valley, where a powerful all-weather military plane was waiting. We streaked south to another military base near Las Vegas. Art Jones met us there, and wearing dark glasses, we drove to Las Vegas in a car with tinted windows for the flight to Los Angeles and then on to Dulles in Washington, D.C. All three tickets had been taken out in the name of Jones. Nobody tumbled and we managed to get out undetected. Conditions of secrecy for the meeting between Leon and J. Edgar Hoover had been met.

Skipping over the cloak-and-dagger machinations of the flight, Art Jones said to Hoover, "The press hasn't the least idea we're here."

I had assumed the meeting would be in the formal office, but I was mistaken. We were escorted by the agent to a door that led to the real inner sanctum of J. Edgar Hoover—a replica in miniature of the large formal office. Here again, protocol ruled. Leon was seated directly across the desk from Hoover, so that they could continue taking each other's measure, I assumed. Art Jones and I sat on flanking chairs, and when I glanced back, the agent was seated behind us against the

· · ·

wall. He had pulled out a notebook, and a poised pen was at the ready. Getting down to business in a hurry, I thought.

Instead, Hoover took off on a rambling monologue that began with Lyndon Johnson. "LBJ was an across-the-street neighbor from me for nineteen years when he was a congressman and a senator and even vice president," Hoover began. "He was treated very shabbily as vice president, and he was bitter about it. He confided in me, and I can tell you he had reason to be bitter. When Lyndon came back from Dallas after the assassination, one of the first things he did was call me. He said, 'I want you to stay on with me. There are hard times ahead.'" Hoover paused as if on the brink of imparting an important revelation. "Then the president said, 'I want you to assume a good share of my protection. I know this is a Secret Service responsibility, but I have some qualms about the job they're doing. I'm not criticizing them, but their protection alone isn't enough to satisfy me.'" Hoover said with authority, "I promised the president that the FBI would be in the picture." Reluctant to divulge an important and inside state secret in so many words, Hoover confirmed the FBI's role in protecting the president by saying, "President Johnson and I still have lunch every month in his private upstairs luncheon room."

Without warning, Hoover switched the subject to the Kennedys. Leon glanced at me sideways as if to say, "When in hell are we getting to Nevada and *my* problem?" I shrugged in a gesture of helplessness. As far as I was concerned, Nevada's problem could wait. I was hearing history straight from the source, and I didn't want it to stop.

"I don't want you to get the wrong idea about my relationship with the Kennedys," Hoover said emphatically. "Joseph Patrick Kennedy was an old friend of mine, and I used to go to Hyannis Port often to visit with him. The stories that old scalawag could tell about his rum-running days. And Honey Fitz, too, Rose Kennedy's father. That was a pair to draw to." Hoover shook his head in nostalgic admiration.

· · ·

Then he became serious. "I remember the Kennedy kids growing up. From the beginning, the old man wanted young Joe to be president. Joe was the eldest son. From day one, he was being groomed for that." Hoover's voice fell with genuine sadness. "Then young Joe was killed in the war, and his legacy fell to Jack. Jack didn't have as much strength as Joe. He leaned more to the intellectual and the arts.

"Bobby Kennedy was a mean little kid. I never thought he would amount to much even then, and he still doesn't amount to much." The corners of Hoover's mouth turned down. "That long hair of his. Sloppy dresser. I looked up the barber who cut Jack's hair and still cuts Bobby's hair. He told me their shirt collars were black underneath from dirt. Now, you would think kids raised as rich as they were would be cleaner." Hoover started to digress, saying, "Those beatniks he attracts wherever he goes. Thank God they aren't old enough to vote." Then his face flushed as he remembered something. "Do you know what he did? When Jack made Bobby attorney general, Bobby had technical jurisdiction over this office . . . over *my* FBI. One day Bobby came slouching down that hallway outside. Then he dared to come into my outer office wearing those dirty sneakers and dirty jeans. He ignored my agents at the door to *this* office, my private office, and flopped himself down in *that* chair." He pointed at me and the chair in which I was sitting, opposite one corner of the desk. "Then he leaned back in his chair, raised his legs, and *put those dirty sneakers on my desk.*"

Nothing Bobby Kennedy could have thought of would have tormented that epitome of immaculate manners and attire more. "This punk kid had the temerity to tell me I was going to have to integrate the FBI. I told him that everyone knows I have Negro agents. But only if they're qualified. I won't pick anybody—Chinese, Japanese, Negro, or anyone else—unless they are qualified. Then that little bastard says, 'I don't think you are demonstrating a cooperative attitude.' I

· · ·

told him that if he wanted a new director of the Federal Bureau of Investigation to get one and I would retire." Hoover concluded smugly, "That was the last time he bothered me like that."

Leon audibly cleared his throat and started to speak, but Hoover held up his hand in a signal that he was not finished with what he was saying. "Next to Bobby Kennedy, the most crude, insulting man I ever met was Khrushchev. He speaks English, you know, and pretends he doesn't. When I met him at the White House, he said to his interpreter, 'Tell Mr. Hoover that I don't like the way he is persecuting communists in the United States. It is a denial of personal expression. That is not the American way.'

"That is the moment when I said to his interpreter, 'You tell Chairman Khrushchev that I am thoroughly acquainted with his entire espionage movement in the United States.' The interpreter did not have to translate. Khrushchev understood and stormed away, and I stormed away in the other direction."

Hoover rambled on. This time, it was about the Lindbergh kidnapping and someone called Gaston who lied about a hundred thousand dollars hidden in a lead pipe in the Hudson River. Leon cut short his monologue. "Mr. Hoover, about Nevada's gambling problem . . ."

Hoover leaned back in his chair. "I have nothing against gambling," he said. "I go to the racetracks. I used to lose quite a little bit, but then I decided I had to cut down if I wanted to enjoy the tracks. So now, I limit myself to two-dollar bets and the most I lose is five or six dollars a day." He reeled off the various racetracks he went to, and did not mention the name of one he was not going to in California "because the governor had promised the racetrack concession to the Alfonso brothers if he won the election, and you know what hoodlums they are."

Suddenly, and without asking, we were in Nevada. It started with Hoover staying at the Sahara resort hotel on the Las Vegas Strip be-

· · ·

cause construction tycoon Del Webb was both owner and an old friend. "That is the only honest place on the Strip," Hoover said. It was a flat-out statement with no equivocation and covered a lot of territory. Neither Leon nor Art Jones, a banker who knew, could have made a blanket pronouncement like that.

In the next half hour, J. Edgar Hoover proved he knew what he was talking about, reeling off names of resort casinos, who the real owners were, how many "points in the joints" they owned. "You take Caesars Palace," Hoover said by way of example. "Sam Giancana owns that and the place is filled from top to bottom with hoodlums and ex-convicts."

When he got around to the Desert Inn, our campaign headquarters, and owners Moe Dalitz and Ruby Kolod, both campaign contributors, I could feel Leon flinching without actually seeing it.

"With help from our informant inside the Desert Inn," Hoover said, his lidded eyes fixed unblinkingly on Leon, "we were able to get films and wiretaps showing distribution of gambling winnings skimmed off the top. I believe you know what 'skimming' means, Governor. Winnings never counted for taxes due the State of Nevada and . . ." He paused and then added in reverent tones, ". . . our federal government."

Neither Leon nor Art Jones volunteered a word, and Hoover went on. "The Desert Inn was not singled out for this kind of scrutiny by the FBI," he said. "Our informants were in place in nearly every Strip casino. When we exposed the films, we were able to identify the couriers, men and women, and followed them to Cleveland, Detroit, New Jersey, Miami, and so on. I can assure you they were not carrying oatmeal in those black bags."

Hoover rambled on for a while with some revelations about Las Vegas that Leon already knew. Hoover was at first surprised and then patronizingly delighted that the governor-elect of Nevada at least

· · ·

knew something. "Governor, I like your attitude and your way of doing things," Hoover said. "Be assured that the FBI will work with you in cleaning that filth out of the good state of Nevada. I am even prepared to give an order that our film and wiretaps be made available to you."

Fortunately, I said nothing, but Leon did. "Mr. Hoover, I know you have a busy schedule. We've taken enough of your time." He got to his feet and we followed suit. "I want to thank you for your offer of cooperation."

I caught the slight emphasis on the word *offer,* but it did not occur to me until later that Leon had accepted Hoover's offer but not FBI assistance.

"It has indeed been a pleasure to talk with you," Hoover said, standing up. "My assistant, Duke DeLauer, is waiting for you in his office."

A photographer materialized out of nowhere to take a group picture, partly for public relations and partly for the record. I was becoming suspicious of everything by now.

"Your photographer's right on target," Leon said to Hoover.

"If he wasn't, I'd send him to Anchorage."

Hoover's last words were ominous and directed to Leon. "We know you can clean up your house, Governor," he said. "But don't let what is going to happen now stain *your* administration. Make sure politically that it reflects back to the Dean Cooper administration."

The meeting with Hoover's chief assistant, tall and hawk-faced Duke DeLauer, started out to be a repetition of our session with J. Edgar Hoover. DeLauer asked Leon bluntly how he had gone about choosing prospective members of the Gaming Control Board that wielded the powerful whip hand over Nevada's legalized gambling industry. Leon explained, "Integrity and a background of absolute honesty. A traffic ticket can knock you off the board."

DeLauer nodded. "I know. We've checked them out."

Leon regarded him with incredulity. There was a touch of irritation in his voice when he said, "How'd they come out?"

"Fine," said DeLauer.

Exactly as Hoover had done, DeLauer offered Leon copies of the wiretaps and films of couriers filling their black bags in casino counting rooms and delivering them to syndicate heads in a dozen eastern and southern crime centers.

Instead of a yes or no answer, Leon asked DeLauer, "Are you prepared to give me the names and photographs of FBI informants in our gambling casinos?"

DeLauer jerked upright in his chair as though he had been prodded. Then he regained his composure and said in a grave tone, "That I cannot do, Governor. If our Cosa Nostra informers were flushed out, they would be killed in a minute."

"I know that," said Leon. "That is why I don't even want to know that they exist." Leon was silent for several moments. He had withdrawn into his isolation chamber. When he raised his head, his decision had been made. "That is precisely the reason I cannot accept your offer of filmstrips and wiretaps," he said. "I can surmise that the FBI got permission to wiretap through a Department of Justice order. I can also guess that our local Nevada telephone companies were reluctant to accept that order. Wiretapping is illegal and our telephone companies don't want to get caught up in any indictments, which would be manna from heaven for the press. That is the reason I cannot accept your offer. Governors are not immune when it comes to breaking the law."

DeLauer did not argue. "I understand, Governor," he said. "I respect your position."

When they stood up to shake hands, Leon said, "I know a lot more about what's going on in Nevada than I did before. Let me sort this

· · ·

out with my Gaming Control Board and my personal staff." Leon shook his head with obvious doubt. "If I can't clean up my own house, I'll take the FBI up on its offer."

"We have confidence you can get the job done," said DeLauer reassuringly.

I thought to myself, "I'm glad *you* have confidence. Leon can't clean out the hoods without your help and he won't clean them out with your help. To make things worse, you've fingered a dozen contributors to the governorship campaign, one congressman, two U.S. senators, and a hundred legislators, who are just going to love their governor for cutting their campaign purse strings. You're asking him to cripple the economy of a state by closing up a dozen hotel-casinos, because the fact of the matter is that their owners are the only ones who know how to run a gambling joint without going broke. You're asking him to take away the jobs of a few thousand people who work for the hotel-casinos. You're asking him to cut his own political throat, when he could have gone a long way in government. And if he goes down in disgrace, you're wrecking the reputation of his family, *my* family. Don't you realize it's too late to change the situation? Thanks for nothing."

Outside the Department of Justice, there was an official car and driver waiting. We dismissed them and walked in silence down Pennsylvania Avenue in a mist-soft rain. A ribbon of red lights from home-going cars stretched from the green-domed Capitol at one end of the Mall to the sandstone obelisk of the Washington Monument rearing into the sky at the other end. Its summit was marked by tiny red, tapered, blinking lights. We passed the cross section of the world's peoples going home at end of day, voicing accents of French, German, Spanish, British, and a dozen unrecognizable tongues.

My mind went back to a time before when I was living in Washing-

· · ·

ton, bringing back memories of war years and wonderings of what the very near future held for brothers scattered halfway around the world. Now, another kind of conflict confronted one of those brothers and another kind of uncertainty loomed over us.

"What the hell do we do now?" said Leon, breaking our silence.

20

"Is this what we worked our hearts out for?"

The agonized lament emanating from the office of the governor, in this case Leon, was not exclusive. It was probably being uttered from Alaska to Florida by newly elected governors buried under an avalanche of executive and social obligations.

Leon was ensconced now in the executive chambers of the state capitol in Carson City. The governor's office was lofty and white ceilinged and old. Wood paneling had been added in recent times, and the massive easy chairs were of brown leather worn by generations of politicians to a softness so yielding that one ran the risk of getting trapped in its depths. A bronze bust of Abraham Lincoln in Romanesque toga was the only statuary—he was the one who had admitted Nevada to the Union at the time of the Civil War, when he needed additional votes in Congress. A portrait photograph of Leon's family and a black and white picture of a Basque sheepherder were all that adorned the walls. More adornments would come with time.

What triggered the agonized lament for Leon was living up to his campaign pledge of meeting individually with each and every agency and department head in state government. I could not help thinking that Leon had made altogether too many campaign promises, including the private meeting with J. Edgar Hoover and the FBI. Now, he was having to pay the piper.

The Hoover revelations, at least, had been put on the back burner for the time being. "He has to understand that we're going through with a change of administration," Leon said. After the meeting with the FBI, we had concocted a statement and released it even before we had left Washington, D.C. I had taken an end run on the capital press corps by phoning it to the wire service bureaus for United Press and Associated Press back in Reno. The statement from Leon said, "A working relationship has been established with the FBI in getting to the roots of accusations about mob infiltration made against a segment of Nevada's legalized gaming industry."

We bolstered the governor-elect's statement by injecting intrigue and suspense: "Evidence of a highly confidential nature has been presented to me for evaluation and further investigation. If our findings here in Nevada indicate that eventual action is warranted, *then that action will be taken by the State of Nevada.*" This was to put the FBI on notice that the issue of state's rights was involved here. Federal intervention, anathema in Nevada, was a last resort. The "highly confidential" part was also misleading, on purpose. It would keep every gambler in the state on edge wondering what and how much Leon knew about him. When I asked Leon why he had refused the FBI tapes and wiretaps, he said, "If I took them, the FBI would have a hammer over my head to clean house right now. Hood backgrounds or not, these are our people and gambling is what keeps the state alive. I've got to have time to decide how to come at this. The statement puts things on hold. It's all we can do until the transition from Dean Cooper to me is done with."

The transition involved the promised meetings between the governor-elect and "each and every" agency and department head in

· · ·

state government. The very word *transition* became a nightmare. Leon must have had a thousand head-to-head meetings around the clock over the next two months. He learned about the workings of state government. Actually, he learned more than any governor should know. Jurisdictional disputes and power grabs covered over with insinuations, jealousies, and hatreds were heaped on his desk and poured into his ears. He had neglected to take into account the housekeeping factor. This finally led to his dismay on finding out what being elected governor boiled down to.

What got him back on track was the arrest of the chief justice of the supreme court on a drunken driving charge. The charge was eventually dismissed, but the chief justice, John Burbank by name, felt impelled to make a formal and judicial written explanation to the governor. It was apparently a work of art, and rumor had it that the explanation was better organized and written than any opinion the chief justice had handed down to date.

But he never got a chance to deliver it. When he walked with nervous tread into the governor's office, Leon with glasses on was bent forward over his desk making notes on the first draft of his inaugural address.

"Morning, John," said the governor without raising his head. "Sobered up yet?"

The chief justice was experiencing some difficulty making his mouth and vocal cords work. Finally, he managed to whisper out a word.

"Sarsaparilla."

Leon raised his head and peered at the chief justice over his horn-rimmed glasses. "Did I hear you say 'sarsaparilla?' I haven't heard that word since I was a kid."

"Sarsaparilla," the chief justice whispered. "That's all I drink now."

Leon regarded the quivering mass of judiciary standing before him.

· · ·

139

"John," he said gravely. "You look to me like you need a stiff shot of whiskey. It's in the sideboard in back of you."

A few days later, Leon was having one more of his promised meetings with agency heads. This one was with the director of the Division of Fish and Game. The director looked distraught. His agency had been caught in the middle of a public controversy over a disease making the rounds of state fish hatcheries. The disease apparently made the fish swim in erratic patterns, which made them difficult to catch and supposedly dangerous to eat. The director of Fish and Game had just gone through a technical and lengthy description of the dilemma facing his division.

After listening patiently for half an hour, Leon decided to end the session with a question. He did so with a straight face. "Is it true that these whirling fish are carriers of venereal disease?"

The director of Fish and Game recoiled as if he had been slapped. "Governor," he said, his voice trembling with anger, "whoever told you that is a damned liar."

Another interview was with a groundsman who was bucking for his boss's job as superintendent of Buildings and Grounds. The interview had not been asked for by Leon, but he felt he had to grant it to keep another unthought-out promise, that the "doors to the governor's office would always be open to every Nevadan."

The groundsman's name was Billy Budd and he had convinced himself that the way to get his boss's job was to convince the governor of his own erudition, or as it turned out, command of malapropisms.

His first one was philosophical. "Governor," he said, speaking of a personality change in his boss, "people change from one epic to another."

When the governor blinked, Billy Budd elaborated. "He has lost his relaxability."

· · ·

A little later, he spoke of the love of nature that led him to gardening: "Mother Nature is more powerful than modernism." I assumed he meant getting back to nature is better than being materialistic.

Again, about his boss: "It is my personnel opinion that he has an ionastic mentality." I assumed he meant that his boss had an iconoclastic bent.

Billy Budd outdid himself and lost his bid for promotion when he told about meeting a brown bear in the mountains. "The same day, would you believe," he said, "I ran into a bear of the same consistency."

Leon scribbled a message to me as I was taking notes at a table in the back of the executive suite. His secretary dutifully brought the message back to me. It said, "Would you get rid of this guy before I lose my already fragile command of the English language?"

Other encounters were not so distressing and Leon was not as patient. Word had gotten out that in his budget message to the legislature, Leon was going to ask for an increase in gambling taxes. Del Webb, the high-powered construction magnate, had built Bugsy Siegel's Flamingo resort hotel in Las Vegas. When he saw how much money the Flamingo was making, Webb had built a casino of his own. He had also become an overnight authority on casino financing. When he called Leon and told him that gambling could not absorb a tax increase, Leon told him, "Now, you listen to me. I'm no dummy like those legislators you're handing shit to about what tough shape the casinos are in. I've been a gambling attorney and I know what goes on. You guys are on a free ride. You can afford triple the tax I'm asking. In fact . . ." Mr. Del Webb had already surrendered.

There was no naysaying the fact that Leon had almost single-handedly rebuilt the Republican party in Nevada. Now that their man was governor of the state, and therefore solidly ensconced with the

· · ·

money and power structure that ruled, the citizenry were no longer afraid to use the word *Republican* when applying for a job. They were coming out of the woodwork everywhere. It had been a long time since Republican gatherings and dinners had drawn anything but flies. Now, Republican women were vying with each other to organize dinners with celebrity speakers. Leon had his own ideas about who one celebrity speaker could be.

A few months before, he had gone over the state line to hear a talk by someone in California who was being billed as a comer in politics. Reaction to the new face in California politics, though, was anything but unanimous. One-time movie actors with political aspirations were old hat in California. They came and went like the ocean tides along the Pacific shoreline. This one was different, Leon insisted. His political philosophy was right—Republican and conservative. His talents as a speaker were manifold. In fact, Leon insisted, he had never heard anyone in politics who could communicate a message with such charm and conviction. The man's name was Ronald Reagan.

"Reagan is going to be the next governor of California," Leon said to us, his core group, during the campaign. "Don't kid yourself about that."

George Friar was doubtful. "But he's an unknown. We need a floor show to draw the crowd we need for this bash."

"Ron Reagan *is* the floor show," Leon insisted. "He doesn't need any help from anybody. Wait until you hear him. You'll see."

Peck Poulson, our public-opinion pollster, was now part of Leon's administration. "I've got my doubts about using the 'conservative' tag to get the money people here," he said.

"To hell with the conservative tag," Leon said. "We bill this one as a 'hands-across-the-border' thing." Leon was getting impatient. "Ronald Reagan and I are going to be working together. There's no

· · ·

50 percent on a personal relationship like this one. We're either 100 percent committed to each other, or nothing. Anything less and we can look forward to a long memory about an 80 percent relationship. I say it's going to be 100 percent from the beginning." He paused, deliberating about whether to say what he wanted to say. He had to know that our reaction would range from incredulity to outright guffaws, but he made his decision and said, "Ronald Reagan could be the next president of the United States."

21

While he is in office, not after, it is *de rigueur* that a governor be placed at the head of every invitation list worth the name. The day he is voted out of office, his name is automatically scratched from the list. No offense can be taken when a governor is thus relegated to oblivion. This is a hallowed practice and must be treated as an American tradition.

If the governor were to accept even a third of the invitations he receives, he would weigh three hundred pounds in a year. The problem of choosing which invitations to accept and which to decline and for what reason rests on the shoulders of the governor's private secretary, not the first lady. The first lady, however worthy, cannot be expected to know all the political nuances involved. Can this host be counted upon for a big campaign contribution next time around? Will other potential contributors be present at this dinner? Is that hostess hated by a wide circle of acquaintances, and if so, can she be counted upon to cut the governor to pieces for his conduct at dinner? The governor must never forget that first political rule: choose your enemies carefully. If she is known as your enemy, and everybody hates her, she can help you more than your friends can.

Then there are the celebrities of stage and screen, who cannot help you a bit politically or otherwise. But it's more fun to go to their suppers and spend time with them than with some stuffy old dowager who has a bag full of money.

Rena Chenault was one of the former. She was a French chanteuse, a little past her prime, but she had done all right in Paris in her day. No Piaf or Maurice Chevalier, but good enough to be recognized anywhere in France and booked into Las Vegas. She had a compact figure, not overlarge breasts but you knew they were there. Her eyes were blue and her skin was fair, with sort of a boiled-onion look, and that night she was wearing a low-cut, clinging silk ensemble of blouse and slacks. She was not particularly pretty, but her tremendous vitality made up for that. She ran and bounced around like a rubber ball, her mouth wreathed with a devil's grin and her speech laced with ribaldry. Although she pretended not to understand English very well, she chose her errors with precision, a comedienne's timing, and a native sense of humor.

Her villa, really a Mediterranean cottage in style and size, was off the ninth hole of the Desert Inn golf course. Inside, the white walls were inset with mosaic tiles, and elegant French furniture graced the hardwood floors. The glass doors that led to the patio were ceiling high, and at night the patio was bathed in soft lights set in trees with weeping branches and blossoms. An ornamental pool lined with aqua Italian tiles and underwater lights of rose and blue was the jewel in the crown. The patio was a cone of soft pastel under a sky of midnight black.

"My favorite governor!" Rena screamed when Leon was ushered through the front door. She bounced across the room and into the

· · ·

foyer exactly as if she were performing on stage, gathering Leon in her arms with a body press. Leon returned the embrace with ease. By this time, he was getting pretty good at radiating sex appeal.

Wrought iron tables set in an interlocking chain were tastefully set for dinner on the patio, so that a guest was seated within talking distance of several people at the same time. Pert waitresses dressed in short, severe black skirts and starched white blouses and cuffs moved in quick, sexy steps, serving cocktails and hors d'oeuvres and then a delicate French supper of jellied fish and chicken accompanied by French champagne.

Except for Rena Chenault's explosive bursts of laughter, conversation was politely subdued in tone and so disjointed that all one could remember afterwards were short exchanges.

"If the governor wagged a finger, Rena would bounce right in bed with him," someone said when Rena effusively greeted Leon.

"She knows better," someone said. "Lafe's her boyfriend now. She won't rock that boat."

"You're both wrong," someone else said sardonically. "She'd screw the governor for insurance's sake, then go home to tell Denise all about it." Denise was a slinky French girl with tawny skin and lynx eyes. She too was dressed in clinging silk slacks.

A man I hadn't seen before stood up to make a toast to Rena. His face was on the pudgy side, but his out-thrust chest, hard hands, and watchful eyes betrayed someone not to be taken lightly. I learned later that his name was Bob Mathews. He obviously knew Rena and knew her well.

"To our hostess, Rena Chenault," he said in a gravelly voice. "The Perle Mesta of Las Vegas."

"Who is Perle Mesta?" Rena asked ingenuously.

"She's a *Washington* bitch," someone said.

Rena's eyes narrowed for an instant, judging whether that meant

· · ·

she was a *Las Vegas* bitch. She decided not and smiled at the upraised glasses.

"Don't talk to me about Mafia muscle," said Lafe Jacobs. "The Mafia muscle is nothing compared to the conservationist muscle."

Lafe Jacobs was a little man with a sharp-boned Jewish face, blue eyes, and a genuinely attractive smile when he was not angry. When he was angry, which was most of the time, his eyes popped, his mouth twisted, and his face became as distorted as a madman's. He was so angry now that his mouth was actually trembling.

The reason for his anger was no secret. Lafe had been telling his sad story to anyone in Las Vegas who would listen. He had built a resort casino on the shores of Lake Tahoe. The resort was his downfall. The loftiest, oldest, and biggest pine tree of all was situated smack-dab in the middle of the driveway leading to the front entrance. Lafe had tried to get permission to have it cut down and removed, but the League to Save Lake Tahoe heard of his sinister plot and moved to block him. After a bitter fight, they won in a walk. Abused and frustrated, Lafe finally sold his profitable Knights Castle and moved to Las Vegas, where he was now building a resort hotel called Pompey's Palace in Roman decor.

"Those bastards think a tree is more important than people," Lafe said. "I used to love trees. Now I hate Joyce Kilmer."

"I worked for the big banker Harry Regen once," said Rena. She also had a line out to hook the job of the governor's representative in Las Vegas. "He was a gentleman."

"Is that a criticism?" asked Leon.

Rena made a mock slapping motion at Leon.

"He made me a present of two condomsiniums," Rena said, muffing the new word.

"I'd be careful how I pronounced that word if I were you," said Leon.

"You are a *terrible!*" said Rena with the French pronunciation. She turned to a young man named Michel. *"Faites quelque chose, Michel."* Michel ran inside and came back with an airy wrap for Rena's shoulders. Michel was an effeminate little Frenchman with a tightly fitting sailor's shirt and bell-bottom trousers. According to Rena, he was a fairy. Everyone at the table knew his background except the man opposite him, a casino owner named Ben Goffstein. He was trying to fix Michel up with a date.

"I'm going to prove to you how much of a friend I am," the casino owner said. "How about Annette? She's a sex kitten if I ever saw one. Hundred dollars a pop when she's not cocktail waitressing. She could have anyone."

"No, zank you," Michel said nervously. "No, no."

"I was on a radio show with Charles Boyer and Maurice Chevalier," said Rena. "I say: after I wake up in the morning I take a douche. I mean bath, you know. But *douche* is the word in French. Charles nearly died, and the interviewer look at me just as if I had said 'fuck.' "

"You're hard to please, Michel," said the casino owner. "How about Marte? She goes for five hundred dollars for a round-the-world trip, and I promise you it is a trip you won't regret taking."

Michel stamped his foot. *"Non. Non. Stupide!"*

"This state is hypocritic," said Lafe. "You want our money but you won't give us equal social status. You're all Jew-haters."

"Lafe," his lawyer, Fred Peterson, said. "You're like all the rest of the Jews. You think the world hates you."

"You're my lawyer," said Lafe. "If you want to be my psychiatrist, you should go to medical school."

"Michel, I even offer you my wife," the casino owner said. "She knows some good tricks."

"Rena," Michel screamed in agony. "Tell him! Tell him!"

Rena leaned over and whispered in the casino owner's ear. He

· · ·

nodded in understanding and said, "Michel, why didn't you tell me? I've got a swishy cousin you would really have gone for. But he's lashed up with another guy."

"Now he tells me," said Michel.

"I think I'll run for Congress and tax every one of you Nevada bastards out of business," said Lafe. "Those Lake Tahoe bastards treated me like I was a member of the Mafia. One of those bastards even asked me in a meeting: 'Mr. Jacobs, is it true you are a member of the Mafia?'"

"So what did you say to that?"

"I said: 'Why, you son of a bitch. I can ask you the same question and see how you answer it. For your goddamn information, I'm cleaner than anybody in this state.'"

Charlie Baron, who had offered to "disappear" a newspaper publisher for Leon, was sitting near the watchful man who had toasted Rena Chenault at the beginning of supper. His black hair was, as always, slicked down. He was elegantly dressed. His narrow face was smiling as he told his story, but his black eyes never really smiled. Every so often Charlie Baron and Bob Mathews would raise their eyes to look at the top floor of the Desert Inn. The heavy drapes were drawn but shadows were moving back and forth. Something was going on up there.

"This young man comes to me to apply for a job as a sales rep," related Charlie. "I listened to him talk about his credentials for a while, then I interrupted him with, 'Do you drink?' The young man flushed and said, 'No, I don't.' So I asked him, 'Do you gamble?' The young man says, 'Lord, no. Of course not.' So I ask him, 'Do you have a chick on the side?' The young man was really shook, and he said, 'Absolutely not!' So I says to him, 'For Crisake, what the hell have you got to look forward to?' I dismiss the young man with 'Let me think it over and I'll get to you.'"

· · ·

Charlie Baron was embarrassed that his story was running long, but everyone was smiling and Leon encouraged him to go on. Charlie cleared his throat and said, "Well, a month goes by and I get a call from the young man out of this hick town up north and he says, 'Mr. Baron, I just wanted to let you know that I've started drinking and I've put down a few gambling bets. But I haven't been able to find a girl yet.' So I say to the young man, 'You got a job. Come on out.'" Charlie Baron grinned. "The young man's working for the Desert Inn now. But he better be smart. If I ever catch him gambling, I'll fire his ass."

The stranger with the watchful eyes, Bob Mathews, said, "Charlie, there's a lot I've got to learn about the gambling business. You'll have to teach me."

Charlie nodded his head accommodatingly. "I suggest you ask the governor. He knows it all."

Leon accepted the compliment with a nod of his head. "Not all, Charlie. I've got a lot to learn."

"If the governor's gambling agents are any sign of how much he knows," said Lafe with a sharp edge in his voice, "you won't learn anything."

Leon regarded him without smiling. "Why do you say that, Lafe?"

"One of your boys comes into my Lake Tahoe joint once and says to me your gambling control board has a report on one of my people dealing second cards at a twenty-one table. I ask him, 'What's the dealer's name?' He says, 'We can't divulge that.' I look at this idiot agent and say to him, 'Then how in hell am I supposed to fire him?' And your genius of a gambling agent says, 'That's your affair.'"

"How did it turn out?" asked Leon.

"It didn't," said Lafe. "To satisfy the son of a bitch, I have all the decks in the joint checked out and put all my dealers through a lie detector test. I tell your genius agent what I've done, and he says, 'That

· · ·

doesn't mean anything. Our man saw it done.' So I tell him, 'Use your head, you son of a bitch. What owner is so dumb that he's going to let a dealer cheat for a couple of lousy bucks and put a billion-dollar gambling license in danger?' "

"I'll have the incident checked out," said Leon.

But Lafe, remembering the incident, was really angry now. "While I've got you, Governor," he said, "let me tell you another little story. This one's about your buddy with the big points in the Desert Inn, Moe Dalitz."

There was an instant freezing of faces at the table. They belonged to Charlie Baron, whose eyes had suddenly become very dangerous; Leon, whose expression was one of olympian disapproval; and surprisingly, Bob Mathews, who was apprehensive and wary.

"Moe Dalitz comes to visit me when I'm building my Pompey's Palace on the Strip," Lafe said, angry enough to signal that he would not be stopped. "Dalitz says to me, 'We'd like to help you with your financing.' I say to him, 'The financing is fine, Mr. Dalitz. Thanks, but I don't need help.' Moe Dalitz says to me, 'Well, we know better, Mr. Jacobs. We know you need money.' I say to Dalitz, 'Who's we?' Mr. Dalitz says to me, 'My friends and me.' I say to Mr. Dalitz, 'Who are your friends?' He says to me, 'That's none of your business. I came to offer you money.' I says to Moe Dalitz, 'What in exchange for . . . a loan?' Dalitz is mad now, and he says, 'What the hell you talking about? A loan? For a percentage is what I mean. A piece of the action.' So I says, 'Mr. Dalitz, thanks. I can get along without you.' Moe Dalitz says to me, 'All right, I'm taking the gloves off. I'm telling you we get a piece of this joint.' And I says to Dalitz, 'I'm telling you no.' Moe Dalitz says to me, 'You son of a bitch. We're taking it. This joint will never open if we don't.' So I stands up and says to Moe Dalitz, 'Get out of here, you motherfucking son of a bitch. And don't try anything. I'll be waiting for you.' Well, Dalitz burned down my warehouse and tried

· · ·

to arrange a strike of my contractors. He and his friends threatened my life. But I opened my Pompey's Palace by the skin of my teeth. They can't touch me anymore."

In the silence that followed, I remembered our walk in the rain down Pennsylvania Avenue after our meeting with J. Edgar Hoover. The expression on Leon's face was as baffled now as it had been then.

22

To this day, I cannot remember when the political life we were leading began to go crazy. Perhaps it was Rena Chenault's bizarre dinner party that triggered the insanity. Maybe it was just what political life turned into somewhere along the line. Or simply that being governor or an aide to a governor had opened up a facet of Las Vegas that we didn't know existed.

It wasn't knowing hoodlums. They were predictable. Their word was good and more to be trusted than the word of the three-piece-suit businessmen who were moving into town in droves. Their word wasn't good for twenty-four hours.

The old guard of Las Vegas hadn't changed much, except to be overawed by big money and glittering hotels and the latest floor show featuring Sinatra, Sammy Davis, or Liberace. The mores of the old guard had been set early, particularly among the Mormons. If one had been raised around them, he learned that Mormons didn't change. Feeling threatened by the licentiousness that was nibbling at their town's vitals, they became even more respectable and conservative.

They were getting outnumbered, though, by the social set that had grown up around the hotel-casinos. These were the high-salaried

· · ·

hotel managers and their staffs and the slick Los Angeles–type businessmen who had set up shop in Las Vegas to make a rich living off the multitudinous needs of the Strip's resort hotels and the downtown Glitter Gulch casinos. Casino managers, floor and pit bosses, and the elite roulette and baccarat croupiers who had learned their trade at Monte Carlo were well behaved. They were all too aware of the penalty that would be inflicted upon them by their syndicate bosses. They were conspicuously absent from occasions that were breeding grounds for public spectacles.

Some entertainers considered themselves exempt from rules of conduct. Frank Sinatra, who owned a piece of the Sands, was one of these. He should have known better. But his Italian temper, drinking himself to saturation, and God complex led him from trouble to trouble. He reached his zenith one night when he demolished the presidential suite at the Sands, then hijacked a baggage cart and made a mess of the hotel lobby and casino. He overturned the dinner table of a floor boss who refused to give him carte blanche at the gambling tables, trying to protect Frankie from Frankie. The floor boss was big and knew how to use his fists. He put Frankie to sleep with one punch.

Las Vegas's new social set also considered themselves exempt from rules of conduct. Its playground was the Strip where *everything goes* and unfaithfulness was the name of the game. Husband and wife accompanied each other to a Strip occasion. Husband and wife peeled off and each found a bed partner for the night. It was all taken for granted and it was considered poor taste to make an issue out of the practice. So and so's husband wouldn't make trouble if you screwed his wife, but her boyfriend might.

The wives were invariably good-looking women with inviting eyes, swelling breasts, and flaring hips. They were dressed to the teeth in silk and diamonds, the latest in Paris fashions, and masterfully ap-

· · ·

plied makeup. The biggest complaint of the single girls in the new social structure was that of unfair competition from wives.

An attractive young governor like Leon was fair game for the predators. Whenever he spoke at a Strip dinner, political or charitable, it would be to a full house. Since he had made it a practice to time his appearance minutes before the cocktail hour ended, dinner was target time. The waiters ran themselves ragged delivering napkins to him. The napkins bore the name, address, telephone number, and available hours of exotic wives.

When this napkin routine first started, Leon looked a little befuddled. Then he learned from neighboring governor Ronald Reagan of California that it was part of an old institution called "a prestige lay." Soon he began to take it in stride by opening the napkin, reading its contents, raising his eyes to meet the sultry eyes of the sender, nodding his head courteously and smiling, and handing the napkin either to me or to one of his aides for safekeeping. This elaborate procedure was considered a class act by everyone in attendance, be it husband or wife or mistress.

The only time I saw Leon get thrown off his suave, even keel was when a waiter handed him a different sort of napkin. Leon opened it, read the contents, and looked puzzled. He showed the napkin to our poll man, Peck, who had accompanied us to dinner.

"Who in hell is this creep?" Leon asked Peck.

"He's the chancellor at the new university, if you want to call it that, in Las Vegas," said Peck. "Name of Dawson."

Someone was waving airily at Leon from his seat at the other end of the table. He looked to be gangly with a Van Gogh beard, Caesar haircut, and red-rimmed eyes. Leon did not return the wave.

"If I never see Las Vegas again," said Leon, "it'll be too soon. Listen, in this town, there are only two priorities—a buck and a lay. And

· · ·

they're interchangeable. I have no prejudices against either, but when they become the ruling passions in your life, you're in trouble." Leon thought about what had leapt without preamble from his mouth, then said, "This town is so ripe for a housecleaning. But there's no one big enough to do it, including yours truly, the governor."

We were having breakfast together in his room. If he had uttered these words within earshot of a waiter downstairs in one of the restaurants, his true sentiments would have been all over Las Vegas in a day.

"You ain't heard nothing yet," I said. "Let me tell you about last night."

"How late did you guys stay up?" Leon said. "You look awful."

"I feel worse," I said. "We really tied one on after the fight."

Four of us had flown down in the governor's private plane to see the heavyweight fight between Sonny Liston and Floyd Patterson. It didn't turn out to be much of a fight, but at least Patterson was matched against the first world's champion to fight in Nevada since the early days of Corbett-Fitzsimmons and Johnson-Jeffries. The convention center was full, tiered rows of seats rising to the sky, and the crowd outside was well sprinkled with old pugs with beaten-down noses and flattened face contours. Patterson had looked good coming down the aisle with a towel over his head and a light terry-cloth robe open in front to show his rippling muscles. But when Sonny Liston came down with his head concealed under an ominous hood, he resembled an executioner with an axe, moving toward the chopping block in the Tower of London. Which is just what he turned out to be. When Patterson was cut down, he looked relieved.

After the fight, Leon had gone to bed, having been propositioned by three creepy con men in the time it took to have one drink. "This is impossible," he said. "See you in the morning."

· · ·

I had had another drink with two of our campaign workers, Chet and Swede, then another, and another, until I lost count.

"A couple of hookers came and joined us," I told Leon, "Chet getting hornier the more he drank."

"How about you?" asked Leon.

"No," I said honestly. "Booze works the other way for me."

"Okay, okay."

"Chet made a deal with this nifty little blonde," I said. "But Swede said he wasn't paying that much and went to bed. Not to be deterred, Chet made a deal with both of them and took them upstairs. He tried to put this black-haired witch in my bed, but I was too drunk and told her thanks but no thanks. Honest I did. So Chet screwed her in his bed while the blonde sat on my bed trying to get some life into me. When Chet got done, he took the little blonde to his bed and screwed her, too."

"This is a sick story," said Leon.

"It gets sicker," I said.

I took a stiff swallow of black coffee. "After the two broads left," I said, "Chet started to get dressed. 'Where in hell are you going?' I asked him. 'After a broad,' Chet said. He went out the door with nothing on but his pants. I thought to myself, 'Oh, my God, Chet's going to get into big trouble.' I threw on some clothes and followed him. He'd punched the button for the elevator and was talking to the elevator boy. 'Where do I find a doll?' Chet asked. The elevator boy held up his hand and said, 'Look no further.' The boy went down and came back in a flash with a hooker. 'That will be a hundred dollars,' the elevator boy said. 'Not for me it won't,' Chet said. 'I'm not paying no one hundred dollars for a screw.' The elevator boy said, hopefully, 'Fifty?' They settled for fifty bucks."

"Go on," said Leon. "I can't wait."

· · ·

"Neither could Chet," I said. "He started to lay her on the floor right in front of the elevator. 'You can't do that here,' the elevator boy said. Chet said, ignoring him, 'I can't see why not. There's only three of us here,' and he proceeded to screw the hooker."

"I don't want to hear any more," said Leon.

"There's not any more to hear," I said. "Chet got up, kissed the elevator boy on the cheek, and went back to the room."

Staring out the window, Leon said, "I suddenly feel the need for a long, long sauna."

"I suddenly feel the need for Papa's mountains," I said. "It's been too long."

"You're on," said Leon.

Two nights and three days and the quiet company of our father cleansed our senses of the bruising they had taken from blaring orchestras, clanking armies of slot machines, intoxicating perfumes, and turgid flesh. The silence of the mountains covered us like a mantle, especially at night when the only sounds were of a high wind in the tops of towering pines, the lonely yipping of a coyote, and the sigh of the campfire as it settled into ashes.

Not everything was perfect, though. Our father was not the same. Something had happened to him. His long steps were shorter, his boots began to drag in the dirt on steep climbs, and the forever bronze of his face and hands had an underlying pallor.

My first reaction was anger at Leon for inflicting politics upon our family. Besieged by telephone calls and strangers at the front door, our mother bore the harassment better than our father would have, but she was beginning to look irritated. Our youngest brother, Mitch, who was "holding down the fort" in the law office, was at the point of exhaustion. The long hours were taking their toll.

Leon's wife, Janet, had been a political widow through the long

· · ·

weeks of the campaign. When Leon was elected she had tried living in the antiquated mansion with their children, and gave up. She had moved the family back to their modern ranch-style home. Now, while the mansion was being restored, she was caught between two homes. The strain was showing visibly.

Our father had been spared most of the furious inauguration activities. Leon had delegated to me the task of "getting him to something." The inaugural ball, replete with black tie and tails and formal gowns, was absolutely out of the question. The formal inauguration held on the front steps of the capitol was a close second. With much pleading and arguing, our father finally consented to attend the brief and private swearing-in ceremony at the supreme court justices' inner sanctum.

Leon and I decided to ask our father what was wrong when we were huddled around the last early morning campfire, eating bacon and eggs and sourdough bread off of tin platters and drinking strong coffee out of tin cups. He looked at us out of gray eyes that not long ago had been as sharp as an eagle's but had suddenly grown old and filmy. He said it all in one sentence that only a sheepherder who has walked a hundred thousand miles could really understand:

"My legs have lost their value."

· · ·

23

"At 4:00 A.M. on the morning of November 27, 1966, a stretcher was *not* carried into the Desert Inn in Las Vegas. A tall, shambling man wearing a hat and a trench coat with the collar pulled up and speaking with a Texas drawl did *not* escort the stretcher into . . . and so on . . ." George Friar's sonorous voice trailed off, then began again, "Is that in substance our public stance, Excellency?"

Leon was leaning far back in the leather, horsehair-stuffed executive chair that a hundred years of Nevada governors had occupied. The heels of his cowboy boots rested on the mirrored mahogany surface of the executive desk. "We aren't taking a stance," he said almost inaudibly. "As far as the governor's office is concerned, the presence of Howard Hughes in Las Vegas is no more of an occasion for an official statement than that of any other visitor. Actually, that's what he's here on—a brief stay in the salubrious climate of southern Nevada. It isn't the first time. From what Skinner has found out, Hughes has been coming to Las Vegas since early times."

Leon was not impressed by the fact that one of the richest men in the world had deigned to visit his state. That was the Basque in him, I knew from living in Basque villages in France. They were not impressed by anybody. If Jesus Christ himself had walked down the main street of the village, nobody would have given him a second glance.

When John Kennedy was assassinated and the press was rounding up reactions from officials everywhere, I had drafted one for Leon, who was on the road in the rural counties. I had written that Kennedy, whom I personally admired, had been a great president. "No!" Leon said heatedly over the telephone. "I didn't think he was a *great*

· · ·

president. I didn't even think he was a *good* president." When Richard
Nixon was torpedoed by Watergate, Leon said, "That'll teach him not
to turn his campaign over to his subordinates." And later on, when
Nelson Rockefeller needed an up-and-coming *western* political star
to balance his presidential bid, he offered Leon a chance at the vice
presidency in trade for his public support. Leon told him bluntly that
Senator Barry Goldwater, Rockefeller's opposition, was his friend.
Leon proved his friendship later and paid for it in spades. When
Goldwater was being treated like a leper by Republican leaders in his
run for the presidency, Leon met him at the Las Vegas airport, telling
angry Nevada Republicans, "I could never look the man in the eyes
again if I deserted him now." Shaking hands with Goldwater at the
bottom of the tarmac did not help Leon's election.

The governor's office remained aloof while Las Vegas and the national press were agog with all the theatrics of Howard Hughes's
arrival. That arrival was embellished so much that in the end, nobody could determine whether Howard Hughes was carried into the
Desert Inn on a stretcher, walked in under his own power, or flew
into the hotel with the Buck Rogers spacebelt he had just invented.
Hughes's getting ensconced on the ninth floor of the hotel—which
contained the suite we had used for campaign headquarters south—
was further embellished by rumors and news stories that *both* the
eighth and ninth floors were fully equipped with electronic communication equipment so that Hughes could keep in instant touch
with his worldwide empire. Sophisticated medical equipment was
also supposed to have been installed to care for Howard Hughes's
reportedly failing health. A small army of electronic technicians and
medical attendants and bodyguards—called the Mormon Mafia by
cynical locals—had also been installed. Supposedly.

When these rumors reached the governor's office far to the north in
Carson City, Leon showed his first flicker of interest in the arrival of

· · ·

Howard Hughes. "Something doesn't fit here," he said by the way in a staff meeting. He was talking to Bill Skinner in particular. "Can you go down and find out what the hell's really happening down there?"

"I don't have to go to Vegas to find that out," said Skinner. "I can do it by telephone."

"How?" Leon asked.

"I'll call Bob Mathews," said Skinner. "He's Hughes's number one man now. He was also in the Bureau at the same time I was. We worked some touchy assignments together."

"The Bureau?" asked Leon. "You mean the FBI?"

Skinner nodded as if everyone should know what *the Bureau* was.

Later, Leon learned that Bob Mathews had been not only a dangerous-assignment type of agent for the FBI, but a counterespionage agent for the OSS in the European theater during World War II. It was said he could kill a man using just his hands. Nobody believed that one until he very nearly killed a burglar with his hands in Las Vegas.

Leon called another staff meeting for the next day to hear Skinner's report. "The arrival of Howard Hughes was not a spur-of-the-moment thing, Bob Mathews tells me," Skinner said. "It's been in the works for months. That's why you saw Mathews at Rena Chenault's party. Mathews was working out reservations for Hughes at the Desert Inn. That isn't easy. It takes time and juice to reserve two entire floors on the Strip, even in December."

"That's one of the things that doesn't fit," said Leon. "December."

"The stretcher business and someone being carried into the Desert Inn was true," Skinner went on. "Nothing new. It's an old FBI trick. Also, the electronic and medical equipment, technicians, bodyguards, and aides really are in place."

"Is Hughes really that sick?" asked Leon.

"No," said Skinner. "He's a little weak, but he's not going to die."

· · ·

"How long are they going to stay in the D.I.?" Leon asked. Something was on his mind.

"That's what doesn't make sense," said Skinner. "They're booked for nine days. Only five days left to go."

"Why did Mathews book the Hughes people for only nine days?"

"That's all the time Moe and Ruby would give them," said Skinner. "The holiday season is upon us. So are the high-roller gamblers."

"So the Hughes crowd has got to move say a half million dollars worth of equipment out in five days," said Leon.

"Hughes has got something else to move," said George Friar, who had come into Carson City to hear Skinner's revelations.

"What's that?" Leon asked.

"One . . . half . . . of . . . a . . . billion . . . dollars . . . for . . . the sale of . . . Trans World Airlines," said Friar in dramatic tones.

"Right," said Leon. "And he has to do it in a hurry, or Uncle won't leave him very much of it." Leon's brow was furrowed in puzzlement. "Something is going on here. Pros like Hughes and his people don't get into situations like this."

The ponderous door to the executive chamber opened hesitantly, and Leon's private secretary peeked in. "There's a man on the phone named Bob Mathews wants to talk to you, Governor. I told him you were in conference but he said it concerned Howard Hughes and it was urgent and important."

Leon bit his lip and looked at Skinner. "Will you field the call? I've got a feeling this is one I should duck."

Skinner nodded his head in agreement and went out. There was no conversation in his absence except for George Friar's question to himself: "Now why would Robert Mathews call the governor of Nevada on urgent business?"

Bill Skinner was back in a moment. "You're not going to like this,

· · ·

161

Leon," he said. "Moe Dalitz and Ruby Kolod have told the Hughes people they have to vacate their rooms, or two floors worth of rooms actually, five days from now. As per agreement when Mathews made the reservations."

"High rollers?" asked Leon.

Skinner nodded. "They'll be here on schedule."

"So how does that involve the governor's office?" Leon asked. "That's in-house business."

Skinner took a deep breath. "Bob Mathews says that Howard Hughes wants you to intervene. He wants you to call Moe Dalitz and Ruby Kolod and tell them to back off. He wants you to tell Moe and Ruby that nobody kicks the Hughes Organization out of anywhere. You can attribute that statement right to The Man himself."

Leon listened patiently. "That's not Howard Hughes talking. That's Bob Mathews trying to cover his own ass."

"You mean . . ." George Friar began.

"From everything I've heard about Howard Hughes, he doesn't ask *anybody* to run interference for him," said Leon. "Including governors and presidents."

"Mathews is lying?" asked Friar.

"Yep," said Leon. "He blew it."

"Then I tell Bob Mathews that you aren't going to call Moe and Ruby?" asked Skinner.

Leon nodded. What Bob Mathews had asked was not that much of a favor, really. But Leon had been quietly furious at Moe Dalitz and Ruby Kolod for coming personally to the headquarters' suite on election night with their "congratulate our candidate" pronouncement. That line had gotten around Las Vegas and Reno in a hurry. We had tried to stop its flow with the revelation that Moe Dalitz and Ruby Kolod had contributed a lousy two thousand dollars to Leon's campaign. But nobody would believe it. Within a month, Moe and Ruby's

· · ·

reputed campaign contribution had climbed to a million dollars and only God knew how high it would reach in the end. Former governor Dean Cooper's people had made sure of that. I had wanted to even the score with the revelation that Dean Cooper's money raisers had taken a cool bundle of cash from an unnamed hood when Cooper attacked J. Edgar Hoover and his FBI as Hitlerian and Gestapo-like. But Leon had stifled my ardor. "We won the election," Leon had said. "That's the bottom line."

Skinner delivered his message and came back. "Bob Mathews said all right, if that's the way you want it. But The Man isn't going to like it."

Leon chuckled. "I don't suppose he will. I'd give a lot to be there when Mathews tries to talk his way out of this one. Bob Mathews's ass is in a sling."

Then the incredible happened, in less time than it took us to wind up the rest of the conference agenda. We had worked late, and the tall, arched windows outside the governor's office were black with night. The capitol was empty except for us, so we could hear the telephone ringing in the outer office. The secretary had gone home and the phone went unanswered for a long time. Finally, Leon got up impatiently and went to his own desk and picked up the telephone.

"Yes, Bob," was all he said before he started listening. He listened for a long time, pausing only once to cover the receiver with his hand and say to us, "It's Bob Mathews."

Just before he hung up, Leon said to Mathews, "No, I really don't foresee any problems. But I can't be sure until I've talked this over with my Gaming Commission and Gaming Control Boards. Tomorrow." Leon paused. "Nine o'clock at the Governor's Mansion, check," he said. "Here's the number for my private line. I'll be in my study there."

Leon's head must have been racing with the avenues the telephone

· · ·

call had opened up. He stood by his desk a good while before he turned to us.

"The Man, as you like to call him, is solving his own tenancy problem," Leon said to us. "When Mathews told him about the eviction notice, Hughes didn't bat an eye. He told Mathews, 'I'm not moving. I'll just buy the joint.'" Leon let that announcement sink in with all its implications. Then he said, "Howard Hughes is going to call tonight to tell me his plans personally and see if I have any objections." Leon added, as if in afterthought, "He does his business at night, you know."

"*Deus ex machina,*" George Friar said solemnly.

My brother Mitch had come into the executive office in time to catch Leon's exchange with Bob Mathews and his announcement to us.

Faces turned toward Friar in puzzlement.

"It's from the Latin," said Mitch, who had studied classical theater. "It implies that the gods intervene in the affairs of men."

Leon gave Friar a weary look. "I wouldn't attribute divinity to Howard Hughes," said Leon. "But for the time being, he'll do."

George Friar was not much off the mark even if he was showing off his erudition about Greek gods intervening in the affairs of men. I doubted though whether he was clairvoyant enough to foresee the full implications of the coming of Howard Hughes to Nevada. That could mean not only the state's welfare but Leon's political future. I knew Leon saw that.

· · ·

The first thing to be established was whether Howard Hughes was serious about buying the Desert Inn out of pique. Leon did not trust that line at all, but he couldn't be sure. Hughes had a quixotic background. After that, there was the question that nobody had asked— whether Moe Dalitz and Ruby Kolod were willing to sell.

Las Vegas was a rumor mill and the matter of credibility hung over every rumor. The credibility specter was something to be considered and delicately questioned. As Jim Murphy said from bitter experience as a reporter trying to run down a story, inquisitiveness was a misdemeanor in Reno, a felony in Las Vegas, and a capital crime on the Strip. It could get you rubbed out.

Whether Howard Hughes was serious about investing in Nevada gambling would be answered for us when Leon emerged from his private study in the Governor's Mansion. It was 9:30 P.M. already, and the call from Howard Hughes had come through on Leon's private line at 9 P.M. sharp. That it was Howard Hughes calling was revealed to us by one of Leon and Janet's very young daughters, Molly.

We four brothers had been talking in the family room when Molly yelled in a piping voice, "Dad! Some guy named Howard Hughes wants to talk to you."

Leon swore and disappeared into his study. "How did you get in here?" we heard him ask Molly. She came running out of the study and the door closed behind her. "He talks funny," was all Molly had to say before scooting up the stairs to her bedroom.

Whatever Leon talked about with Hughes must have been thorough, because a half hour went by before Leon opened his study door and absentmindedly beckoned to us from the doorway. We were the only ones of his kitchen cabinet who had been asked to come to the mansion. George Friar was hurt at not being invited, but Leon was wary that he would reveal prematurely what had been talked about with Hughes. For posterity's sake. George liked too much to

· · ·

reveal his links to the famous. Bill Skinner was not hurt. In fact, he did not want to be privy to revelations until Leon was damned well ready to tell him.

Skinner warned Leon that whatever he said to Howard Hughes would be taped, and taped very well. Hughes was not called an electronics wizard for nothing. Skinner said he could return the compliment by taping what Hughes said to Leon. Leon thought it through and decided not.

"It'll show through my voice," Leon said. "I don't want Howard Hughes to hear that because it will say I don't trust him. That could mean the instantaneous end of this relationship."

"You're leaving out something," said Gene with an edge of sarcasm.

Leon looked the question and Gene said, "What if you hear this cosmic guilt in *his* voice?"

"Hughes wouldn't give a damn if I did," said Leon. "That's the difference."

In the restoration of the Governor's Mansion, Leon had taken particular pains with the study. I think it was the only room in the mansion he cared about. The dining room was used only for state dinners, the lofty, domed living room for official receptions, the extra bedrooms for visiting governors and even one president, Richard Nixon. The family room had some attraction because it contained a pool table—nostalgia from a Carson City pool hall that had once been our hangout. The children's rooms were on the second floor and were supposed to be private, but they never were. Leon and Janet's children lived with a parade of unknown and unwelcome visitors.

The study was paneled in dark wood and looked deep and old fashioned. The walls bore no signed photos of dignitaries. Those had been put up in the waiting room and executive office in the capitol. Family pictures dominated his study, our own family growing up,

· · ·

a gilt-edged wedding picture of our mother and father in Reno in 1920, a photo portrait of our mother taken in a Bordeaux studio before she left France right after World War I, two photographs of my father in the Sierra with his sheep. The rest of the photos were of him and his wife, Janet, and their own family. Leon underwent a subtle change when he was holding forth in this room. It was as though he was drawing strength of family from those three generations of family photos.

There was also a little fireplace in the study, and on this winter's night a small fire was burning down inside. Leon stood with his back to the fireplace, looking almost over our heads.

"Let's see if I can put this together chronologically," he said. For a while, the conversation seemed to duplicate the one Leon had had earlier that day with Bob Mathews. No problems foreseeable. The Gaming Commission and Gaming Control Board would be meeting tomorrow to act on Hughes's application for a gambling license.

"What about legal procedure?" Mitch asked. "Fingerprints and background check and all that?"

"The Commission will have to go along with me," said Leon. "It's one in a million odds against this happening again—a man with more money than the Mafia willing to get into Nevada gambling. Getting fingerprints is flyspecking. Howard Hughes has been fingerprinted a thousand times and his background checked back to his first burp. Why play games with him?"

"You'll get some heat from the press," said Gene. Our brother had come up from Las Vegas to be on hand when Leon found out what was going on.

"Screw the press," said Leon. "They'd give me heat if Saint Peter applied for a license."

"Jim Murphy wants the beat on this one," said Gene. "He says we owe it to him. His personal opinion is that Howard Hughes will be

· · ·

bad for the state. He'll turn Las Vegas into a respectable little old family gambling town, and Jim will have nothing to write about."

Leon grinned. "Get him on the line when we're done here," Leon said to Gene. "Jim Murphy has never turned us around." Leon asked cautiously. "What's Jimmy the Greek doing with the Hughes rumors?"

"He says it's six to five against Hughes buying the D.I.," said Gene.

"I told him he was a lousy oddsmaker," said Leon. "Jimmy should have listened harder."

"Well, what did Hughes say?" said Mitch. "Is he or isn't he?"

"I asked him first shot out of the barrel," said Leon. "Was I correct in assuming he was serious about owning and operating a gambling casino. He said 'Yes' with no equivocation or conditions."

"You know what they say," said Mitch. "It takes a gambler to know how to run a gambling joint. Is this Hughes's first time in?"

Leon nodded. "First venture. He thinks it might be fun. I told him I'd handled gambling clients in private life and it kept occurring to me that owning a casino was like having your own bank, the only difference being that your hard cash is out on the tables instead of in the vaults. Also, no cash flow problem since it's already hard money. Hughes agreed and told me that one of his finance people had called gambling a 'cash cow.' Go milk it when you need it."

Leon muttered something about "a telephone handshake, Texas style, instead of a bunch of signed and notarized papers. You know, I think I'm going to like this guy."

"What does he sound like?" asked Gene.

"Texan," said Leon. "Sort of a special drawl. His voice is higher pitched than I expected."

"What did he ask *you?*" I said.

"He did ask for some advice. I gave it to him straight. The advice will be run back to me, but the syndicate will have to live with it."

My brothers and I leaned forward in our chairs. This was to be

· · ·

the beginning and the crux of what Howard Hughes's coming to Nevada could mean. Leon said he had told Hughes he was right about keeping the dealers and croupiers and pit bosses. Good ones were hard to find, and the ones at the Desert Inn were trained gambling workers. They had been carded and checked out by our Gaming Control Board. The board was double-checking every one of those cards tonight. Leon paused for impact. Something else. "I told Hughes that what I said didn't mean he shouldn't fire anybody. I told him I would strongly urge him to replace every man in the money-counting room with his best, most-trusted numbers people. Immediately. Also, I urged him to replace every one of the couriers who take the money from the pit to the counting room."

"Jesus!" said Gene. "The shit will fly in the Strip joints."

"I couldn't care less," said Leon. He had told Hughes he would be surprised how fast a hundred thousand dollars a day can be misplaced between the casino and the counting room. Skimming was the name of the game, he had told Hughes.

"Did he ask you about J. Edgar and his boys?" Gene asked.

Leon said he told Hughes that J. Edgar would learn about the stop in skimming the day the honest count started. So would Frank Costello and Vito Genovese and Lucky Luciano.

"J. Edgar Hoover will sleep well when he hears what we're doing," Leon smiled. "But J. Edgar will *not* sleep well tonight. His favorite conquest up to now was John Dillinger. Now, with Moe Dalitz and Ruby Kolod and the rest of the Strip gang going honest, J. Edgar will not be content."

"What about Moe and Ruby?" Gene asked. "Everybody's forgetting them."

Leon said that Hughes had told him Bob Mathews had sounded out Moe Dalitz and Ruby Kolod and that they "seemed inclined to go." He was quiet for a while. "I'll have to talk with them, too. I have

· · ·

to know for certain. It's too important to the state to go by hearsay on this one."

"I'm going to miss Moe and Ruby and Charlie Baron and all the rest of the crew," said Gene bitterly.

Leon was regarding Gene with poorly concealed astonishment. He may or may not have told Gene what had been tormenting him even before we had talked to Hoover and the FBI. But I had no hesitation. "For Christ's sake, Gene," I said. "Can't you see that Howard Hughes's coming to Nevada could do our job for us? Cleaning out the hoods?"

"Right," said Leon. "I think I'm seeing light at the end of the tunnel."

With time, the relationship between Leon as governor of Nevada and Howard Hughes, the billionaire tycoon, became stronger despite the strange medium of long-distance telephone.

In the second telephone talk, Leon told Hughes there was a rumor, unverified of course, that the Sands hotel might be interested in selling. Within a month, the purchase was consummated. Unknown to Hughes, Leon had an ulterior motive. The shadow figure who really owned the Sands was a genuinely no-good hoodlum named Meyer Lansky. In his beginning years with the syndicate, Lansky formed one half of the "Bug and Meyer" squad of underworld executioners. The other half of the killing combination was of course the late but unlamented Bugsy Siegel. With the purchase of the Sands, Nevada's Gaming Control Board was saved the almost impossible task of getting rid of still another Mafia figure.

Leon had his private talk with Moe Dalitz and Ruby Kolod and came back with news that should not have come as a surprise. Moe Dalitz had told him, "Howard Hughes can have the joint anytime he wants. I'm tired, Governor. All my life I've had to look over my shoulder to see if someone was aiming a gun at me. It would be one of my own who was pointing that gun, or it would be the FBI. I want done

· · ·

with that. I want to retire. Right here in the town I helped to build, though I will never be able to have bragging rights. It's time for me to play golf when I feel like it, to sit in the sun and pay this state back for what it has given me. I want to be respectable."

Within two years, Howard Hughes, through his parent Summa Corporation, had picked off seven Las Vegas hotel-casinos owned either openly by the syndicate or through a chain of front men reporting to the Mafioso families in New York City. Finally, Howard Hughes was landlord preeminent on the Las Vegas Strip, and Leon had satisfied his promise of cleaning up his own house before the FBI had to do the job.

Before the coming of Hughes, Leon had quietly been working on a concept of corporate gaming. This would have put hotel-casinos under the added scrutiny of the Securities and Exchange Commission. The corporate gaming bill would not have had the chance of a snowball in hell of passing through the legislature. Payoffs and threats to vulnerable lawmakers would have killed the bill in committee. It would never have seen the light of day, and the Mafia ownership of the Strip would have remained intact. After Howard Hughes had finished his buying spree, payoffs and threats died of their own weight and the Nevada legislature made corporate gaming law.

Leon as governor reciprocated in kind for the burden Howard Hughes had lifted from his shoulders. The parent Summa Corporation that Hughes had formed to have dominion over his kingdom erupted in a power fight between newcomer Bob Mathews on one side and two long-timers with Hughes—Bill Gay and Chester Davis—on the other. From what Howard Hughes told Leon, Mathews had sent him a letter saying that Chester Davis and Bill Gay had blown the TWA sale. Obviously, Mathews was trying to undermine Hughes's confidence in Davis and Gay. Chester Davis plotted his counterattack quietly, without fanfare. He told Hughes that Mathews had been play-

· · ·

ing fast and loose with the billionaire's money, buying two resort-hotels that were losers from the start and building himself a million-dollar home in Las Vegas. Privately, Hughes rejected Mathews's claim and accepted Davis and Gay's documentation. Hughes signed a proxy and gave it to Davis and Gay. The proxy, telling Mathews that he was fired, was delivered. Mathews went into a panic when he saw his dismissal in writing, claimed that the proxy was not valid, and went to the extreme of hiring a handwriting expert who would testify that Hughes's signature was a forgery. Davis and Gay reciprocated with their own handwriting expert. "It's like a murder trial," Leon told us after talking with Hughes. "Choose your own psychiatrist."

By this time, it was somewhat clear that the three principals would never make peace. But Hughes wanted impartial confirmation. He called Leon and asked him as governor to bring the three men into a meeting, determine for himself whether they could work together, and if not, to tell Bob Mathews that he was fired.

Leon met with the three in a suite at the Arab-owned El Morocco hotel-casino on the Strip. The meeting was never destined to end in peace, especially after Chester Davis told Mathews, "Bob, I'm going to carve your balls out."

Since election night, Leon had told our inner circle that the El Morocco was totally unpolitical and therefore the place to stay. Moe Dalitz and Ruby Kolod had been unhappy about the move. With all the Hughes publicity hitting headlines, they wanted the meeting to be held at the Desert Inn. Leon explained to them that it was impossible for him to get out of his room at the Desert Inn. "I can't even go down to breakfast without getting made. Last time, I got hit twenty-five times in twenty-five minutes, for special favors I cannot recall." Moe and Ruby understood.

The mediation meeting at the El Morocco took an entire day. Any one of a hundred sources had leaked the place and nature of the

· · ·

meeting to the press, so the balcony corridor outside the suite was jammed with newspapermen, radio reporters, and television crews. The meeting went on so long that by evening, Jim Murphy opened the door and said to those inside: "It took you guys three hours to decide on Courvoisier for after dinner. How long do you figure it will take to settle one of the most involved corporate disputes in history?"

In the end, Leon could see that there would never be peace between Bob Mathews on one side and Davis and Gay on the other. "When I told him the old man had fired him, he refused to believe it. But he knew I had never lied to him. He took it like a pro."

The warfare between the three principals was not to end there, however. Later, when Howard Hughes disappeared on a Thanksgiving night, in the same manner and on the same holiday on which he had arrived in Las Vegas, the fight broke out again. Bob Mathews claimed that Hughes had been kidnapped by Chester Davis and Bill Gay and taken by a hospital plane to the Bahamas. He leaked the news that he was organizing an armed force to invade the Bahamas and rescue Howard Hughes. The leaked plot was not as crazy as it sounded.

Once, months before, Bob Mathews and I were having drinks in the early morning hours, since Mathews was obliged by condition of his employment to call Howard Hughes every morning at 4 A.M. Mathews, a little in his cups, began to tell me how he and a gangster named Johnny Roselli had been hired by the CIA to assassinate Fidel Castro. I never got a chance to hear the end of *that* one after telling Mathews, "Bob, you're telling me things I don't want to know." The rumor mill had it that there actually was an attempt by them to kill Fidel Castro, but it misfired. Johnny Roselli disappeared and was reputed to be encased in a barrel of cement and dropped into a river somewhere. If he was, the deed was probably done by the Mafia. They did not like mixing politics with crime.

· · ·

Mathews's purported invasion of the Bahamas was aborted by Leon by way of a phone call from Vice President Spiro Agnew, vacationing in the Bahamas.

"Howard Hughes is neither dead nor kidnapped," Leon told us. "Ted Agnew talked with him in the Bahamas. Hughes told Agnew that he had indeed fired Mathews. I asked Ted, 'Can I tell Bob Mathews that?' Agnew said yes, and to tell Mathews he was sorry, that he always liked him."

Respected hotels started opening in Las Vegas, and the first of them was none other than a member of that holy hotel chain, the Hilton. After that there was a land rush, and finally, the biggest hotel in the world opened, the MGM Grand. It was built by Kirk Kerkorian, that self-made, tough little man who had clawed his way up from nothing to something. Jim Murphy's prophecy was fulfilled, and the city of sin, Las Vegas, had become "just a little old family gambling town."

I have always liked the little human byplays that go on while empires are being disputed. The Hughes empire mediation meeting in that obscure Las Vegas hotel was no exception. We didn't learn about it until the dust had settled and we were gathered together at a kitchen-cabinet meeting in Leon's private study. George Friar told us about it.

"I have a friend, a classmate in law school," Friar said, his voice settling into the narrative mold. "He'd been tempted for a long time by a gorgeous blonde secretary in his office. He was a lawyer and a superior court judge, so I have reason to believe he meant it when he said he had never been unfaithful to his wife.

"Finally, he could resist temptation no longer. He and his gorgeous

· · ·

secretary agreed on a rendezvous in Las Vegas. They covered their tracks meticulously, even to the point of separate flights to Las Vegas and individual reservations at an obscure little hotel named the El Morocco, which I in an unthinking moment had told him about. It was an off-the-beaten-track establishment, or so they assumed.

"Everything went off well. Beautifully, in fact. They landed in Las Vegas, went separately to the El Morocco, and checked into their separate rooms. His room was, unfortunately as we will see, room 201. He had no way of knowing that our illustrious governor was in room 204, that the governor for political reasons disliked too much exposure.

"My friend and his gorgeous blonde secretary were in room 201 together at 2 P.M., and presumably they had coupled by 5 P.M. At 6 P.M., he chanced to poke his head out of the door, wondering what the commotion outside was all about, and found himself staring into a CBS television camera.

"In the next room, and two rooms after, were: our illustrious governor and myself; the three executive committee members of the Howard Hughes organization, Bob Mathews, Bill Gay, and Chester Davis; Ed Morgan, a Washington attorney; and Morton Galane, a Las Vegas attorney. Some fifty or seventy journalism, television, and radio men from all parts of the world were waiting outside on the balcony corridor.

"My friend slammed the door shut and said to his secretary, 'If this is your idea of a joke . . .' Anyway, my friend the judge and his secretary were trapped in room 201 throughout our vigil, until 6 A.M. the next morning. They could not order room service for fear of being photographed as local color. There was no going out because they did not want to be frozen on film for his wife's use in divorce court."

George Friar had to stop because he was doubled over with laugh-

· · ·

ter. Then he said, "My friend the judge telephoned me in my office a day later, when he was safely back in San Francisco. He said, 'You've got a crummy sense of humor.' When I had explained my innocence, my friend relented and told me the whole story.

"After inquiring about his health and the current status of his marriage, I asked him about his secretary. My friend said, 'She used to be a good typist. Now, she sits and stares at the typewriter, perhaps permanently.' "

I t was a Sunday and I had driven from Reno to Carson City by way of the steep mountain grade leading to Virginia City, stopping there for a respite from politics by visiting a writer friend.

At the Governor's Mansion, I learned that Leon had gone over to his ranch-style home to play tennis. He and his wife had contemplated selling the sprawling house and grounds when they moved into the mansion, then decided against it because nothing is permanent in politics. I didn't dream that the cliché was to be revived freshly for me this very day.

I sat down in a lawn chair near the swimming pool and watched Leon play doubles. He and one of our old friends were playing two hotshots from Las Vegas, and so it was a match worth watching. Leon had a big serve and his net game was his forte. The Las Vegas pair were no slouches, either. They had the advantage of year-round tennis weather, and it showed. But in the end, they lost, because Leon simply refused to lose.

Leon and Janet's children took over the court and I joined the grown-up players for sandwiches and root beer in the shade of the patio. A July sun in Nevada should be taken in small doses. For no reason at all, or so I thought then, I remembered Tex Maynard and Leon working on their campaign tans an eternity ago.

So much had happened in the three years since then. Tex Maynard had dropped dead. Leon had been elected, Howard Hughes's empire headquarters had moved to Nevada. The Mafia had moved out, though one could never be certain which respectable front men for the syndicate still remained. Las Vegas's hoodlum image had changed. The FBI and J. Edgar Hoover were assuaged. Leon's program for Nevada was all but complete: a healthy surplus in the treasury, thanks in good part to honest counting rooms in the casinos. State employees had job security instead of a spoils system. A medical school had been added to the state university in Reno, helped by a huge gift from Howard Hughes, who had a medical center of his own. A community college system for Nevada's isolated little towns was well on its way, thanks again to Howard Hughes, who had been touched by a small cow town's raising money to help itself and had matched what it had raised.

There had been rough times, too. After the assassination of John Kennedy, public officials had become fair game. Leon had not escaped near shootings. A state trooper had shot it out with a would-be assassin hiding outside the mansion's garage. My brother Gene had called one night from Las Vegas with a police warning that Leon was to be killed the next day by the Black Panthers. Leon hated security, but his aide, Bill Skinner, went armed with his pistol and FBI training, and stuck to Leon like a stamp. There was no incident.

After our lunch, Leon said, "Pete, I want to talk to you a minute."

We excused ourselves from the tennis players and crossed to the

· · ·

porch adjoining the house. There was a swinging chair in a fairly secluded corner and we sat down there. The silence was broken only by the ping of a tennis ball, a coughing from someone coming up for air in the swimming pool, the murmur of voices from a poolside table where Leon's wife, Janet, and a friend were visiting.

Without any preliminaries, Leon said, "What would you say if I told you I'm resigning the governorship this week?"

I was so stunned by the audacity of the announcement that I exclaimed, "Do you mean to say you're going to resign the governorship?"

"Shh! They don't know about it over there," he said, gesturing toward the table with the tennis players and the table where Janet and her friend were sitting.

"Why?" was all I could muster. "I don't understand."

Leon told me in no uncertain terms. "You know I talked to Kirk Kerkorian a few months ago and he indicated he wanted me with him," said Leon in a low voice. "Well, I saw him Friday, two days ago, and he dropped it on me. He wants me to be president of MGM and the whole outfit, Western Airlines, International, and some merger that involves $300 million. The merger has to be finalized *now,* and my decision made *now.* By July 14, in fact."

In the intensity of a political campaign, everyone except the candidate runs the risk of losing his identity. This is the way it must be if the candidate is to win the election. To submerge one's self is the sacrifice that must be made for the candidate. He alone preserves ego and the rest are dispensable baggage. I had seen it happening to me through the draining months of Leon's campaign. To save myself, I had mentally moved a thousand miles away from his aides, his supporters, the capitol, and particularly Leon. It had been a near thing, but I had accomplished it. It was only when I felt sure that my identity

· · ·

was intact that I went back, but with free mind and will to contra-
dict the king, to oppose the king, to fight the king, even to laugh
at the king. When I fought him bitterly over a question of principle,
he quit speaking to me. I was patient. After the first battle of wills, I
had learned that if I were indeed right, I would hear my own words
coming back at me from the king.

But this crisis was so confounding, at least in my mind, that I found
myself parrying for time.

"Can't Kerkorian wait until your term has run out?"

Leon shook his head adamantly, "No! The corporate world moves
too fast. It's now or never."

"How are the people going to take it?" I asked. Until this moment,
I had never realized how stupid *that* sounded.

"That doesn't bother me a bit," said Leon. "In this game, your
friends stay with you. Your enemies carve you up, whatever you do.
The rest of the people don't give a damn. They will forget about you
in two weeks."

"How are you going to do it?" I said, faltering, because I had recognized that what he was saying was true.

"We'll have a press conference Wednesday of this coming week,"
said Leon. "I want the top reporters and editors there. It'll be a quick
job of organization."

"But their reaction."

"I'll handle that," said Leon. "They'll see the sense of it. If they don't,
I don't give a damn."

"How about our brothers?"

"You can ask them yourself," said Leon. "Here they come."

Gene and Mitch were emerging from the house along with an old
rancher who had always been a Republican stalwart. He walked as
though his legs had been fitted to a saddle when he was a child, and

· · ·

the lines in his face showed Indian blood. He had blue eyes and a fatherly grin that had swept him into office as state controller during our election campaign.

"Pete's got doubts about my bailing out," said Leon.

I could not believe what I was seeing. They were regarding me as if I were a traitor. I nodded challengingly at Gene, who looked belligerent. "I think Leon ought to go with it," he said. "This is once in a lifetime."

My brother Mitch did not need prompting. "I was stupefied when Leon told me," he said.

"About his bailing out?" I asked.

"Hell, no!" said Mitch. "I want Leon to get out of politics so bad it hurts."

Expecting support from a man I had always regarded as the epitome of the public servant, I nodded at Wilson McCann.

Wilson looked at me evenly. "If I were Leon, I would do it today," said Wilson. "This would shake up those bastards who look down on politicians. To hell with them all. They kiss up to you only when they want something. They don't give a cow turd for you."

I was feeling outnumbered. "What about the people out there?" I said. "How will they take it if the man they voted for bails out for bucks?" I said.

"The Democrats won't say much," said Leon. "They'll be glad to get me out of the way. The Republicans don't care now. We're not the minority party anymore. Candidates are a dime a dozen."

"Why can't Kerkorian wait?" I said.

"It's now or never," said Leon. "Pete, you don't understand the magnitude of this thing."

"What is the magnitude?" I said. "In bucks?"

"Kerkorian and I have to talk about that tomorrow in Vegas," said

· · ·

Leon. "It'll be healthy. That's for sure. Shares in the corporation that will be worth a few million dollars in two years. I'll have a private yacht and a DC-9 of my own. I don't know what the salary is, but probably around a million a year." He paused and spoke with a conviction I had to accept. "The money doesn't mean that much to me," he said. "I've never cared about money that much. It's the challenge. I don't think you understand how big this is."

Leon was not convinced he had convinced me. "Listen, Pete," he said. "It's the best time for me to bail out. I want out. I've got my program through. Nobody can fault me about working. I've worked four years in a little over two years, pulling double shifts day and night. Now, I'm bored with it, like every other governor before me. Personnel problems. Crappy detail work. There's no challenge in it. Think of the challenge in a big corporation like this."

Wishing my head would clear, I tried again. "What do Janet and the kids think?"

"Get out before I'm boxed for good," said Leon. "Wendy said to me, and she's got a lot of sense, 'Dad, it's about time we thought of ourselves. This life is no good. We have no privacy.' And little Joe said, 'Whatever you choose, Dad. But, it's a hell of a thing to expect a kid to be the son of a governor for more than four years.'"

I was about to let it go for the moment, until the next day could bring me clear thinking. White-haired Wilson put his rough cowboy hand on my shoulder and said, to make it easier, "I remember Ted Carville. He was district attorney and judge and governor and senator, and when it was all done, all the people who got rich because they had influence with him wouldn't throw him a bone. He was a lawyer with no clients. Hustling for divorces to pay the rent and groceries. Politics is a no-good life, and no thanks for it, either. The only way to win is to die in the saddle. if you live, you end up on the trash heap."

· · ·

"If I'm going to leave politics in a year," Leon said, "why not leave now, go with Kerkorian, and come out winners? The time element is the thing."

My night was tormented with indecision. Imagined headlines and the disgrace of a governor resigning. An unheard-of breach of trust. To take a cushy private job. Our children and our children's children would have to live with it.

And on the other side of the argument, I told myself that I had been getting more jaundiced with politics as time went by. Why *should* Leon stay on as governor? For a few good people who were worth it and a lot of false friends who weren't worth it, who wouldn't lift a finger to help us, no matter what. For those to whom politicians were dispensable trash.

"You were right, Pete," said Leon's voice, calling from his hotel room in Las Vegas. "When it came down to the wire, I knew I couldn't walk out on the governorship. I've turned Kerkorian down."

"How did he take it?"

"He was deeply disappointed—his words," said Leon. "But he wasn't surprised. He said loyalty—in my case to the office and the state—was the reason he wanted me in the first place."

"Will there be a second chance?" I asked.

"I doubt it," said Leon. "If there is, it won't be the top spot. And you know I won't settle for second."

There was a long moment of silence, and I knew Leon was mulling over his head-to-head meeting with Kerkorian. "I don't know," he said. "But I guess I do know. You have to do things right. There is a right way and there is another way. And this is right. I'm comfortable. I can live with it. I've never shirked my responsibility or gone back on a commitment, and that came home to me in this meeting with Kerkorian, so I'm not looking back now."

· · ·

The image that was in my mind was of a tall pine falling very slowly to the forest floor. When it struck the earth, the thudding impact shook my entire frame. Leon's words over the telephone were empty of sound, as if they were coming from another world.

Our father was dead.

I remember nearly nothing of the drive from the university campus in Reno across the long green valley to Carson City. The only image that remains is that of the high horizon of the Sierra to the west, and an illusion of my father walking with giant strides along that mountain rim.

My mother and my sister Suzette, the nun, met me in the screened, ivy-covered porch that was the entrance to our family home. I held my mother, but she was stoical as always and needed neither words nor displays of sympathy. The starched black nun's habit that enveloped my sister could not conceal the exhaustion and emotion that shone with a dull light from her eyes. It was she who had cared for our father in the long and lingering dying time. His body, purified by a lifetime in the mountains, would simply not let him go. The last time I had touched him his long-muscled arms were as hard and unyielding as granite.

I went alone into the bedroom where our father lay. Our family had just begun to gather. Leon was the only one there, and for the first and probably last time in his life, his eyes were wet with tears.

I had dreaded the moment when I would have to look at my father wasted in death, but there was no getting out of it. When I did, I gasped aloud, thinking I was seeing an apparition. He lay so that his body was at an incline from the waist upwards, exposing his wide shoulders and a chest that only mountain men possess. His arms were crossed at the wrists in front of him, revealing starkly those long-fingered hands shaped by work and plunging horses at the end of a rope. I raised my eyes to his face, and thought I was losing my senses.

· · ·

His face was as bronzed and smooth as if it had been newly sculpted by sun and snow and the ceaseless wind of desert and mountain. For some unfathomable reason, his white hair seemed to be streaked with black as it had been when he was a man in his prime.

"When I think of the hundreds of times I could have been with him in the mountains instead of a lousy office . . ." said Leon.

I knew what he was really thinking of, the long periods when our family home was reeling with politics and our father would flee to the mountains. "I never told you, Leon," I said. "But once when we were up there, he said to me, 'I know what your brother thinks, that I hate politics. I didn't like all that high-toned stuff that went with it, but it was never the politics that drove me away. I couldn't believe an immigrant's son could ever be a governor. I didn't want Leon to get hurt.'"

Leon did not answer, but kept looking at the floor. I knew that he needed what our father had told me.

There were sounds coming from the rooms in front of the house. Before the rest of the family could come into the room, I said to Leon, "There's something else I want to tell you. Remember a couple of months ago, when you and I were here, just sitting with Papa. He hadn't said any words in a long time and we thought he'd lost his speech. Then out of the blue, he said to us in that strong voice he used to have: 'You boys better saddle up the horses. We got a long ride ahead of us today.'"

Leon looked up, remembering, and I said, "You know, until that moment, I thought he was going through the tortures of the damned in that bed and I used to pray he would die right away. But he wasn't going through hell. He was reliving the good parts of his life, and horseback was one of them. I remember how he used to swing into the saddle. You only see it a few times in your life and never in these

· · ·

motorized days—that effortless familiarity that goes only with men who have lived their lives in the saddle."

That I said to Leon. To myself, I said, "You're right, Papa. You've got a long ride ahead of you today. It's the way you wanted to go. Our ride is just beginning. We've got a ways yet to go."

Three

. . . .

26

Suddenly, politics wasn't the least bit fun anymore. In the time we had been there, even the most serious of situations had contained a grain of humor that we could look for and seize upon for escape. We had fallen into that political pit all politicians dread. Before, our escape had been to keep reminding ourselves, "If you can't laugh in this game, you'll be a dead man in six months." Jack Kennedy, with his saving Irish humor, honored that rule.

Politics had turned mean. The reason was that we were in the fight of our lives. We were not prepared for it. Winning a gubernatorial campaign had made us think we were political sophisticates. Now we were in the big leagues, outclassed, outfinanced, and outnumbered. We had not thought our situation through. This was no local race confined to our state's frontiers. We had forgotten that elementary lesson that each state in the nation was entitled to two United States senators, and a senator from Nevada had just as much power and clout as a senator from New York. The fact that Nevada was the least-populated state meant nothing in the equation.

The country's financial and political powers kept close watch on each precious senator. They would pour a ton of money and heavy political artillery into a senatorial race to see that their man won, to make sure that their senator could continue to do them favors that meant millions upon millions of dollars.

Our opposition was an incumbent United States senator who had been doing favors for the financial and political giants for a long time. Over a span of three six-year terms, a sitting senator can amass a mountain of due bills, which he will collect in campaign contributions next election time.

. . .

The giants were being flown into Nevada by chartered airplanes. There were so many that they resembled an endless squadron of B-29s in a World War II bombing raid. They came to conservative Reno, but mostly they went to "everything goes" Las Vegas. There, they could not only pay off political debts to their senator but have a few nights on the town in the process.

These nights on the town were not small-time. The best-looking, most-endowed call girls in the country made the Strip and downtown Glitter Gulch their hangout and they were available at the crooking of a thumb. The visiting potentates did not even have to pay for their rooms. The luxury suites were waiting for them, compliments of the senator and the house. Before they dragged themselves wearily back onto the chartered planes that would take them back to Washington, they would, of course, have left their tokens behind, bundles of money for the senator's political war chest. It was very easy to launder a check into hard cash at any cashier's cage at any casino, and no one would be the wiser. The stream of chartered planes bearing supporters and money came to be known as the golden galleons of the Spanish Armada, and the word on the street was that our opposition had a war chest like Fort Knox.

As if that were not enough for us to confront, the Spanish Armada brought celebrity Democratic senators in to give a speech at a fundraising banquet and get interviewed by the newspapers, radio, and even television, which was catching on like wildfire. All faithfully implored the citizenry to support their invaluable colleague and return him to the U.S. Senate.

And as if that weren't enough, then came *Air Force One* bearing the president himself—Lyndon Baines Johnson.

"Don't minimize the influence of that plane," George Friar reminded us. "Every time the wheels of *Air Force One* touch ground, there go a thousand votes to the opposition. In California, it's ten

· · ·

thousand votes every time the wheels of *Air Force One* touch down."
California or Nevada, the impact evened out.

On top of everything else, our opposition was Senator Jack Horner,
who embodied the deadly combination of being a Mormon from
Mormon country—Las Vegas.

Why were we even in this race? How could we have gotten ourselves into a situation like this? Leon was governor and comfortably
and unbeatably so. He had no further aspirations at the moment.
The bright young candidate the Republican party had chosen to run
for the United States Senate suddenly found it impossible to forsake
his clients, who formed the burden of his law practice. The real reason, George Friar said, was that the bright young candidate's heart
pumped not blood but piss.

At the last moment, there were no Republican candidates for the
United States Senate. In truth, it was too late to find even a sacrifi-
cial lamb. The party would not recover for a long time from losing a
United States Senate seat by abject forfeit.

So Leon offered himself up as the party's sacrificial lamb. He did
not believe it was the sacrifice it seemed to be. He had a hunch that
he could beat Senator Jack Horner. Taking on not only an incumbent,
but an incumbent with huge seniority, running against a two-to-one
voter registration and a war chest rich as anyone could ask for in what
was shaping up as a landslide election by President Lyndon Johnson
over challenger Barry Goldwater, it was no wonder that none of us
shared that hunch.

· · ·

27

"One plus if you do get elected to the United States Senate, which I doubt," said George Friar through a mouthful of dust, "you will be four thousand miles away from your constituents."

"We could be just about that far away right now," said Leon, wiping off his goggles. "Where in hell are we?"

Since the July day when the Republican candidate had defected, and an angry Leon had filed for the United States Senate race, we had logged approximately a hundred thousand miles by most of the means of transportation known to man—single- and twin-engine planes, car, four-wheel-drives, pickups, and, as of this moment, a mule-drawn hay wagon that had picked us up when our truck had gotten stuck in the sand.

We had made political stump stops at cow towns, mining towns, and ghost towns that no politician in Nevada history had ever visited before. At each stop there would be an open-air rally with fireworks, barbecues, picnics, six-man football games, what went for political banquets in dining rooms of old hotels with the paint peeling off the boards, all arranged by Abner. Once, because the only cafe in town was too small, we had been hosted in a billowing tent that threatened to take off in the windstorm that was raging on the desert.

In communities where there was no airport, we landed on two-lane highways and wide dirt roads. The most heart-stopping trip of all was when an early blizzard swooped down on our little plane and it bounced around the sky like a butterfly.

At every stop, Leon used variations of the same theme: "The Republican party, outnumbered as we are, has a chance to make political history with a victory in what is prophesied as a Democratic land-

· · ·

slide year. Well, it may turn out to be a landslide in some misguided states, but not here in Nevada. I've been through a tough campaign before, but none so gratifying as this one in overcoming the obstacles we face. We are on the ten-yard line and we are going over."

Cheering words for the troops who had paused to hear Leon—prospectors with a stubble of beard on their faces, come to town for supplies, small-town merchants with long aprons, hookers short on sleep blinking down from their balconies through bleary eyes, and once, five hundred steers in a cloud of dust being driven right through town by yipping cowboys with bandannas covering their mouths and noses.

We were as bad off in the polls as bad could be. That was borne out to me when I ran into a newsman with whom I had worked on a few stories some years back. He had left the newspaper world to become a flack for Senator Jack Horner in Washington, D.C. We had been good friends back then. We had a private drink away from prying eyes and vowed we would still be friends when this campaign was over. We bet a dinner on the outcome, he saying that Jack Horner would beat my brother Leon by thirty thousand votes minimum. From the way the polls were going, it looked as though he was right, but I bet anyway, out of loyalty.

That was the first of two meetings my newsman friend and I had during and after the campaign. We did not know it then, but the second meeting would be the last we would ever have.

Desperately now, Leon was scrounging for enough forlorn votes in the boonies to whittle away at the margin that our opposition, Horner, was piling up in Las Vegas. There seemed to be little chance that Leon's "prophecy" would come true. It was the same situation as last campaign, but so far no miracle such as Leon's family hour on television had materialized. We would probably win well in Reno and northern Nevada, get whipped soundly in Las Vegas and southern

· · ·

Nevada, and hope for enough votes in the cow counties to squeeze out a win.

"When you're losing," said Leon in an endless litany, "suck in your gut and put a smile on your face and look winners." Despite that perennial smile, Leon was changing in front of my eyes. He was becoming harder and more cynical as our bad-news campaign wore on. He was becoming a political animal, fighting for his very life. It didn't pay to cross him. Organized labor found that out. He told them at their annual convention: "I will not tolerate your demeaning the office of governor. If you are willing to talk reasonably instead of playing games, I will continue to arbitrate your disputes. If you are set on playing games, I will leave these negotiations, but I will leave with a public statement that collective bargaining in Las Vegas, because of you, is dead."

Barry Goldwater had almost blown us out of the water with his offhand remark that it was okay to use tactical atomic weapons. Militarily, he probably made sense, but the civilian population had no way of knowing that he meant *atomic* rifles. That word *atomic* was the trigger word that sent shivers down spines. When Goldwater topped that by saying "extremism in the pursuit of . . ." he was tagged forever with the label of extreme right-winger. He waited two years before explaining what he *should* have said election year: "Cicero said it first."

Keeping to his vow, Leon nevertheless went to the Las Vegas airport where Goldwater's plane was coming in. By then, the Republican officeholders of all the western states were avoiding Goldwater like the plague. Leon was to be the only Republican officeholder in the West to stand by Barry Goldwater in his darkest days. Richard Nixon also stood up to be counted. He toured thirty-six states for Goldwater. Despite Goldwater's getting whipped anyway, the two of them captured the GOP leadership for the conservatives.

In Nevada, Leon went to the airport in Las Vegas knowing that

· · ·

it might well be costing him the election. Even our own campaign team was arguing with him right to the instant Goldwater's plane touched down. Nevertheless, it was an electric moment when Barry Goldwater emerged from the plane, straightened up at the top of the gangway, and saw Leon waiting at the bottom, waiting to shake hands with him. Goldwater's lean western face showed no expression whatever. This meeting, he knew, went beyond plastic political smiles. He came down the steps and they shook hands. At that moment, a friendship was forged that would last Leon the rest of his political life. Cameras whirred and clicked. Jack Horner had made sure of that. That night, the *Las Vegas Tribune* would run an eight-column shot of that meeting on its front page. Jim Murphy, who covered the story, said in an aside to me, "Your brother is so dead that the only thing you should worry about is what you're going to put on his tombstone."

Leon's campaign planks had validity and deserved newspaper space. We had thought out and worked out positions with care. George Friar said that our platform, like all political platforms, "started with principle and moved to the political." Newspapers in Reno and the small counties must have thought our press handouts were valid, because they used them faithfully.

But something was going wrong in Las Vegas.

We read and reread and weighed the planks:

—Foreign aid should be diverted to our own needs and social programs. We have an obligation to the elderly and the handicapped. Right now, a lot of us are working to support those who won't support themselves.

—The federal government is already taking 42 percent of every dollar earned in the United States. Yet, Senator Jack Horner wants to *up this,* if you can believe it.

—By the end of the decade, there will be a $30 billion shortfall in the national budget. We could be headed for a deep recession.

· · ·

195

—Our Senator Horner wants centralization of power in Washington. Do we want Washington to tell us how to dress, eat, spend, die?

—Unless we are attacked, never will there be another Vietnam without congressional approval.

—Our Senator Horner is for gun control.

"That one alone will kill him in the cow counties. Can you imagine those cowboys giving up their six-shooters? Add this to it: Senator Horner proclaims that nobody owns him. That's right. He peddles himself by the installment plan."

Such was the substance of Leon's campaign for the United States Senate. The planks made for a solid if not brilliant conservative platform from which Leon could jump with impunity.

But something was going wrong in Las Vegas.

The *Las Vegas Tribune,* which had by far the largest circulation in southern Nevada, at first used the handouts after they had been rewritten and expanded upon by their top political reporter, Jim Murphy. The placement of the stories was fair, the same page and the same space that the *Tribune* was giving to Horner.

And then, almost imperceptibly at first, stories about Leon were cut by one paragraph, then two paragraphs, then four paragraphs. As the weeks went by, even the one-paragraph stories were buried in the obituaries.

Among our campaign crew, the blame was at first laid at Jim Murphy's door. Jim was a liberal and Horner was a liberal, and Leon Indart was the archfiend conservative. But neither Leon nor I believed that Jim Murphy was so blatantly doing the job on us. Political philosophies had nothing to do with Jim's demonstrated sense of fair play. Leon laid down the dictum to our campaign crew not to say one word of complaint or worse to Murphy whenever he came up to our headquarters room in the El Morocco Hotel.

Finally, it was Jim Murphy himself who, short of condemning his

· · ·

own editor, revealed to us what was happening. Something was going wrong with Jim Murphy, too. His Irish face was pale and pinched and the black eyes behind the horn-rimmed glasses blazed too often.

"We can drop the pretenses," he said to the room. "It doesn't take clairvoyance to see that you're blaming me for the news-side treatment, and you're pissed." He swept the room with one scathing look. "If you think that little of me after four years of living together, you can go screw yourselves."

George Friar hung his head. "Apologies, good sir." Friar held up his big hand before Jim Murphy could respond. "Whatever you're going to tell us, Jim," he said, "don't incriminate anyone over you. That way, you can answer your editor's or your publisher's inevitable inquisition. But if I'm reading this right, you don't know the whole story yourself."

Gratefulness peeped out from Jim Murphy's eyes. It was the first human reaction that Jim had ever let escape in our company. "Here it is," Jim said, spreading his hands. "Up to a few weeks ago, I was doing my usual thing with your quotes and your handouts." He looked at me. "You don't fool me with the technique you invented—a positive lead graph to lower my defense and a gut shot in the second graph." I smiled conspiratorially at Jim and said nothing. "I write my own stories," said Jim, "and they're legit. My . . ." Jim caught himself. "When I'm done writing a piece, I send it on to . . . the editorial side. They're the ones who decide if the story should be cut to meet space limits."

Jim stopped and looked down while he made sure he was phrasing it right. "I can usually anticipate how much space the paper's got. In the time I've been there, I've never had a story killed and I've never had a story cut by more than a graph." Jim raised his eyes and looked at Leon evenly. "Then one story I wrote about a speech you made got cut by two graphs. I didn't say anything to . . . the editorial side.

· · ·

Breaks of the game, I figured. Then my next story on you gets sliced by three graphs. Since I won't write more than six graphs, even if it's about the second coming of Christ, that's half of the story cut out. I was miffed, but I kept my mouth shut. My next story, and it was a good shot, was cut to one lousy graph and placement was the obits, as we say in the news game. This time, I was hopping mad and I had a showdown with the editorial side." Jim threw down the pencil he twirled constantly in his fingers. "Oh, what the hell. You know who I'm talking about. Mike Moore. He's the guy I turn my stories in to."

"So what's up, Jim?" I said, speaking up because as a reporter I had gone the rounds with Mike Moore. "Is this a personal vendetta?"

"I don't know," said Jim. "He didn't say."

"What *did* he say?"

"He said, 'That's the way the cookie crumbles.'"

"Oh, for Christ's sake!" George Friar exploded. "The profundity of the fourth estate." Friar leaned forward over the table. "What's coming up next?"

"It's come up," said Jim with an empty voice. "I turned in my story last night. As you can see today, the story is invisible. It's been junked."

Leon interposed for the first time.

"Is this a permanent state of affairs? You mean we're going to get blanked?"

"I asked Mike Moore that," said Jim, "a few minutes ago. He said, 'Do me a favor, Jim. Don't ask questions about what the gods on Olympus decide.'"

"Meaning?" said Leon.

"Yes," said Jim Murphy. "From here on out, you are an invisible candidate. The *Las Vegas Tribune* doesn't even know you exist."

Leon was silent through the burst of denunciation and swearing

· · ·

from the campaign crew. "I think it's time I had a little talk with Mr. Mike Moore."

"Do me a favor, Governor," said Jim Murphy.

"Don't worry," Leon said. "What was said here today goes no further."

"It doesn't matter," said Jim Murphy. "Just give me a phone call when your meeting's over with. I want confirmation of what the powers of the *Tribune* are going to do. I need justification."

"For what?" said Leon.

"I'm going to resign," said Jim.

"I'll spare you the trouble," said Mike Moore, editor of the *Las Vegas Tribune*. His desk was at dead center of the newsroom, surrounded by a dozen smaller desks marked by their reporting duties: *Sports, Society, Valley, Regional, Mining,* and so on. With the exception of the *Society* desk, which was occupied by a middle-aged woman with frizzed hair and a pencil stuck into it over her ear, the reporters were men. Most were bareheaded and short-sleeved with their neckties open. One reporter getting on in years wore an old-fashioned snap brim hat tipped back on his head.

The newsroom was typically noisy with the bursts and clatters of already old Underwood manual typewriters, and it was as smoky as a pool hall. Everyone, even *Society,* was smoking cigarettes that dangled from lips, were stuffed in corners of mouths, held in nicotine-stained fingers, or crammed into big ashtrays already filled with butts. Nobody bothered to speak to his neighbor. Concentration on the story was the name of the game.

Even Mike Moore went on editing stories and marking them up for the printer while we waited. His handwriting with the heavy leaded pencil was illegible. He waited until he was good and ready, and then

· · ·

raised his head as if noticing us for the first time. His first words belied the act he was putting on.

Waving us into the two wooden chairs in front of his desk, he started over again. "I'll spare you the trouble of saying it: You're not getting fair play. So what else is new?" He leaned back in his chair, thrust out his considerable stomach, and locked his hands behind his head.

Leon regarded him with judging eyes. "We're not complaining," I said. "Equal treatment by the *Tribune* has killed many a candidate."

"True," said Mike Moore, regarding me coldly through his thick bull's-eye glasses. "And it has made many a winner."

Leon made a gesture of impatience that covered both Mike Moore and me. "Now that I've heard it confirmed," he said, "I'm curious as to why. The *Tribune* and I, and you and I, have always gotten along well. Even in your endorsing editorial for Dean Cooper in the governorship thing, you helped me by damning him with faint praise."

Mike Moore allowed a small smile to play across his lips. "Was it that obvious? I must be losing my touch." He unclasped his hands, put his meaty elbows on the desk, and looked at Leon. "I'll tell you why. Whatever I do to you this time is not personal, Governor. I happen to like your style. And if the truth be told, I like your politics, too. But this newspaper happens to be Democratic and liberal."

"You mean your publisher is," said Leon.

"That's right. He backs winners. He can't afford to make an enemy out of a United States senator."

"But he's running the risk of making one," said Leon. "Because the next United States senator from Nevada is sitting across the desk from the editor of the *Las Vegas Tribune*."

"Wishful thinking," said Mike Moore. "But good luck."

"What if I do beat Horner?" said Leon. "Where does your boss, or you, stand then?"

· · ·

"We'll be the best backer you ever saw in a newspaper."

"That's not very admirable," said Leon.

"It may not be admirable, but it's political," he chided Leon. "Don't show your naiveté. You need growing up."

Leon's eyes had gotten chillingly cold.

Mike Moore stood up to tell us the session was over.

It was over all right.

"The word is that your publisher has passed the word down to you to gut me," Leon said. "He has the right to do the job on me politically. But he better not try gutting me personally. You can tell him that from me."

"I have the right to do what I want with the news," said Mike Moore. "As far as you're concerned, you're invisible."

"We'll see," said Leon.

"We'll see?" Mike Moore repeated. "You ain't seen nothing yet."

Next morning, when Abner went to the *Tribune* to lay out a half-page ad, he was informed that the *Las Vegas Tribune* would not be accepting any of Leon's political advertisements for the remainder of the campaign.

The editor was right about our not having seen anything yet. But as it turned out, neither had he.

· · ·

28

Washington, D.C., was bathed in the bright sun of October, when there is both warmth and an autumn nip in the air. Abner and I were sitting on a bench at Pennsylvania Avenue Square, but so far we had been oblivious of the history surrounding us. Finally, my conscience got me to my feet and I wandered around the square, reading the words of such as George Washington, John Adams, Daniel Webster, and, to my surprise, Walt Whitman, who was not a founding father. Only tourists do this. The locals, and I had been one once, are too rushed or don't care.

It was lunch hour and government employees were popping like squirrels out of the nearby doorways of the great stone buildings that housed Treasury, Interior, Justice, and Commerce. Typically, the rush took on the dimension of an exodus.

The day before, we had left Reno on the first leg of the transcontinental flight to Washington. When we crossed Nevada, the gray-brown mountains seemed brutal rising out of the morning mist. When the mist began to burn off, dry lake beds that frequent the Nevada landscape were white in the glare of the morning sun. Alluvial desert fans were like artists' washes on a canvas and the horizon stretched out forever, as barren and unpeopled as a moon surface. I had caught myself thinking: Let it stay that way forever.

When we had passed over Virginia's dun fields and gray forests of beech, birch, and oak, the Washington Monument obelisk rose again for me with the simple dignity that I once had grown to love.

My reverie was interrupted by Bill Skinner's appearance. He looked

. . .

Washington with his dark wool suit, gray fedora hat, and the flat document valise he was carrying. Our eyes met, and the expectation in Abner's and my eyes must have showed, because Skinner broke his rule of silence on a public street. "Got it," he said. "The whole works."

So much hinged on the contents of that valise. What we hoped so desperately to find had brought us across the country to the nation's capital and had driven us into playing spy rendezvous games on Pennsylvania Avenue.

But this was no game. Two weeks before, a friend from Skinner's FBI days had called. He had been tracking the Senate race between Jack Horner and Leon. He was incredulous when he could find no press mention in Nevada of a Senate hearing on the relationship between Senator Horner and one Bobby Baker, a one-time Senate page boy who had risen meteorically to the powerful position of secretary to the Democratic majority party in the Senate. According to Washington newspapers, Baker gave marching orders to Democratic senators on how to vote—in the name of President Lyndon Johnson. Along the way, he had managed to pile up a fortune of two million dollars.

This much was picked up off the wire services by one lone newspaper in Reno and none in Las Vegas. Since the budding scandal had nothing to do with Nevada, it simply wasn't newsworthy. When more pieces of the scandal began to leak out, Las Vegas's name came up. But the wire service stories died there. Nobody was eager to mention anything that would damage Nevada's already dented image.

Skinner's former FBI friend told him that eastern newspapers had managed to pick up enough leaks from the Senate investigation into Bobby Baker to show that he was somehow linked to a chartered airline flight to Las Vegas for a fund-raising event.

That morsel was enough to send Skinner into his old FBI mode.

· · ·

He told Leon as much as he knew, and Leon as governor asked the Senate Rules Committee for a transcript of the hearing. One glance through the transcript showed that much of the testimony was being suppressed. Before news of Leon's request could spread far enough to ensure permanent destruction of the record, Skinner raced to Washington, D.C., with Abner and me as backup.

But neither Abner nor I nor Leon nor anyone else was ever to find out how Skinner managed to pirate the original uncut transcript of the Senate hearing out of the records. We did not hang around in Washington long enough to examine the transcripts. We three were on our way home to Nevada on the first flight.

I n the security of his study at the Governor's Mansion, Leon opened and scanned the sheaves of transcript one by one before passing them on to us.

"This is dynamite," said Leon. "But can we use it?"

"It's sworn testimony," said Skinner testily. "It's all documented."

"I didn't mean that," said Leon. "I meant will there be a backlash from Nevadans who don't like our senators being kicked around."

"Oh, for Christ's sake," said Abner. "It's the election."

"All right," said Leon. "Let's go ahead."

E verything was waiting for us at the Strip's El Morocco: a massive table piled high with green-covered transcripts, two desks, two typewriters, four ashtrays, a few cartons of cigarettes, and the room-service number for our meals. Adjoining rooms held beds on the off chance we would ever get time to take more than a brief nap.

Abner and I sighed in resignation, took off our jackets and draped them over our chairs, and started reading and typing. It would be two weeks before we would see daylight again. When that time was done,

· · ·

Leon made a regal visit to our common working room, choked on cigarette smoke, and picked up the first draft of the television script that was aimed at the heart, head, and tenure of U.S. Senator Jack Horner:

> A little more than a year ago, an incident of corruption in high Washington circles rocked the capital of our nation.
>
> The incident had to do with one Bobby Baker—a salaried employee of the U.S. Senate—whose manipulations with political influence made him a millionaire in a few short years.
>
> At home here in Nevada, we at first read about the incident as something that was confined to a small clique in Washington. Then the pieces of the scandal began to leak out—and *some of the pieces were linked to Nevada.*
>
> For the first time in the history of our state, a senator from Nevada became suspect in the nation's eyes—because of his actions in the Bobby Baker investigation.
>
> That man was the junior senator from Nevada—Jack Horner.
>
> What I am going to do is present to you the official record of Mr. Horner's actions throughout the investigation and his personal association with the key figures involved in the Baker scandal.
>
> Mr. Horner—as a senator from Nevada—has an absolute duty to wash away the cloud of suspicion that lies over his own integrity *and the integrity of the state of Nevada.*

Leon's mouth puckered. "Pretty strong stuff," he said. "Do we condemn the whole state for the sins of one son of a bitch?"

"Horner as a senator represents the people of a state," I said.

Abner disagreed. "Okay, Governor. Kill it. Horner's nailed. That's enough."

Leon picked up the script and read on:

· · ·

Let's take a close look at the central figure involved in this scandal, Mr. Bobby Baker.

Coming out of South Carolina when he was only fifteen years old, Bobby Baker went to Washington in 1943. His first job was a page boy for the Senate. But he was a boy in name only. In the town where he was raised, he had earned a quick reputation as an operator.

Leon pulled off his glasses. "Has he got a rap sheet in South Carolina?"

"The police say yes," said Abner.

"Any felonies?"

"No," Skinner said.

Leon took his heavy pencil out of his pocket and struck out the preceding line. "Let's keep it backed up by the record."

As witness after witness in the Senate hearing testified, Bobby Baker had two driving ambitions—power and money. On the surface, he was dapper and bright and ingratiating to those who could help him. Beneath the surface, he was ruthless.

Bobby Baker made it his business to find out where the skeletons were in the U.S. Senate. He knew who owed money. He knew who had a weakness for drinking and girls. He knew where money could be made in undercover deals. He knew which senators had a weakness for money. In Washington, he was a one-man Gestapo.

Leon sighed and pulled off his glasses again. "This is sworn testimony?"

"Yes," Skinner and Abner said almost together.

"It makes it look as though the whole Senate is on the take," said Leon.

· · ·

"No!" said Abner. "Just the bad apples."

"They had it coming, Leon," I said. "It's about time they were flushed out."

"Of course you're right," said Leon, "but as in our first campaign, I don't particularly like riding a white charger into Washington. Let me think it over."

Bobby Baker climbed quickly. By 1955, he reached the job he had been aiming for—secretary to the majority party in the Senate. *This much is official record:* In eight years' time, he used his political influence in the government to pile up a fortune of more than two million dollars. He amassed stocks in banks, insurance companies, a pipeline firm, a food chain store, and a vending machine company with the exclusive right to sell food and beverages in some of the biggest defense plants in the country.

"*This* is what I want to see," said Leon, visibly pleased for the first time.

It was a saying on Capitol Hill in Washington that Baker had as many as ten senators in his pocket for any important vote.

"Barry Goldwater will enjoy that one," said Leon. "Bobby Baker was LBJ's errand boy. That much I know."

As witnesses testified, Bobby Baker used his influence and friends and associates to negotiate lucrative government contracts with a built-in kickback in cash or stock.

He had large stacks of cash money on hand, which he doled out in exchange for favors. And finally—*in the words of the Senate Rules Committee that investigated him*—he used party girls and entertaining, and I quote, 'as part of his business promotion

· · ·

apparatus,' where individuals were induced into certain business arrangements as part of that promotion.

"Beautiful! Beautiful!" said Leon exultantly.

He was a partner in financial deals with a handful of unscrupulous senators, lobbyists, and businessmen engaged in government contracts.

On September 10, 1963—Bobby Baker's tarnished star began to fall. A Washington vending company *filed a civil suit* charging that Baker—for a big cash down payment and a monthly retainer—had used his influence in getting *a competitor company a government contract*. When this story broke, it was the beginning of the end for Bobby Baker. Senators and members of the press began to dig into his affairs. Baker was forced to resign as Senate secretary.

The U.S. Senate ordered a full investigation of Bobby Baker and the incredible network of his deals. Curious things began to happen. Very soon, suspicion revolved around the actions of one man in particular—Senator Jack Horner of Nevada.

"Welcome to the exposé, Jack baby," said Abner.

On December 6, 1963, the *Washington Daily News* broke a story with this headline: BAKER'S PALS TOOK FREE RIDE TO LAS VEGAS.

The lead paragraph in the story read:

"Friends and associates of Robert G. (Bobby) Baker studded the passenger list of a free flight by Riddle Airlines from Washington, D.C., to Las Vegas to attend a fund-raising dinner for Senator Jack Horner of Nevada."

Now, just exactly what kind of people were on that flight? I'll

· · ·

tell you what they were. Influence peddlers, lobbyists, special-interest boys, and government-agency fixers.

I have here in my hands a copy of the manifest listing the names of passengers on the Horner flight to Las Vegas. Until now, this manifest has never been made public.

Leon looked quizzical. "But it was introduced as evidence at the Senate hearing, I hope."

"Right," said Skinner. "There's seventy-four names on the passenger list. Twelve of them were mentioned during the Baker hearings."

Leon went through the manifest, out of which we had pulled the names of the twelve passengers who were questioned in the Senate hearing. They included a lobbyist for a national coal association, another who swung a contract for the new football stadium in the capital, a secretary for whom Bobby Baker bought a home, a call girl who would soon be deported to Germany, a consultant for an airline and missile construction company who picked up the sixteen-thousand-dollar bill for Jack Horner's flight to Las Vegas.

Out of the Senate hearing into the machinations of Mr. Jack Horner's good friend, Bobby Baker, a sordid story unfolded—influence peddling, kickbacks, fraudulent loans from the Small Business Administration, and forged income tax returns.

"And I thought our state was supposed to be the only sin state," Leon said wryly.

When the investigation leaked to Washington newspapers, it was the beginning of the end for Bobby Baker. He was forced to resign as Senate secretary. He was finally found out and stripped of the power he had converted to money.

The conclusions from what you have heard here I leave to

you, my fellow Nevadans. Ask yourselves in your own mind how deeply Senator Jack Horner was involved in the Bobby Baker scandal.

You the people whom he serves in the U.S. Senate have the absolute right to demand an explanation.

The record is absolutely clear that many of the passengers on Jack Horner's money-raising flight to Las Vegas were close friends and associates of Bobby Baker.

Mr. Horner has refused to answer any questions concerning that golden galleon flight to Las Vegas. On the contrary, his actions are aimed at protecting Bobby Baker . . . his good friend.

It is Mr. Horner's duty to wash away the cloud of suspicion that lies over his integrity . . . and the integrity of our State of Nevada.

I pledge to you that when I am elected . . .

Leon's voice trailed off as he began his personal political pitch. He took off his glasses for the last time and let them dangle from his fingers.

Finally he said, "I can't articulate many minuses, but I'm still apprehensive about going with it."

"For Christ's sake!" Abner exploded. "What do you have to lose? Peck's polls show you're getting your ass beat off. This script is your only hope for salvation. And it might not be enough."

Leon winced almost imperceptibly, unable to accept the possibility that he might lose. "How will they come back at us?"

"The usual way," said Abner. "They'll yell smear and accuse you of taking the low road."

"We haven't painted you as a Boy Scout," I said. "The strategy here isn't to make the voters like you. The trick is to make them hate Horner for what he's doing to Nevada."

· · ·

Leon shook his head. "I don't buy that. Everybody in the country has taken a crack at Nevada."

"All right, then," said Abner. "Make them hate Horner for posing as a Mormon goody-goody and then turning them around. You forget something, Governor. Las Vegas is a negativist town. They're always kicking someone in the balls."

Leon weathered the barrage and made up his mind. "All right, let's go with it." He focused on Abner. "Let's get it out of the way in a hurry. Do we do it live?"

"Hell, no," said Abner, horrified. "We tape it in Los Angeles. Hollywood. We're using props to back up your text. Drawings of the seating arrangement in the plane from Washington to Las Vegas, as many actual photos of those passengers as we can get. That chick that was Bobby Baker's secretary, for sure. Charts showing the bucks for Horner piling up. This can't be one-dimensional."

Leon nodded in my direction. "Abner's right," he said. "We can't take a chance on leaks. Brothers going at the same time to Hollywood will start the rumor squads going. Let's decide on dates and places for airing this thing, and you lock up the times."

Leon paused at the door and said aloud, "Pete, go see Sister Sue and ask her to get her shock troops on their knees. I've got a feeling we're going to need all the help we can get."

· · ·

29

Leon's premonition was right. We were going to need all the help we could get. But it had nothing to do with backlash denunciations of Leon as a smear artist and screams of low-road politics. We had put all apprehensions but one on the table.

The *one* we overlooked was detonating the dynamite we had in the can so that people could hear it and read it and see it. Out of morbid curiosity, I first tried to buy time at the television station owned by the publisher of the *Las Vegas Tribune,* where Leon had been declared invisible by editor Mike Moore.

The station manager of KOLV greeted us with mingled hostility and curiosity, and the answer was of course *no.* He fumbled around with reasons like "no time available until after the election." When I was going out the door, he realized he had not played his hand well. He called me back and made a show of poring over his time availabilities. Watching him go through his act, I decided this man had no future at all in theater. After several more minutes of scrutinizing his schedules, he made a yelp of happy discovery and said he had one half-hour slot free, at that. I shared his joy.

"We'll have to see the film first," he said. "To make sure there'll be no mechanical difficulties in airing it. How soon can you get it to us?"

And to make sure our Senator Jack Horner, his press aides, his lawyers, and the entire Democratic party have time to prepare a rebuttal and a counterattack, I thought to myself. I told the station manager I would get the film to him sometime in December, neglecting to add that what I really meant was sometime after the election, and walked out.

. . .

In a few minutes of telephone calls, the enemy camp would be alerted to the fact that we had something in the can. But they didn't know what. With their guilty consciences, the uncertainty would be driving them nuts, I hoped.

I went directly to Hank Romaine's television station. Like his newspaper, the *Las Vegas Herald,* it had a small audience, but at this point, any audience at all would be welcome. Which planted the seed of another idea.

At first, it looked as though we would be striking out again on television time slots. Hank's television station manager was hesitant about making *any* commitments on time. He had a hunch what the tape was aimed at and was terrified of a lawsuit. I asked him to call Hank, whose hatred of the *Las Vegas Tribune* and its editor, Mike Moore, was almost psychopathic. I reasoned that any man who would risk his life to ship arms to Israel would not lack for courage, and I was right.

Hank asked to speak to me. "I want you to give me your word that what you've got in the can won't break me," he said.

"Every word of it is sworn . . ." I stopped there, not wanting to use the word *testimony* just yet. That would be for Leon as a lawyer-governor to do. ". . . in front of a committee of the United States Senate."

The newspaperman side of Hank pricked up its ears. "Do I get a break on the story?"

"Not only that," I said in sudden, blinding inspiration. "We want to buy enough space to run the whole text. Twice."

"A done deal!" Hank remembered the television time request and the money it would bring in there. "How many half-hour segments?" he said.

"Oh, I think five half-hours between next Monday and election

· · ·

day ought to do the job," I said nonchalantly, guessing that Leon and Abner would be finished at the Hollywood studio and on their way back to Las Vegas by then.

Hank could not conceal his gasp quickly enough for me not to hear it. "That's good thinking," he said. "If you're going to do the job on Horner, do it good."

"Do you want to see the tape before it's aired?" I asked, covering the fear in my voice.

"Naw," said Hank. "Just bring me the text in time for me to write my story and my ad people to set it in type."

I booked our times so that showings would be like the Chinese water-drop torture, but also to make sure the evidence of Jack Horner's misdeeds would have time to reach every Mormon hamlet in the entire Las Vegas Valley. That was an inspiration, too, given birth to by a sudden wondering just how faithful the Mormon faithful would remain to their senator when they saw and heard about the company he kept in politics.

The one remaining television station in the state of Nevada was in Reno. It was no trouble at all booking five half-hour time slots there, too, especially after they learned that that was what Hank Romaine's television station in Las Vegas was doing.

We had nothing to fear from Senator Jack Horner's campaign in the rural counties. He had barely deigned to make one pass through that huge geographical and thinly populated expanse. But just to make sure, I booked five half-hour segments at every radio station in the boonies.

That would pick up their afternoons and evenings for two weeks to come, before Election Day.

30

"What's coming off here?" Peck said in his squeaky voice. He was bent over our conference table so intently that his bespectacled eyes seemed to be two inches away from his polling sheets. The poll was not formalized. It was an eleventh-hour sampling of votes in metropolitan Las Vegas and surrounding valley communities, which we had written off because they were so heavily Mormon. The last scientific poll had been taken two weeks ago and had shown little change from the polls taken before that. Those polls had showed Jack Horner winning in a walk in Las Vegas and southern Nevada. Reno and northern Nevada and the cow counties had held to their earlier leads for Leon, but they were not enough to carry Leon in.

Then the television barrage had been launched. Horner was stung, as we predicted. When he got on television to smear and denounce Leon's show, his face was empurpled and his voice almost hysterical with passion. By contrast, Leon's exposé of Horner's personal and financial finaglings had been low key, convincing, and eloquent. Under Abner's coaching and direction, Leon had been sitting on the edge of a desk whose polished top was neatly arranged with charts, artists' drawings of the seating inside the airplane from Washington to Las Vegas, and select photos of passengers of doubtful reputation. It added up to a damning revelation of the activities of a Nevada senator, but there was class to it also.

"Well, what's happening?" George Friar asked in a voice that trembled with expectation of disastrous news.

"There's a shift going on," said Peck. "But what's important is that it doesn't show any signs of letting up."

"For whom and against whom?" Friar asked impatiently.

. . .

Peck was totally immersed in his mathematical mind. "For Leon," he managed to mumble.

Leon strode decisively up to the table and asked in a stern voice, "Where is it happening?"

"Reno, the north, and the cow counties first," said Peck. "Not a big shift there, but our lead is bigger than we expected." He made a clicking sound with his mouth and said, "The big shift is in Las Vegas. Not only here, but the valley towns. Two weeks ago, they were solid for Horner. Now, they're shaping up to a Mexican standoff."

"A Mormon standoff," said Abner, his voice tremulous with disbelief.

No one dared to voice the last and most important question, until Leon did. "How do you project the election now?"

Peck looked up for the first time and swept the room, eyes burning with intensity. "I know I will live to regret what I'm going to say," he said in an uncommonly even voice. "But unless everyone is lying to us, the election as of this moment is a toss-up."

31

Along the way, an old politician had said to me, "There's only one steadfast rule in politics. The unexpected is the expected."

For me, that sums up Election Day and Election Night and their aftermath. Even now, in memory, the events of that long day, that long, long night, and the time that followed add up to a disjointed dream where the unexpected became the norm.

Our first journey into politics had ended where it began, at my

· · ·

mother's rambling old house in Carson City. Our second journey had begun there too, and now we would see where it would end.

Autumn had finally caught up with northern Nevada. An early snow had whitened the spine of the Sierra that loomed to the west. No going there to cut and carry down Christmas trees on our shoulders from Papa's old rangeland. Winter's early arrival had provided the cold snap necessary to turn the cottonwood trees into great spreading bursts of golden leaves and the sentinel poplars into shafts of flame.

The Admission Day celebration had been held only a few days before, and the faint smell of horse still lingered in the air. The parade had gone down Main Street and the politicians who were running for office this year were present to a man. That included Leon seated on the backrest of a convertible and U.S. Senator Jack Horner on a horse. He had taken riding lessons in Las Vegas when he got into politics, and the old cowboys who had been raised on horses squinted but did not smile at him when he rode by waving his hat the way Tex Maynard used to do. But Jack Horner was no Tex Maynard. He had a barrel chest, short legs, and a fleshy face. He looked mad and darted venomous glances at Leon in the big car marked "Governor of Nevada."

The old politicians say too that one can tell by crowd noises how his campaign is doing. If that is so, Leon was in good shape. The bursts of applause that marked his passage down Main Street were loud and genuine. Horner's paid shills had been placed strategically along the parade route. To recently trained ears like mine, his applause was constant, but it lacked spontaneity.

The family home had been equipped much like it had been the first time, on Election Night for the governorship, only more so. There were television sets in the spacious living room and the parlor in the guest wing of the house. One room in the guest wing would again be the nerve center, equipped with Leon's private phone and a bank of telephones to gather results from voting polls throughout the state.

Peck's sheets listing towns and precincts were spread out in a semi-circle on a desk that also held three of those private lines to his scattered poll watchers. George Friar had an armchair and a little table with a telephone of his own. His legs were crossed and his fingertips touched together beneath his chin. He was deep in thought. Skinner was holding down the southern end in Las Vegas. He had literally stationed himself in one of the waiting rooms outside the county clerk's office, where the voting boxes from the precincts would be brought for counting. Skinner had somehow managed to finagle two telephones, one so he could talk to Leon in the family home in Carson City, the other for taking calls from the hand-picked poll watchers he had stationed at every precinct in Las Vegas and its neighboring communities. Some of the bigger precincts had voting machines now, so there was little chance of chicanery there. And the voting places in Westside where the black population was congregated were manned by blacks who had come over to Leon's side, actually registered Republican, and volunteered to be poll watchers on their own ground. They *looked* like they meant business, and the people for Horner knew that they did indeed *mean* business. That brought another measure of relief to our side. Still, Skinner, with his FBI antennae vibrating, was unexplainably apprehensive and that bothered me.

The family home began to fill up early, what with campaign crew, party people, and reporters—excluding Si Price, whom Gene had met at the door and turned back. Si Price was furious. He would wreak revenge in his stories if Leon lost. George Friar said he would do it even if we won.

The thing that bothered me the most about preparations for election night at the family home was the champagne, brought by party people. The bottles had not been opened and were chilling in a huge silver container filled with ice. When Leon saw them later, he was just plain irritated. On my part, I was superstitious. That is a Basque trait that I had learned to treat with respect. The presence of the champagne before the fact was to me premature and an invitation to bad luck. But of course, I could say nothing.

Leon had gotten a head start on us by turning on television at his own home for a few minutes before leaving. By the time he walked into the family home after the polls closed at 6 P.M., he knew what was happening in the eastern and southern United States. It was not good. The predicted Democratic landslide was in motion, President Lyndon Johnson was beating the daylights out of challenger Barry Goldwater, and Republican office-seekers were being bowled over like tenpins.

"It's a rough night out for Republicans," Leon said with a forced grin on his face as he made a courtesy tour of the living room and dining room. He went into the kitchen to greet our mother, who was heating French hors d'oeuvres. From there he could go through the alley connecting the two wings of the house and duck through the door leading to election nerve center. Our numbers man, Peck, was on the phone to Skinner in Las Vegas, and George Friar to our main poll watchers in Reno. Leon whispered to Peck, "Skinner?"

Peck nodded and turned his full attention back to the telephone and whatever Skinner was telling him. Leon waited until Peck hung up the phone and then asked, "What's out of the southland?"

"Skinner says the turnout was big in Vegas and the valley towns."

Our brother Gene came into the room in time to hear Skinner's report. "Damn!" he said. "I was hoping for a flash flood." What he didn't need to say was that with two-to-one registration, a big turnout was good for Horner, a Democrat, but not for Leon, a Republican.

"Registration and Barry Goldwater are hanging like albatrosses

· · ·

around your neck," Gene said bitterly to Leon. He had been solidly opposed to Leon's public greeting of Barry Goldwater at the Las Vegas airport.

"I'm not so sure of that," said Leon. "Take a second look at Goldwater's vote in the West, not the East. He's not getting beat that bad."

"But he *is* getting beat," said George Friar. "And that has to hurt our race."

There was an audible groan from the guest-wing parlor and the living room, where nearly everyone was gathered.

"What's happening?" asked Leon.

Our youngest brother, Mitch, came through the parlor door into the nerve-center room. "First statewide results," he said. "Horner's beating you pretty bad, Leon." Mitch added lamely, to take the sting out of his news, "It's still early."

Leon, acknowledging the gesture, said, "I hope you're right."

Leon crossed the room and closed the door into the parlor, as if he were shutting off the television announcements coming from the parlor into the nerve center. "I'll get my returns from Peck," he told the room. "He's more scientific than those tube jockeys."

It would be a half hour before Peck was willing to make a report. He had been juggling telephones without stopping. No hellos or good-byes. A mumbled word or two. Hurried jotting down of figures on his master sheet. Pick up another ringing telephone and repeat the process.

"It's Horner," he said. "But not by as much as the tube says." He was silent for a moment, deciding whether to say what was in his mind. "Something . . . is . . . going . . . on," he said, dragging each word out slowly.

There was another, louder groan from the living room and the parlor. "The troops need comforting," said Leon and ducked through the alley door so that he could reach the bigger group in the living

· · ·

220

room first. I followed him. Our mother was dipping dough balls in hot grease, a French treat we had always loved growing up. She made Leon stop to taste one. But it had to cool before he could put it in his mouth. My mother's little game gave her time to find out from the best source, her sons, what was really going on. She looked the question instead of voicing it. That was *her* Basque superstition manifesting itself.

"Don't give up, Mom," said Leon. "I'm telling you, I know best how I'm doing."

When he crossed through the high double doors into the living room, Leon was met by moans, a few genuine sobs, and a few not so genuine. He held up his hands and said, "Don't give up. I'm telling you. Our strength isn't in yet."

"Oh, Leon," someone cried out. "It's hopeless."

"Listen," Leon said in his commanding voice. "A candidate has to know his own campaign best. We're not beaten. This is going to be a tight one. This one will go down to the wire."

The moans and sobs quieted, but there was little conviction in the sounds that supplanted them.

Leon could not have anticipated how right he was. Before the night was over, the tide was to turn three times from loss to victory to loss to victory . . . It was not until the early hours of morning that Peck's droning voice, almost worn out by then, began to sound finale to the vote count. "Pershing County complete, Lyon County complete, Elko County complete, Humboldt County complete . . ."

By then, the election-night faithful had gone home and we had convinced our mother she should go to bed. Only we brothers, George Friar, and Peck and Abner were still up, unshaven and hollow eyed with exhaustion.

At 6 A.M. every county was complete except the most important one—Clark County. Leon had won every county by a handful of

· · ·

votes, a few hundred or a few thousand, except one—the one which contained Las Vegas and its considerable number of precincts.

By then, Peck and the television stations agreed that Leon had a comfortable if not overwhelming lead of just over a thousand votes.

"What's going on down there?" Leon said into the telephone line that connected him to Bill Skinner. His voice was taut with tension.

"The valley precincts are all in," said Skinner. Leon held the telephone in the air so that we could hear. "You didn't lose them by much at all, and that's surprising. Mormon country, you know. I guess the faithful have deserted brother Jack Horner."

"We know," said Leon impatiently. "But what about Las Vegas proper? The city precincts."

"Something's strange," said Skinner. "I thought they were all in, but they're not. The county clerk and the sheriff say they won't declare Clark County complete until all the votes are counted."

"Why the hell not?" said Leon. "They have voting machines in the city precincts. Those things should have kicked out their totals hours ago."

"That's what I told them," said Skinner. "They got pretty nasty. They say the vote tallying is their jurisdiction, not mine, not yours, even if you are governor."

"Jesus," said Leon. "Don't leave that courthouse until Clark County has been declared complete." He hung up weakly. His brows were deeply furrowed, which was the signal he was worried about something.

We waited in the nerve center for another fifteen minutes. When the phone rang, it actually startled us. I picked it up.

"This is Clark Wheeler from the National Election Service," said the voice on the other end of the line. "Am I speaking to the governor?"

"No, his brother."

"You'll do," said the voice. "Your brother has been declared winner

· · ·

222

by the National Election Service. That's us. The margin of victory is one thousand and eighty-four votes."

I thanked him. "It's all over, Leon," I said and gave him the message.

"That's my count, too," said Peck. He laid down his pencil and stretched. George Friar leaned back in his chair and yawned. My brothers exchanged glances with me. I was to remember later that nobody said the word *congratulations* and the victory champagne was still untouched.

"Let's go downtown and get some breakfast," said Leon.

"Good idea," said Gene.

"I think I'll stick around for a while," I said. "I'll hold down the phone."

Leon looked at me. "Still superstitious?"

"I guess so. I just don't trust that town since the hoods left."

They left the house, their footsteps echoing strangely in what had been a noise-filled atmosphere for so many hours. They came back looking refreshed, in time to hear the phone ringing. I picked it up.

"This is Clark Wheeler at the National Election Service again," said a voice. "Things have turned around. The county clerk and the sheriff just found two thousand votes. Your brother has lost the one thousand lead he had, and lost the election by fifty-four votes."

I relayed the message to Leon. His eyes blazing, he picked up the receiver. "Where did they find the missing votes?"

"Absentee ballots."

"They're supposed to be counted first."

"Well, they weren't this time," the official voice said. "Sorry about your losing."

"Think nothing of it," said Leon.

As soon as Leon hung up the phone, it rang again. Skinner was calling. His voice was strung tight as a violin string. "All the time we thought we were ahead," Skinner said, "there was a little drama going

· · ·

on in this courthouse. I didn't tell you, but I had planted an informant in there. He was disguised as a janitor."

"Go on," Leon said tersely.

"Do you remember that little potbellied stove in the corner of the county clerk's office, for heating in the old days?" Skinner asked. "Well, that stove was pretty busy for at least one hour. My janitor said they were burning papers, but he couldn't see what papers. We don't need to be clairvoyant to guess they were burning absentee ballots cast for you. Someone, I don't know who, was holding those ballots back for an emergency. Well, there was an emergency, all right."

"Will your man testify to that?" Leon asked.

"Testify to what?" asked Skinner. "Burning papers he never got a close look at?" Skinner's voice became sheepish. "Besides, my man is an ex-con. He was all I could get. His testimony would have no credibility. And the ballots are all ashes."

Leon was grimly silent. "So we'll never know," he said in a voice drained of all emotion. "It's the age of voting machines, and an old potbellied stove turns the trick."

But there was someone who did know. When it was all over, I ran into my flack friend again. I couldn't bring myself to pay off my campaign bet with a dinner, but we had a drink. His parting words were, "Some day, I'll tell you how we did it to you."

I didn't want to know. He went back to his flack job in Washington and I to the ivory tower. I guess I could have forced the meeting, but what good would it serve? I had had it.

The second campaign venture ended where it began, around our mother's Spanish Mission table in the old family home in Carson City. It was an ending we could not have anticipated. It was after rage—at least for me—had subsided enough to think rationally.

· · ·

I never did see rage in Leon. He had thrown up a "never look back" barrier against the past and what might have been.

Mitch was relieved. Now, he would not have to bear the crushing load of the law practice alone. But it was a mixed feeling, I could sense. He had learned he could handle the practice alone and even the most demanding clients were satisfied in his protecting hands. Gene, after swearing violent revenge, had reverted to his easygoing "who cares?" lifestyle and his own relaxed law practice.

The final combatant, Sister Suzette, had taken the fact of a lost election worse even than I. For one who had clung so long to her Christian belief in the best in everyone, the fact of a probably stolen election had been an excruciatingly painful revelation. She would come out of it with a more realistic attitude about the failings of humanity.

My mother had so far concealed her feelings about Leon's losing the election. I watched her as she served coffee to us four brothers in her best china cups, but she was displaying no emotion. At that, none of us looked the worse for wear after what we had been through— a victorious election, a lost election, a court challenge, and a failed recount, because how does one count ballots that do not exist, that have been burned to a cinder? We knew the election had been stolen. But where was the proof?

"At least we've got nothing to be ashamed of," said Leon. "We ran an honorable race. We lost the election. But we kept our political reputation intact, and that's what will be important in the long run."

My mother, undeniably grayer now but still unlined, said, "They cheated you, didn't they, Leon?"

"We can't be sure, Mom," said Leon, to calm her.

"The gangsters didn't do it, did they?" she asked, not letting go.

"No," said Leon. "They hate cheaters worse than we do. That's not

· · ·

225

the way they conduct themselves. They're not in the cheating business."

"Jim Murphy called," I said. "He wanted me to tell you he was proud to be covering you, win or lose. He'll be there if there's a next time."

"Howard Hughes had a note hand-delivered to the office," Mitch said. "It read: 'Whatever you do, I'm behind you. If you decide to leave politics permanently, I want you with me.'"

Leon shook his head. "No, I've been down that road. That's nice of him, but I have to be my own man."

"Are you really leaving politics for good?" asked Gene.

"I've got a stomach full of it now," said Leon. "But it would be a shame to waste everything we've learned, dirty tricks and all."

"Does that mean . . ."

Leon nodded. "I'll be back."

"Another shot at Horner?" asked Gene.

"Nah. Six years is too long to wait. When that election comes around again, his own people will dump him."

Leon was right. His own people did, not even letting him survive a primary. When it happened, there were no tears wasted on my part.

"I hear Senator Allen may not run again," said Leon. "He feels he's served his time. Eighteen years is a long hitch."

If that was true, the election was only a few years away. And if I was reading Leon correctly, he really had made up his mind to run again. He was irrevocably hooked. His political career would end in the U.S. Senate. After that, who knew? The saying that every U.S. senator is a potential candidate for president did not become a truism by accident.

My brother would be in the Senate. I would not be with him. That

· · ·

would be the final and permanent loss of identity. The political fire that burns in the bellies of political candidates did not burn in mine. I had a ways to go on horseback, too, like my father. But not down the path of politics. I'd traveled that path and I had seen as much as I wanted to see.

I am having this recurring dream. I have been away and I have come home. I am walking up Robinson Street from Main Street, and it is of course familiar, as I pass all the houses I know. The Cavell house of gray stone. The white-pillared Chartz house with its sweeping balconies. And I reach Minnesota Street.

I turn left toward our family home at 402 North Minnesota Street. The house with its high hedge and white frame wings and its two cherry trees that gave white blossoms in the spring, that my mother loved so much, is no longer there.

Instead, there is a totally unfamiliar house of no character, nondescript, standing where our house was.

There is an old man walking toward me on the sidewalk and I stop him, give him my name, and ask where my family's house is.

And he says, "No house of that name was ever here."

My heart stops and I say, "But my family lived here."

And he says, "No one by that name ever lived here. Nor anywhere else in Carson, either, in my lifetime."

· · ·

THE BASQUE SERIES

A Book of the Basques
Rodney Gallop

In A Hundred Graves: A Basque Portrait
Robert Laxalt

Basque Nationalism
Stanley G. Payne

Amerikanuak: Basques in the New World
William A. Douglass and Jon Bilbao

Beltran: Basque Sheepman of the American West
Beltran Paris, as told to William A. Douglass

The Basques: The Franco Years and Beyond
Robert P. Clark

*The Witches' Advocate: Basque Witchcraft
and the Spanish Inquisition
(1609–1614)*
Gustav Henningsen

*The Guernica Generation: Basque Refugee
Children of the Spanish Civil War*
Dorothy Legarreta

Basque Sheepherders of the American West
photographs by Richard H. Lane
text by William A. Douglass

A Cup of Tea in Pamplona
Robert Laxalt

Sweet Promised Land
Robert Laxalt

Child of the Holy Ghost
Robert Laxalt

Basque-English English-Basque Dictionary
Gorka Aulestia and Linda White

The Deep Blue Memory
Monique Urza

Solitude: Art and Symbolism in the National Basque Monument
Carmelo Urza

Korrika: Basque Ritual for Ethnic Identity
Teresa del Valle

The Circle of Mountains: A Basque Shepherding Community
Sandra Ott

The Basque Language: A Practical Introduction
Alan R. King

Hills of Conflict: Basque Nationalism in France
James E. Jacob

The Governor's Mansion
Robert Laxalt

DATE DUE

GAYLORD | | | PRINTED IN U.S.A.